TED TAYLER

DEAD RECKONING

BOOKS

By Ted Tayler

The Freeman Files

Fatal Decision

Last Orders

Pressure Point

Deadly Formula

Final Deal

Barking Mad

Creature Discomforts

Silent Terror

Night Train

All Things Bright

Buried Secrets

A Genuine Mistake

Strange Beginnings

Dead Reckoning

A Normal November

Into the Sunlight

Tame the Storm

One True Friend

Whispered Truths

A Morning Murder

Quick to Anger

Red Herring Season

Gathering Clouds

Still Standing

Vinci Books

vinci-books.com

Published by Vinci Books Ltd in 2025

1

Chapter One

Saturday, 25 August 2018

ALEX AND LYDIA had to make an early start. The train journey to Edinburgh Waverley involved two changes and took over seven hours, whichever way they approached it. Alex offered to drive overnight because Lydia wanted as much time with her mother as possible, but Lydia judged the extra hour they might gain with Eleanor wasn't worth the effort.

"I like my bed too much," she had said as they drove back to Chippenham from the Old Police Station on Friday afternoon.

"I enjoy sharing it with you," said Alex.

Somehow, they dragged themselves out of bed to make it to Bath Spa station to catch the train.

"I called Eleanor last night to say we would arrive in Edinburgh by a quarter past three this afternoon. Providing there were no delays," said Lydia.

"How long does it take to reach her place from the station?" asked Alex.

"Twenty minutes on the bus," said Lydia. "Eleanor's happy for us to stay with her, thank goodness."

"You stayed with her in Craigmillar the last time you visited," said Alex. "Her house is big enough, isn't it?"

"I didn't have you with me last time," said Lydia. "I didn't know how she felt about us sleeping together."

"I get it. Eleanor is your mother after all's said and done, even though you're twenty-five. We didn't have this problem with Chidozie. It made more sense for us to book our accommodation that weekend."

"With the eye-watering price of our train fares today, saving the extra cost of a hotel bed for the night was more than welcome," said Lydia. "We're not made of money."

"It means we can risk treating Eleanor to another fine dining experience tonight," said Alex. "Do they serve haggis in August?"

"Ugh," said Lydia, "haggis is an acquired taste. Despite the number of Burns Night suppers, my Dundee parents forced me to attend, one I never acquired. We'll avoid the restaurant where Chidozie and Rosa took Eleanor. It sounded fantastic, but variety is the spice of life."

"It was *that* expensive?" grinned Alex.

"Eleanor didn't elaborate on the phone, but I reminded her that Chidozie and Rosa were used to the costs of restaurant meals being far higher in the Netherlands. Edinburgh prices wouldn't have seemed excessive to them."

"Your father is a wealthy man, Lydia. You couldn't have missed that while we were in his company. He bought his place in Dubai at a great time. Heaven knows what it's worth on the open market today. I can't wait to visit."

"That's something I need to discuss with Eleanor this

weekend. If possible, I'd like us to arrange our trip to stay with my father to coincide with hers."

"Even though Eleanor told you she and Rosa got on well, you still have reservations about them spending too much time together."

"Two's company," said Lydia.

"Five provides safety in numbers," said Alex. "Less chance of awkward moments."

"My thoughts exactly," said Lydia.

No sooner than they got comfortable in their seats, they had to grab their things and get off at Bristol Temple Meads, the first of their scheduled changes.

As they boarded the train to Birmingham New Street, Lydia's thoughts returned to yesterday afternoon.

"What did you make of Martyn Street?" asked Lydia. "I'd ruled him out as a suspect."

"Gus took Luke to the Wilton café for their first meeting with Jackson and Street. Their reports in the files didn't point towards Martyn being the killer. He lost his rag at something Gus said, but neither Gus nor Luke made much of it. The witnesses who contributed to the murder file described Martyn as a hard-working giant with a quick temper. Most painted him as slow-witted or backward, but he fooled everyone. Martyn was far more capable than many people imagined. Gus led him through the sequence of events unfolding when he left the engineering factory. Gus gambled the solicitor wouldn't jump in to suggest his client didn't have to answer. Whether Martyn has genuinely erased stabbing his mother from his memory or not, I don't know. A court will decide. It will help if Salisbury police discover the remnants of the bloodied clothing and the murder weapon Martyn admitted having hidden. Gus believes we've got enough evidence for a guilty verdict."

"We don't always see the results of our labours, do we?" said Lydia. "I mean, actually going to court for the trial and helping to find the young woman Gus mentioned after you guys returned to the office."

"You mean Maureen Glendenning," said Alex. "Gus thinks Bourne Hill are the right people to take that search forward. Luke and Neil did most of the leg work yesterday, trying to find her in the UK or Spain. I only heard what they told Gus late yesterday. What did you and Blessing contribute?"

"Not much," admitted Lydia. "We finished updating the Freeman Files and then searched social media for signs of a Maureen Glendenning. That proved a fruitless exercise. Neil hadn't found evidence of a wedding in the reasonable period he researched in the morning. Just after lunch, Blessing trawled through the recorded deaths since 1968 without luck. It's an unusual surname, so the chances of everyone missing a mention of a Glendenning are slim. By the time you and Gus returned, we had resigned ourselves to accept that the poor girl was dead."

"What about Maureen's child? Did Luke try to learn who adopted the baby? We're assuming Maureen put the child up for adoption, but the mother's name would appear on the paperwork."

"Gus told London Road what we knew," said Lydia, "after he informed them he'd wrapped up another cold case. Gus didn't discuss it with us, but perhaps he thought it better for the fifty-year-old man or woman not to find out. How would it help them?"

"You searched for your birth parents when you were old enough," said Alex. "I wonder if Maureen's child ever started the process?"

"I'd be surprised if Graham Street's name appeared on

the birth certificate," said Lydia. "He was an evil man, wasn't he?"

"He wasn't the only person from the investigation who was a bad lot. That's another side of the Marion Reeves case that feels unsatisfactory," said Alex. "Everyone who deserved to stand trial died before we uncovered the truth."

"Maybe an investigation will find culprits in the sexual exploitation affair that are still alive," said Lydia.

The train pulled into Birmingham New Street just before eleven o'clock. Alex and Lydia switched trains for the final time. Another four hours, and they would arrive at Waverley Station.

Lydia looked forward to meeting with Eleanor again and introducing her to Alex. Because of the type of relationship she'd developed with her birth mother, Lydia wasn't nervous. The nerves would set in when the couple travelled forty miles further north to Dundee to meet the people she called Mum and Dad.

"A penny for them?" asked Alex.

"I was just thinking about what we might do this afternoon," said Lydia. "There won't be much time for sightseeing before we travel into Edinburgh for a meal. Eleanor isn't a night bird. She'll be tucked up by eleven o'clock, so we can't eat too late."

"While you were miles away, staring out of the window, I scrolled through a few places of interest on my phone," said Alex. "We could use the hop-on, hop-off open-top bus service to check out the hot spots. Eleanor will guide us to the best options, and we can get to as many as possible tomorrow morning. If we make an early start, we can fit in lunch somewhere with Eleanor closer to home and then get a taxi to the station to save a few minutes."

"That sounds good," said Lydia.

The train trundled into Waverley Bridge on time. Alex put an arm across Lydia to stop her from rushing for the carriage door.

"Let the eager-beavers go first," said Alex. "Give them ninety seconds to trample over one another in a rush to get off the platform. Then, we'll follow behind them and decide the best exit to catch that bus to Craigmillar."

"You're not a fan of crowds, are you?" said Lydia, gathering her things together.

Alex grabbed his bag and, taking Lydia's hand, led her off the train. She had to admit the worst of the crowds had dispersed as they strolled along the concourse.

"I know it's a Saturday afternoon," said Alex, "but this place is busy, isn't it?"

"Waverley Bridge handles twenty-five million passengers every year," said Lydia. "There have been so many changes in recent years. The main station facilities stand in the middle of a large island platform surrounded by platforms on four sides. There are eighteen platforms, which connect to Scotland, and a range of train franchisees run trains between Edinburgh and every major city in England."

"Were you a trainspotter when you were a young girl?" asked Alex. "You seem to know the place inside out."

"My parents brought me into Edinburgh quite often when I was growing up," said Lydia. "The train was the easiest way to travel. This city was where I was born, after all. When I left school, I wanted to be an actress, and it was a toss-up whether to find a drama school here or in Glasgow."

"What made you choose Glasgow?" asked Alex.

"It was further from Dundee," said Lydia. "I knew I was adopted, and the need to find my birth parents was growing.

So I felt I should get far enough away to find my path if that makes sense?"

"You realised the time had come when you needed to stand on your own two feet," said Alex. "No matter how well-meaning your parents were, they stifled your true character."

"Gus might have preferred it if I'd remained a home bird," laughed Lydia. "I'd turn up to the office in a sensible twin-set over a knee-length tartan skirt."

"You wouldn't look out of place in this building," said Alex. "How long has it been here?"

"Since the late 1860s," said Lydia. "The booking hall floor featured beautiful mosaic tiling when it opened, but there have had to be too many changes in recent years for the original features to be so prominent. It's such a shame. The station no longer allows access to cars because of the heightened threat of a terror attack. The taxis used to drive right onto the concourse. Now they have to queue outside."

"Cars parked next to steam trains right where we're standing must have created a terrific atmosphere," said Alex. "The pollution must have been deadly, but nobody knew it back then."

"The covered escalators over there will take us to Princes Street on the north side," said Lydia. "We can catch the bus outside."

Twenty minutes later, they reached Eleanor's home in Craigmillar. Lydia rang the bell.

Alex didn't have a particular picture of what Lydia's mother might look like. But, when he had met Chidozie Barre, the family likeness was striking. Chidozie was tall, muscular, handsome, and confident. There was no doubt Lydia was his daughter.

Eleanor had a slighter build, and her ginger hair faded

with age. It was more rosy-blonde than copper these days. In a decade, the grey and silvery-white highlights would become more dominant.

"Come in, you two," said Eleanor. "You've had a tiring journey. Sit yourselves down and relax with afternoon tea. Lydia knows where your bedroom is. You can get settled in later."

Alex and Lydia dropped their bags at the foot of the stairs, sank into the comfortable sofa, and did as instructed. Eleanor left them and returned from the kitchen several minutes later with a trolley. The top shelf held three plates laden with food, plus a pot of tea and a small sugar bowl. Eleanor pointed to side plates, cutlery, cups, and saucers on the bottom shelf.

"There are the makings, you two. Get stuck in."

Alex looked at the sandwiches, cakes, and scones on offer. He'd need to walk the three miles into the city to make room for an evening meal. Lydia had already dived in. She was always hungry.

"So, you're the famous Alex Hardy I keep hearing about?" said Eleanor.

"Famous rather than infamous," said Alex. "I'll settle for that. It's good to meet you too, Eleanor, finally."

Lydia had demolished two sandwiches and was deciding which cake to go for next when she spotted something in a vase on the mantlepiece.

"A red rose," she said.

"A single red rose, Lydia," said Eleanor. "Chidozie brought it when he and Rosa visited. It's on its last legs now. I ought to have thrown it out, but I kept talking to it and saying you would be here this weekend."

"He didn't forget what he'd given you when he arrived for your first date," said Alex. "How romantic."

"Mmm," said Lydia. "I hope you weren't encouraging him, Eleanor?"

"Don't be foolish, girl. It wasn't to be twenty-six years ago, and we've both moved on. I'm so glad you and Chidozie found one another. Rosa told me about your time with them at the Lady Eleanor. Despite the name, it sounds like an interesting place. Rosa said that Chidozie was disappointed they were losing their chef."

"A five-star restaurant has snapped up Lucas Romeijn, I imagine," said Alex. "His food was spectacular. Chidozie knew they were lucky to have held onto him for as long as they had."

"Lucas, yes, that was his name," said Eleanor. "He leaves at the end of this month. Chidozie and Rosa were interviewing people to replace him after they flew home. I haven't spoken to them since."

"Where did you take them while they were here, Eleanor?" asked Lydia.

"They took me to The Table in the evening," said Eleanor, "to see how the other half lives. We spent a lot of time here chatting. If it had been just the two of us, I think Rosa would have enjoyed a few hours of retail therapy on Princes Street or George Street. I liked her. We got on well together."

"They invited you to Dubai in the autumn, didn't they?" asked Lydia.

"You know they did. I told you on the phone. Why, what's the matter?"

"Nothing," said Alex. "We got an invitation too. How would you feel if the three of us flew out there together?"

"That sounds a marvellous idea," said Eleanor. "I'd get to spend a whole week with my daughter. And her partner, of course. Are you sure Chidozie and Rosa wouldn't mind?"

"I can't see why," said Lydia. "If you were there alone, they would feel duty-bound to keep you entertained every minute. When they close the Lady Eleanor and escape to Dubai, they deserve a rest after a busy summer. We can let them do their own thing while we three explore Dubai, then get together in the evenings. Us girls can go shopping one day while Chidozie and Alex can chill out by the pool."

"We'll need to stay for two weeks to fit everything in," laughed Eleanor. "You've got it worked out, haven't you?"

"I try," said Lydia.

The afternoon tea took its toll. Alex glanced at his watch as Eleanor wheeled the empty trolley towards the kitchen.

"We can forget the open-top bus ride," he said. "I'd better ring around to book a table. Then, when we get our gear upstairs, shower, and get ready, it will be time to leave."

"How far away is the Castle, Eleanor?" Lydia called out.

"Half a mile, dear. It's worth a visit if you want to take a walk later."

"I've found a restaurant a mile from the Castle," said Alex. "I'll ring and check if we can get a table."

Lydia joined Eleanor in the kitchen.

"It's a beautiful evening," said Eleanor. "People think we don't get warm sunshine here in Scotland. We do, not as often as we would like, but you learn to enjoy it while it lasts."

"Once we learn what time we're eating, we'll plan our night," said Lydia. "Alex was hoping you could point us towards the best places to visit. He's never been this far north before and wants to see the sights."

"You don't need me to tell you it will take more than a couple of hours tomorrow morning to do that, dear," said Eleanor. "I'll come with you if you wish. We can whet his appetite. Maybe you'll both come back again soon."

Alex was standing in the doorway.

"We'd love to, Eleanor. I've booked a table for eight o'clock at the Condita. It's less than a mile from the Castle. I hope that's okay?"

"That's fine," said Eleanor, "it's one of the top ten restaurants in the city. I'd better hunt for something to wear now."

Alex and Lydia carried their bags upstairs to the bedroom.

"Eleanor only has one bathroom," said Lydia. "Perhaps it would be best to catch the bus into the city and get off as close to the restaurant as possible."

"She said the Castle was only half a mile from here," said Alex. "The restaurant claims to be a mile from the Castle. Surely, we can walk it?"

"This is Scotland, Alex," said Lydia. "They have castles everywhere. Craigmillar Castle is half a mile south of this house. Edinburgh Castle is probably two-and-a-half miles away to the west. So either we walk to Craigmillar Castle, look around, and then get a taxi, or we skip that trip for this evening and take a stroll towards Edinburgh."

Ninety minutes later, everyone was washed, dressed, and ready to leave. Eleanor laughed when Lydia explained Alex's confusion.

"I know a shortcut through Prestonfield that will get us to the restaurant inside in forty minutes. As long as you promise we'll get a taxi home, I'm game."

"If we leave now, we'll make it in time," said Alex.

It was almost half-past eleven when Alex paid the taxi fare and tottered up the path behind Eleanor and Lydia. The restaurant meal had been excellent, and Eleanor surprised them by knowing a great bar just around the corner. So much for her being early to bed every night.

Perhaps she was on her best behaviour when Lydia came here before.

Any thoughts of a long lie-in disappeared when Eleanor knocked on their bedroom door at seven o'clock.

"Two cups of tea on a tray outside the door," she trilled. "Breakfast will be on the table in twenty minutes."

Alex groaned. Lydia fetched the tray, and the two coffee-lovers started the day with a strong cuppa.

"We need to shower and get dressed," said Lydia. "We're not at home now."

The smells of a fried breakfast wafted from the kitchen and drew them downstairs well within the twenty minutes allowed by their host. Sausage, fried egg, streaky bacon, baked beans, tattie scones, fried tomatoes, and toast adorned their plates.

"That looks terrific," said Lydia.

"How can you face a cooked breakfast after the glasses of single malt we drank last night?" asked Alex.

"This is the best cure I've come across," said Eleanor. "If you want to see the sights of the city and endure a seven-hour train journey later today, you'll need to line your stomach, Alex. Get stuck in. There's more tea in the pot when you're ready."

"I'd prefer a black coffee," said Alex, "if there's one going."

"There might be a small jar in the cupboard," said Eleanor. "I bought it for Lydia, in case she'd lost her taste for tea since she moved south."

"I'll get us a cup in a minute, Alex," said Lydia. "This breakfast tastes as terrific as it looks. It takes me back to Sunday mornings in Dundee with my parents. We drank tea there too. Coffee became my drink of choice when I left home and moved to Glasgow to study."

"That explains it, heathens," said Eleanor with a grin.

Alex swallowed hard and forked pieces of bacon, sausage, and tomato into his mouth.

"You're feeling human already, aren't you?" asked Eleanor.

Lydia came back to the table with two black coffees.

"The kettle was just off the boil," she said. "You should be able to drink it straight away."

Alex took a healthy swig.

"I am now, Eleanor," he said. "My appetite has just woken up."

After breakfast, Alex and Lydia packed their bags and prepared to leave Craigmillar. Eleanor joined them as they took the bus into the city. She showed them Edinburgh Castle, the Royal Mile and Holyrood Palace Park.

"It's a few minutes before one," she said as they sat in the Palace garden. "They don't fire the cannon at the Castle on Sunday, so you won't wonder what's going on. Many tourists on Princes Street have almost had a heart attack on their first visit. What time's your train?"

"There's one leaving at half-past two that shaves an hour off the journey home," said Alex. "We planned to take you to lunch, but after that scrumptious breakfast, I don't think either of us could manage more than a sandwich."

"Don't worry, dear," said Eleanor. "I can get myself a bite to eat later. Catch the two-thirty train. You'll get back to Chippenham at a reasonable time then. You both need to be wide awake in the morning."

"Gus Freeman will bring back another cold case from London Road," said Lydia.

"I won't come with you to Waverley," said Eleanor. "I can get the bus back to Craigmillar. You can walk it from here in fifteen minutes. Go down Canongate and turn right into Market Street. Ring me when you get home, and promise me you'll come again."

"We will," said Alex.

"Don't forget Dubai," said Lydia.

Eleanor hugged Lydia and Alex before striding towards the nearest bus stop.

"We've got an hour to kill before the train leaves," said Lydia as she and Alex turned towards Canongate.

Alex was scrolling through his phone.

"Caffe Nero and Pret A Manger have outlets on the station," he said. "I could murder a coffee."

"Would you share a toasted sandwich with me?" asked Lydia. Alex nodded.

They reflected on a grand weekend as they boarded the train at twenty-five past two.

"We didn't get to spend that long with Eleanor," said Alex, "but it was fun."

"Tomorrow is another day," said Lydia as she nestled her head on Alex's shoulder. "I wonder whose death we'll investigate this time?"

Chapter Two

Friday, 13 February 2015

"IT PROMISES to be a quiet night tonight, Alf," said Rosie as she peered through the curtained window at the stormy night outside.

"My Joan often asks me why I thought it a good idea to take on a pub on Salisbury Plain," muttered Alf Collett. "There's been a pub here for over three hundred years, I told her. Where else will people go for a drink?"

"Has this place always been called the Traveller's Rest?" asked Rosie.

"As far as I can make out, lass," said Alf. "In the old days, they had stables where the car park is today. Most of the passing trade was on horseback or in coaches dragged by a team of four. The land surrounding this inn was full of farms and smallholdings, with farmers and labourers who welcomed a few pints at the end of the day. Even if it took them a while to get here on foot."

"I take twenty minutes to drive here from home," said

Rosie. "I wondered whether I'd even find the place the first evening I worked here. It's so remote."

"Every class of road, bridle-path and byway has always crisscrossed the Plain, Rosie. If you knew the quickest route to where you wanted to go, it was no problem, but it's harder since the wide-open spaces attracted the interest of the Ministry of Defence."

"When was that, do you remember?" asked the twenty-year-old barmaid.

Alf Collett heard the outside door creak. Joan constantly moaned at him to get a drop of oil on its hinges, but Alf preferred the advanced warning when a customer arrived. Alf checked the large clock behind the bar. Twenty past eight. The first of their regulars had arrived, despite the wind, rain, and occasional sleet that would keep most people indoors.

"Ask Jim," said Alf. He took a pint glass from the shelf and drew a pint of bitter.

Rosie recognised the elderly figure that shuffled through the door from the small square hallway. Jim Thornton was a retired sheep farm labourer and someone who the Traveller's Rest could rely on to turn out in all winds and weathers. The brewery wouldn't get rich on the two pints that Jim allowed himself every night, but he wouldn't give up his nightly visit until they closed the lid on his coffin.

"Not many on the roads tonight," said Jim Thornton as he came further into the warm and inviting room. "It's a darn sight warmer in here than outside. A pint of my usual, please, Rosie."

"On its way, Mr Thornton," said Rosie. "Do you remember when the army started using the Plain?"

"How old do you think I am?" scoffed Jim. "I've lived two miles up the road all my life, and I was born during the

Second World War, but Queen Victoria was still on the throne the first time they used the Plain for exercises."

"Sorry, Mr Thornton," said Rosie. "Alf just thought you might remember reading about when it started. I didn't mean to suggest you were there."

Alf Collett placed the foaming pint on a beer mat on the bar next to their only customer. Jim Thornton handed over a crumpled five-pound note and took a healthy sip of his drink.

"I passed Dave Vickers on his bicycle half a mile back," said Jim. "He's got a better memory than me for facts and figures, young Rosie. I'll tell you what I know, and maybe Dave can fill in the gaps. He'll be here directly."

Alf listened out for the creaking door. Sure enough, Dave Vickers strode through the inner door, cycle helmet under his arm one minute later. A manager of a building society branch in Amesbury, Vickers was in his early fifties, single, overweight, and rosy-cheeked after his cycle ride.

"Golly, it's perishing out there tonight. Evening all," said Dave. "A pint of the usual, please, Rosie."

"I don't understand how you drink cold beer on nights like this," said Rosie with a shiver. "That will be three pounds, please, Mr Vickers."

Dave Vickers moved away from the roaring fire to use the contactless payment machine next to the old-fashioned till on the bar. Jim Thornton tutted and nodded at the two one-pound coins next to his pint glass.

"I can remember when decimalisation came in," Jim moaned. "Forty-odd years ago, a pint of bitter became eight new pence overnight instead of one shilling and sixpence. That's when prices started climbing. It should have been seven pence ha'penny by rights, but the brewery screwed us with a crafty price rise."

"Just over six-and-a-half percent," said Dave.

"If you say so," said Jim. "I know I've got a one-pound coin in my jacket pocket to place alongside these two on the bar when I want my second pint."

Alf Collett could tell where this conversation was heading. Jim Thornton needed to watch every penny as a pensioner. Sheep farming was an honest living, but it didn't give its labourers an inflation-proof company pension when they retired. Jim's state pension and a few savings were everything he had. Jim's wife had worked at a local nursery throughout her married life and wasn't in the best of health these days, which didn't help matters.

"You're a different generation to me, Dave," said Jim. "I thought you had more sense. How will anyone in the future learn the value of money if they tap their way through life without counting the pennies to check they can afford what they're buying?"

Dave Vickers had heard Jim on his high-horse about contactless payments before. Jim was old-school, and Dave hoped cash didn't disappear while people of Jim's generation were still around. Change was painful at any age, but to change the habits of a lifetime was nigh on impossible.

"We'll agree to differ, Jim," said Dave. "I know what I can spend while enjoying a beer on a Friday evening. It's as easy for me to control my expenditure with my phone app as for you to ask your wife for six quid before you leave the house."

Rosie laughed.

"Cheeky young beggar," said Jim. "I don't have to ask permission to pop out for a couple of beers."

Dave took his pint and sat closer to the fire. Alf eyed Jim's glass and prepared to pour his second and final pint for the evening. As Jim took a long swig, almost draining the glass, the outside door heralded another customer.

"Oscar," said Alf. "We haven't seen you in here for a few weeks. Everything alright up at the house?"

Oscar Wallington was the estate manager at the nearby manor house. Alf wasn't sure which regiment Oscar served in, but Oscar left his quarters at Bulford Camp and settled in the area with his family when he'd done his duty. The job at the manor house suited a man well-versed in a disciplined life.

The locals who used the Traveller's Rest reckoned the estate was on the verge of bankruptcy when Oscar took over from the previous manager four years ago. Today, it was in a far healthier financial position, and it wasn't only Oscar's highly polished shoes where the sun shone.

"Best laid plans, Alf," said Oscar. "You know how it is. My wife kept telling me she sticks religiously to this dry January caper. I thought I'd enjoy the extra Scotch we got in for Christmas and New Year and then take a break from the booze in February. After the day I've had up at the manor house, I thought, blow it, I'm dropping by the Traveller's Rest tonight for a wee dram."

"A double?" asked Alf.

"I wasn't aware there was another measure, old chap," said Oscar. "A splash of soda, if you please."

Alf prepared Oscar's drink, and Rosie escaped from behind the bar to warm herself by the fire.

"It could do with another log," said Dave.

"I'm not made of money," said Alf. "It'll be quiet tonight. You can get off home when that fire dies, and I'll close early. Rosie has a tricky drive ahead of her if this weather closes in any further. You appreciate what the Plain can be like this time of year."

"Give that fire a stir with the poker, Rosie," said Dave. "There might be enough life to keep us warm until eleven o'clock."

Jim Thornton finished his first pint and handed his glass to Alf.

"Did you ever wonder what those copper and brass items were hanging in the fireplace, Dave?" he asked, winking at the landlord.

"They look old," said Dave, "but they're for decorative purposes these days, aren't they?"

"Rosie asked why we suffer cold beer in the winter months," said Jim. "One of those Victorian utensils was for warming your beer. Sticking a red-hot poker into a glass of dark, malty beer is an English winter tradition stretching back a thousand years. My grandfather used to drink in this bar and enjoyed sitting where you are now, supping his mulled beer every winter. He told my father he was often troubled with headaches, stomach ache, toothache, coughs, colds, and other rheumatic diseases when he drank cold beer. However, as soon as he started drinking his beer as hot as blood, he stayed in good health throughout the winter."

"It doesn't sound very hygienic," said Rosie, making a face.

"I imagine that was what they used the conical warming vessel on the right-hand side for," said Oscar, sitting on a stool at the bar nursing his double whisky. "Alf's predecessors would fill the vessel, stick it deep in the fire and watch for the foam to form. Then use a tool from the fireside set to help lift it out and pour the warmed beer into a customer's glass. I can't see it making a comeback. Health and Safety would have a field day."

"You still haven't got your answer yet, Rosie," said Jim.

"Ask Mr Wallington when the MoD became so interested in the Plain."

"I was going to ask Mr Vickers," said Rosie.

"I don't know much about those days, Rosie," Dave said. "I learned at school that Salisbury was a prosperous place several centuries ago. Why build a cathedral there if it wasn't? The wealth came from the wool and cloth trade. Those industries declined in the mid-nineteenth century, and Wiltshire had become one of the poorest counties in England by the turn of the century. There were extensive areas of Salisbury Plain where few profitable businesses had survived, so the Ministry of Defence thought they could put the area to better use."

"The training area covers roughly half of the Plain," said Oscar. "The army conducted its first exercises in 1898. From then on, the MoD bought large areas of land until WWII. The one hundred and fifty square miles of land they own makes it the UK's largest military training area. Much of that land is rented to farmers or licenced for grazing. The army keeps fifty square miles for live firing. Public access is greatly restricted or permanently closed in those areas, as you know, Rosie. I'm sure the route you took to drive here tonight was anything but as the crow flies."

"In the dark, it's hard to see crows," said Rosie. "I nearly always get lost, but somehow every lane or track ends up at this pub."

"Our ancestors got a few things right," said Dave Vickers. "They knew the priorities."

"Where do you live, Rosie, if you don't mind me asking?" asked Oscar Wallington.

"Stratford-sub-Castle," Rosie replied. "It used to be a separate village to the north of the city, but it's part of Salisbury these days."

"You live in a cottage next to your old farm, don't you, Jim?" asked Oscar. "Is that far from here?"

"Between here and Chitterne," said Jim. "I passed Dave in Tilshead cycling from Shrewton on my way here."

"I can't imagine you cycling here, Mr Wallington," said Rosie, moving back behind the bar to stand beside Alf Collett.

"No, I've got my trusty old Land Rover Defender outside," said Oscar. "It won't be long before I can take her on the London to Brighton Rally, but she gets the job done. My journey here is around the same as yours, Rosie. Twenty minutes, give or take. My employer's Lodge House lies on the other side of the village of Chitterne."

"It's a sign of the times," said Alf Collett. "The only way a country pub can survive is for people like yourselves to drive from the nearest town or village. Jim here always has two pints and drives home, praying the police aren't waiting for him up at the crossroads. Dave doesn't drive, but you can still be drunk in charge of a bicycle. Many's the night I've locked up as Dave cycles along the road, hitting the grass verge on either side."

"I fell into the hedge one night," said Dave. "A Christmas Eve, I think it was. I was laughing so much I couldn't get up for several minutes."

"Just as well you were wearing a helmet," said Rosie.

"What about you, Oscar?" asked Alf. "Will you want another double scotch?"

Oscar Wallington tapped his nose.

"When you've spent a lifetime learning how to evade the enemy, you work out how to get back to base with no one seeing you."

Jim Thornton rapped his hand on the bar top.

"You crafty beggar," he said. "The Defender comes in handy for that purpose, no doubt."

"She's a four-wheel drive," said Oscar, "and there are a dozen fields between the Traveller's Rest and the Lodge owned by the estate. So I can manoeuvre my way back to my billet, avoiding any places the police might patrol if I've over-indulged."

"I don't think I've ever seen a patrol car out this way," said Rosie, "not since I've worked here."

"My predecessor was fond of a lock-in," said Alf. "Before you ask, Joan would have my hide if I started that game. It has to be ten years since a patrol car idled past the Traveller's Rest looking for someone to nick. As for my licences, they send a young PC during daylight hours to check them."

"Just the one?" asked Dave. "I thought they went nowhere without a colleague."

"The Plain will be unfamiliar territory to many of the youngsters they have working for the police nowadays," said Jim. "I dare them to visit certain parts in the dark, alone, without wondering if ghosts and ghouls hide behind every tree and shrub. I know the area well, and long ago, people rarely strayed more than a few miles from the house where they were born. Sixty years ago, as a young man, I can remember villages within a few miles of this pub populated by only five families."

"Inbreeding going on," muttered Oscar.

"Maybe there was," said Jim. "Perhaps they knew no different. If I developed a thirst after searching for a lost ewe, I might wet my whistle in one of the dozens of nearby pubs that have long since disappeared. When I walked into a bar, everyone's eyes turned towards me. The temperature dropped a few degrees, and conversation died until I had drunk my beer and left. There were rumours of pagan worship in those remote villages and hamlets. I can't swear to any truth behind those rumours, but forget what you believe about the world being a small place. Put yourself in the middle of the Plain, with civilisation miles away. What if a combination of the weather, geography, or circumstances cut you off from the nearest big town? Even the plague if you went back far enough. Who knows what demons might have survived in such a wilderness, real or imaginary?"

"You're a bundle of laughs tonight, Jim," said Alf. "Is it because it's Friday the thirteenth? Do you think something wicked lies in wait outside that front door?"

"I wish I had someone to come home with me later tonight," said Rose. "I'll lock my car doors and turn the stereo up full blast on the way home."

Jim Thornton turned his attention to his pint of bitter. Most of what he just said was a myth, but people underestimated the dangers of the Plain at their peril.

Dave Vickers stared into the fire's glowing embers and wondered if he could afford driving lessons in the spring. He decided it required a fresh pint while he considered. The large clock behind the bar ticked on as the handful of staff and customers sat quietly with their thoughts.

Oscar Wallington ordered another double whisky as the clock ticked to half-past nine. "The last one for me for tonight," he said.

"I don't think Dave and Jim will be far behind you, Oscar," said Alf. "Jim's hung onto that empty glass for long enough."

As Alf slipped a twenty-pound note into the till and sorted Oscar's change, he heard the creaking door. With a sigh, he placed the change on the bar and looked to see his new customer.

"That's all we need," he groaned as he recognised Kendal Guthrie.

The Guthrie family claimed to have farmed on the Plain for centuries. Nobody was too sure when they first moved south from Angus in Scotland, but they lost any trace of an accent several generations back.

Kendal Guthrie was a larger-than-life character and was universally disliked.

At sixty-seven, he was a widower; his wife, Poppy, died eighteen months earlier from a heart attack. The couple had two children. Wesley, married with two sons, lived and worked on one of the five farms currently owned by his wealthy father.

Wesley, at thirty-eight, was two years older than his sister, Helen. She married young at eighteen to Guy Stilwell, a structural engineer, and they emigrated to Melbourne, Australia, four years later. Helen and Guy had no children. Wesley had only seen his sister in the past fourteen years when she flew back alone for their mother's funeral.

Alf Collett patiently waited while Guthrie removed his camelhair coat and looked for an appropriate place to hang it.

"I suppose it's too much to ask that a pub in the back of beyond might possess a coat hanger. This coat cost me twelve hundred quid."

"The wind and rain outside can't tell the difference between it and an old parka," said Alf. "There are several spare pegs on the rack by the door. Take your pick. What can I get you to drink?"

"A gin and tonic. Slimline, no ice, with a twist of lemon. Get the girl to put it together if it's too complicated for you."

Kendal Guthrie strolled to the bar and made a great

show of removing his wallet from his inside jacket pocket. Dave Vickers admired the cut of the dark blue suit Guthrie wore. The building society manager reckoned it would cost him at least a month's wages.

Guthrie watched Alf cutting the evening's first and only slice of lemon. Then he turned to study the person sitting near him at the bar.

"Who do we have here?" he sneered. "A squaddie masquerading as a gentleman farmer. You're a long way from home, Wallington. That Defender of yours outside looks to be on its last legs. Go easy on the whisky. You can't afford to scratch my Bentley Continental GT if you leave here before me tonight."

"My Defender will get me home whatever the weather, Guthrie," said Oscar. "I served my Queen and country for over thirty years, and I was a Warrant Officer Class One for the last thirteen of those years. That's as far as you can get from a raw recruit without a commission. As far as I can tell, the only person you've ever served is yourself."

"Ooh, touched a nerve there, did I? If you fancied a better motor, General, why not do what the estate manager before you did? No wonder the place was losing money. He embezzled over a quarter of a million, or so I heard. A mere twenty grand would be enough for a car that suited a man of your calibre."

Guthrie laughed out loud. Nobody else in the room joined him. Alf knew it wouldn't phase the farmer. It was water off a duck's back. Guthrie relished the fact people hated him. He thought it was because they were jealous of his wealth.

Alf placed the gin and tonic on the bar counter in front of Guthrie and turned away.

"How much do I owe you?" asked Guthrie shifting a wad of banknotes partly from the wallet.

"Four pounds, fifty, Mr Guthrie," said Rosie.

"Ah, the vision of loveliness speaks as well," said Guthrie. "I can see you've not been busy tonight, sweetheart. Can you change a fifty-pound note?"

Guthrie laughed once more when he saw Rosie's head snap around to seek help from Alf.

"Don't worry, sweetheart," said Guthrie. "I've got several of each denomination—even a measly fiver. Put the change in the charity box for Guide Dogs for the Blind. Keep an eye on this one, Alf. She might have sticky fingers like the last girl you had behind the bar. Or was that just a vicious rumour about you and Imogen?"

That set Kendal Guthrie off again. He thought he was highly amusing.

"Well, you can't stop people talking," said Guthrie. "They tell me Joan hasn't come downstairs to work alongside you since Imogen left. You know what they say. No smoke without fire."

"Alf's not like that," said Rosie. "He's been the perfect gentleman ever since I started."

"Imogen did short-change customers," said Dave Vickers. "She couldn't get away with it with us regulars because we're too familiar with the prices. Alf reckoned Imogen was lucky if she got two pounds a night. It was hardly the Great Train Robbery."

"You'd know all about that, wouldn't you, Vickers? Our jovial building society manager offers half of one per cent interest rates. Who does that help? It means people who don't have the first idea about money can borrow it far too easily, while those of us who have worked hard for it get next to nothing for investing several million in your branch."

"I don't set the rates, Guthrie," said Dave. "Blame the Bank of England."

"Funny that, isn't it, General? Dave quickly passes the responsibility on to someone further up the chain. You must have encountered that when you were a serving soldier. Same story, but the other way around. The grunts in the trenches carry the can when something goes wrong in the heat of battle."

Jim Thornton released his grip on his pint glass, stepped away from the bar stool, and lifted his coat from the back of a nearby chair.

"I'll be on my way," he said.

"If the Devil were to cast his net in here tonight, he'd be disappointed," said Guthrie. "All shrimps and no Atlantic bluefin tuna. Jim Thornton, as I live and breathe. What a life, eh Jim? You toiled away for fifty years for Bob Ellison's father, and did you get a gold watch on the day you retired? Did you heck. Now you're spending your last days praying that your poor wife goes first. Does she realise the truth, Jim? Bob told me his old man promised he wouldn't turn you out of your tied cottage until you died. Now Bob has had enough of scraping a living as a sheep farmer and wants to sell the lot, lock, stock, and tied cottages. Fred Ellison was an honourable man; he gave you his word. Nothing in writing though, Jim, was there?"

"Bob won't go back on his father's promise," said Jim. "Not everyone is as devious as you, Guthrie."

"You might have a problem, though, Jim. What do you know of Lower Everleigh? Or farms out at Enford, Ablington, Durrington, and Collingbourne Ducis? Of course, you wouldn't have your finger on the pulse. They're on the latest list from the MoD. Five farms were released for sale to tenant farmers. Little by little, as the General here will confirm, our army is decreasing in size. They don't need the land they amassed before the Second World War. You've got to be quick when you hear a whisper of a release such as that. There's money to be made. I've got my name down for the ones that are the best fit with my portfolio. I won't secure every one of them, but that doesn't matter. Anyway, now I've heard that Bob Ellison's farm is up for grabs, that's one I want, and you know why."

"You own the farms on either side," said Oscar Wallington.

"Give the General a cigar," said Guthrie.

"You wouldn't turn an old couple out of the home they've lived in for half a century," said Dave Vickers.

"That's cruel and vindictive," said Rosie.

"No. That's business, sweetheart," said Guthrie.

"I'm not your sweetheart," yelled Rosie.

"Don't fret, petal. You're too skinny for my taste. That Imogen was a fine-looking woman, but Alf would know better than me whether her performance compensated for the couple hundred pounds she stole from him."

"That's enough, Guthrie," said Alf Collett. "I'm calling time. Ten minutes, and everyone needs to get out. Don't come back, Guthrie. You're barred."

"Hah, they have barred me from better pubs than this dump. If I want a place to drink, perhaps I'll turn Jim's cottage into a roadside tavern for a couple of years. It will take time to get planning permission for residential development for the rest of the land."

"Nigh on impossible," said Oscar.

"You've been out of the army for a while, General," said Guthrie. "Surely, when troops and their families return from the defunct German bases, they will need somewhere to live? Larkhill, Bulford, and Tilshead are right on my doorstep."

Kendal Guthrie waved his wallet as he strolled to collect his coat.

"Money talks."

He was still laughing as Alf heard the front door creak shut behind him.

"He's serious, isn't he, Mr Thornton?" said Rosie.

"I haven't heard a thing from Bob Ellison," said Jim. "I know plenty of farmers, not just on the Plain, have struggled these past few years. Several have got out altogether; the others diversified to survive. Bob's heart was never in it, anyway. Fred struggled to convince him to take over after he retired. While Fred was alive, there was no chance Bob would sell up, but it's been several years since Fred passed. Who knows? Guthrie has had his eyes on that farm for years."

"When did you retire, Jim?" asked Dave Vickers.

"Five years ago, when I reached sixty-five. I was happy to work on, but Bob reckoned I'd done enough to deserve a rest."

"Fred Ellison was older than you, wasn't he?" asked Alf.

"Ten years, maybe," said Jim. "He died two years before I stopped work. So that's seven years ago."

"When did Fred talk with you about the tenancy?" asked Dave.

"He called into the cottage and discussed it with the wife and me shortly after he handed the farm over to his son. He said we deserved to have a roof over our heads for as long as we needed it after staying with him throughout my working life. Fred carried on working until he was

30

seventy. That would have suited me, but Bob put a stop to that. Why, what does it matter?"

"The laws have changed relating to agricultural tenancies over the years," said Dave. "I would contact a solicitor to find out where you stand."

"I can't afford a solicitor," said Jim. "Fred gave me his word. That's good enough for me, and it should also be good enough for Bob. Guthrie likes to stir the pot every chance he gets. One day, he'll go too far, and someone will put an end to it."

Jim wrapped his scarf around his neck and waited until the others were ready to leave. He didn't want to be outside alone with Kendal Guthrie. He'd heard enough from him for one night.

Dave Vickers brought his empty glass to the bar and handed it to Rosie.

"I don't think you're too skinny, Rosie," he said. "Kendal Guthrie's an ignorant pig."

Rosie giggled and collected the handful of empty glasses.

"Take care cycling home, Mr Vickers," she said. "I don't want to see you in the hedge when I drive past. I'll sing at the top of my voice to scare away the bogeyman."

Oscar Wallington was ready to leave, and he went to join Jim by the door.

"We both copped flak from Guthrie tonight," he said. "You're right. It's high time Guthrie got his just deserts."

Dave Vickers didn't pass a comment. He knew he needed to pay a visit before tackling the bike ride home to Shrewton. As Dave headed for the Gents, he noticed Rosie slipping into the Ladies next door. Two minutes later, Dave made his way outside and groaned when he saw the weather had worsened.

Alf Collett waited until the bar was clear of customers and then locked the front door. They hadn't taken enough money to make it worth opening, and Kendal Guthrie had soured what little joy the evening had brought. Alf joined Rosie behind the bar and picked up a cloth to dry the glasses she had finished washing.

"I'll finish these if you want to get off home, Rosie," said Alf.

"We're nearly done. Why do you think Mr Guthrie is so horrible to everyone? Did you see that wallet of his? He had hundreds of pounds, and his watch was a Rolex. Who needs three gold rings on each hand, anyway? It's asking for trouble."

"He'll get what's coming to him," said Alf. "If what Guthrie said to Jim is right, this place could have competition just up the road, which will finish me. Now I've barred him; he's the sort of bloke who would open a pub out of spite, whether or not it made him money. He's a swine, through and through."

Rosie shivered.

"I didn't like how he looked at me," she said. "He gave me the creeps."

Rosie fetched her woolly hat, coat, and gloves from behind the bar, and Alf let her out of the side door.

"Mind how you go, lass," he said. "I'll see you tomorrow."

Alf stood by the door and waited until Rosie reached her car. The barmaid waved a hand as she drove slowly towards the road. Alf waved back. The weather hadn't improved. It was still blowing a gale, and the chilly rain was almost horizontal.

"Friday the thirteenth," tutted Alf as he closed the door.

"Weather like this makes you wonder whether Jim's monsters are on the prowl."

Chapter Three

Saturday, 14 February 2015

"WESLEY?"

Wes Guthrie tried to clear his head. He'd stayed out late, got soaking wet as he walked home, and fell up the stairs at around two o'clock. Millie, his wife, was already awake and downstairs in the kitchen.

Millie cursed him when he finally made it to bed, and when she got up twenty minutes ago, you could have cut the atmosphere with a knife. Wes knew he had a good deal of making-up to do if he could be bothered.

"Wesley? Are you there?"

"Who is that?" he asked.

"Helen, your sister. I know we don't often see one another, but surely you haven't forgotten the sound of my voice."

"Sorry, I had a few drinks last night and am not awake yet. What time is it over there, anyway?"

"Seven in the evening. Guy and I were going out for a

meal. We've found an awesome Italian place on Southbank Riverside."

"Bully for you," said Wes. "What's up?"

"Trust you," said Helen. "It would have been Mum and Dad's fortieth wedding anniversary today. I thought I would call. Dad's bound to be thinking of her."

Wes couldn't think why. His father never gave much thought to anyone or anything except money.

"So, why don't you call him, sis? It will save me the bother."

"No, you don't understand, Wesley. I started ringing him an hour ago with no reply. Do you know if he's away for the weekend?"

"When did he ever go away for the weekend, Helen? Perhaps his phone's on the blink. I'll drive over later. It's too risky for me to drive anywhere yet. Enjoy your meal."

Wes ended the call and staggered to the bathroom.

"Serves you right!" shouted Millie.

Noon had come and gone before Wes felt human enough to drive over to see his father. It wasn't how he would have chosen to spend a Saturday afternoon. He hadn't had a day off since New Year, and after he'd finished work on the farm yesterday, he'd left Tom Dix in charge with instructions not to call before Monday.

"Who is it you're going to see today?" asked Millie as he made ready to leave the house. "The same tart as last night?"

"Don't talk rubbish," said Wes. "I was drinking with my mates. Helen called earlier and said she couldn't get hold of Dad. No idea where the old beggar went in that storm. Let's hope he hasn't wrapped his new car around a tree. I'll be back in an hour."

Wes eased the car into early afternoon traffic on the

A303. Wes, Millie, and the boys lived in Winterbourne Stoke, three miles from Stonehenge, and he was soon turning off the main road towards Durrington. Wes drove past the Stonehenge Inn and took Netheravon Road to Glenhead Farm.

It hadn't always been called Glenhead. Wes couldn't remember whether his grandfather or great-grandfather changed it from New Farm to bring a touch of Angus to Salisbury Plain. Anyway, what idiot decided it was a good idea to call something New whatever? Wes had gone to school in Salisbury, and he knew the New Inn had stood on New Street since the end of the fourteenth century, which made it one of the oldest inns in the country.

Wes continued to consider the irrationality of the study of place names as he negotiated the potholes on the lane leading to his father's farmhouse. He spotted the Bentley parked in front of the double garage. Kendal Guthrie was in residence. His father hadn't yet had a flag designed to fly from the gabled rooftop, but give him time, thought Wes as he pulled up by the main house.

Wes rooted through the pockets of his jeans, hunting for the spare set of keys he'd picked up at home. As he stood outside the large wooden door, his mobile phone rang.

"Did you have a good time last night?"

"Tamsin," said Wes. "Hello, babe. I think you know the answer to that. Look, I can't talk now. I'm standing on my Dad's doorstep. Are you at home? Can I call round in an hour? Less if I can get away from here sooner."

"I'll be here, waiting," replied Tamsin. "Perhaps you can stay longer this time?"

Wes had been seeing Tamsin Meredith for three months. The girl was insatiable. Not that he was complaining. Beautiful, too, with legs that went on forever.

"I told Millie I'd be back in an hour," said Wes. "I'll have to tell her Dad kept me talking. See you soon."

Wes rang the doorbell and listened for his father. Nothing. He could be somewhere on the farm, thought Wes. He rang his father's mobile and realised he could hear its ringtone nearby. Wes frowned. His father went nowhere without his phone. He fumbled with the set of keys and unlocked the door.

"Dad, are you okay? It's Wes. Did you have too much to drink too?"

Wes stood in the hallway and looked upstairs. All was quiet. He took the stairs two at a time and checked the main bedroom, the en suite, and the other rooms on the first floor. There was no sign of Kendal Guthrie. Wes returned downstairs and walked into the spacious lounge/dining room.

"This is like the flaming Marie Celeste," said Wes. "Nothing out of place, but no signs of life."

Wes called out to his father once more as he walked through to the large farmhouse kitchen. He glanced through the windows, trying to spot him in the garden. Wes stood by the butler sink and studied the apple trees overhanging the lawn. Where would his father have gone? Who would know? It was a lousy night, but he'd never sit at home watching TV.

Wes imagined his father had visited someone to discuss business and then drank in a pub that still let him inside the premises. He'd insult everyone in sight, drive home, and because of the weather, use the side door because it was closest to the garage.

Wes turned away from the window and crossed the kitchen to the door leading to the old mudroom. His late mother insisted that anyone, farm worker or local priest, got rid of their shoes before entering the house when there was any risk of mud getting onto her pristine carpets or recently washed flagstone floor.

Wes reached the door and opened it.

Kendal Guthrie lay face down in a pool of blood. He still wore his blue suit, the brand new camelhair coat, and a sturdy pair of muddy shoes.

Wes bent over his father's head and searched for a pulse on the side of his neck. Although he had waited until attempting to drive here, last night's alcohol left him light-headed. Wes knew at once his father was dead. His head swam, and he lurched away from the body and hurried back to the butler sink, where he vomited.

Wes poured a glass of water, drank it, and waited until the dizzy spell settled. He called the emergency services and remained in the kitchen until he heard vehicles coming up the lane. When the front doorbell rang, he took a deep breath and walked through the lounge to answer.

He found two ambulance crew members and two uniformed police officers on the doorstep.

"I'm Wesley Guthrie," he said. "I found my father's body when I arrived here fifteen minutes ago."

"Where is the body, Mr Guthrie?" asked the senior paramedic.

"I'll walk around with you," he said. "My father arrived home, but I've no idea what time. He didn't put the car in the garage. I guess that was because the weather was so dreadful. He must have hurried from the car to this door at the side of the house."

Wes led the three men and one woman to the mudroom door. As they made their way there, Wes flicked through his spare set of keys, hunting for the right one. When he slipped it into the mortice lock, Wes discovered it was open.

The senior paramedic went inside, taking great care not to step into the blood pool. He shook his head.

"Nothing we can do here, I'm afraid. Rigor mortis has set in. This gentleman has been dead for ten to twelve hours, subject to more in-depth tests. He has severe head wounds. There are sharp edges in this mudroom where he could have slipped, fallen, and struck his head as he hurried in from the rain. I can't see any signs of blood anywhere other than on the floor. At first glance, it looks like a tragic accident. How old was your father, sir?"

"Sixty-seven," said Wes. "He was a big man, but he wasn't unsteady on his feet. He kept himself fit throughout his working life. Farming does that to you."

The paramedic returned outside to join his mate.

"I don't know whether it's important," said Wes, looking towards the two police officers, "but Dad would never have left this door unlocked when he went out. So, he had to unlock it when he returned last night."

"Your father was Kendal Guthrie, is that right?" asked WPC Sarah Saunders. "Did he live here alone?"

"My mother died eighteen months ago," said Wes.

"Heart attack, I remember it," said the senior paramedic. "My colleague, Jack, and I came here that day, sir. We did what we could. It devastated your father. Your mother never had a day's illness and then, bang, a massive coronary. Nobody saw it coming."

"It would have been their fortieth wedding anniversary today," said Wes. "My sister called me earlier to say she couldn't get hold of Dad to check he was okay. It would have been an emotional day. I need to ring Helen to let her know."

"Does your sister live locally, Mr Guthrie?" asked Sarah Saunders.

"Melbourne," said Wes. "Moved to Oz years ago. It will be midnight there now. What a mess."

The police officers stood by the open door and viewed the scene inside. Wes moved away towards the garage to call Helen. The paramedics returned to the ambulance and called in their report. When Wes had delivered the news to his sister, he wondered why nobody was doing anything. Everything seemed on hold. What were they waiting for?

A minute later, a car turned off the Netheravon Road and made its way slowly up the lane.

"The cavalry's arrived," said the other police officer, PC Zak Drake.

"Mind your manners," muttered WPC Saunders.

Wes watched as the car drew alongside his Dad's Bentley. A tall, fair-haired driver got out and was joined by his passenger, a stocky, dark-haired younger woman. Wes moved closer to the uniformed officers standing by the mudroom door.

"We'll be with you in a moment, sir," said the driver, who Wes thought looked to be only five years older than him. His colleague was a few years younger than Tamsin, in her late twenties. "I'm Detective Inspector Porter, and my colleague is Detective Sergeant Coleman, by the way."

The detectives spoke to the uniformed officers, glanced inside the mudroom, and then returned to the car. Wes watched as Porter and Coleman donned blue protective suits, overshoes, and hats. The pair disappeared inside, and Wes waited. Sarah Saunders stood outside while Zak Drake fetched two rolls of tape and several wooden pegs from the patrol car.

He cordoned off the Bentley and waited for instructions from the detectives. Sarah could tell Zak was eager to cover as much of the scene as possible with the ubiquitous crime scene tape. The exuberance of youth, she thought. Who said anything about this being a crime scene?

The paramedics received another call-out, and the ambulance reversed away from the farmhouse and disappeared down the lane.

"Right, Mr Guthrie," said Keith Porter, who had emerged from the mudroom. "I'm not convinced this was an accidental death. WPC Saunders tells me your father was fit for his age. If, as you say, he unlocked that door behind us and quickly got inside out of the rain, his first reaction would have been to close the door and lock it. He didn't. If he had done so and then slipped and fell as he made his way to the kitchen, that might explain the serious head wounds."

"Where did your father go last night?" asked Maxine Coleman.

"I don't know," said Wes. "We rarely socialised together."

Wes noticed the glance that passed between Porter and Coleman.

"The weather was dreadful," said Porter. "Are you sure your father didn't leave the door open, anticipating he'd need to get inside in a hurry? WPC Saunders tells us it took you several attempts to find the right key earlier. Difficult in broad daylight, but far more difficult in the dark."

"Take a closer look around you," said Wes. "Everyone on the Plain knew Dad was a wealthy man. He resisted installing CCTV, but he's had security lighting near the house and any farm buildings containing expensive equipment for years. The lights would have come on when he reached the top of the drive and stayed on long enough to reach the door."

"We've checked the mudroom for any signs of a weapon," said Porter. "but found nothing."

"I visited every other room in the house when I arrived, wondering where he'd got to," said Wes, "there's no evidence of a forced entry. Nothing has been disturbed inside."

"Would your father carry cash with him? What about credit cards or a mobile phone?" asked Maxine Coleman.

"You should find a wallet in the left inside pocket of his suit jacket," said Wes. "Dad always carried cash and a lot of it. He distrusted banks and building societies but would have had credit cards. His mobile phone is in his overcoat or his jacket. I heard the ringtone when I called him from the front doorstep."

"Why did you do that?" asked DS Coleman. "Wasn't the bell working?"

"It's a farm," said Wes. "He could have been in one of the barns, in the garage, or walking across the fields."

"Easy to lose track of time when you're walking," said DI Porter. "Did your father wear a watch?"

"A Rolex Submariner," said Wes. He showed the detectives his wrists. "Why wear a watch when you've got a mobile phone in your pocket? It was another status symbol for Dad."

"We found the phone," said Keith Porter. "We'll need to hang on to that. Perhaps it will help us find out where he was last night and who he met. Did your father have any enemies?"

Wes heard the WPC try to turn a stifled laugh into a cough. She was a local woman. Few who had lived on the Plain long hadn't heard rumours. Kendal Guthrie could start an argument in an empty room.

"It's fair to say my father made more enemies than he

did friends," said Wes. "It's one thing to name people who disliked him, and there would be dozens of them; quite another to name someone who would kill him."

"We found the wallet where you suggested he kept it," said Keith Porter. "It was empty, and the Rolex watch was missing. So we could be looking at a robbery that escalated into a violent altercation. As you pointed out, a remote farmhouse owned by a wealthy man will attract every kind of vermin. They might have been after the equipment in the barns, and your father disturbed them when he arrived home. Or they intended to break into the farmhouse, and he returned earlier than expected. Either way, his attacker could be a total stranger."

"They didn't take his rings," said Wes. "I noticed his hands when I checked his neck for a pulse."

"Did you touch anything else, Mr Guthrie?" asked Maxine Coleman.

Wes shook his head.

"If it were a robbery," he said, "and they were prepared to kill my father, surely, they would have taken the rings even if they had to break his fingers to get them off. Dad wore six gold rings, several of them with precious stones. They had to be worth fifteen grand. Dad bragged about them often enough when the price of gold was lower than now."

"Perhaps, the killer didn't want to risk spending too long indoors with the body," said Maxine Coleman. "if it was a stranger, they might not be aware that your father lived alone."

"Maybe," said Wes, "but the killer could have taken the watch and cash to make you think it was a robbery."

"And that's why they left behind the bank cards, rings, and phone," said Keith Porter. "An interesting thought."

"Can you tell us where you were yesterday evening, Mr Guthrie?" asked DS Coleman. "It's standard procedure. We'll ask everyone who could have come into contact with your father the same question."

"I was out drinking with a group of mates," he replied. "Guys that I was at school with in Salisbury. We get together from time to time. I drank too much, as usual, and didn't drive here from our farm in Winterbourne Stoke until I felt safe to drive. My mates and I met at nine o'clock, and Millie, my wife, will confirm that I fell up the stairs at around two this morning. I can remember the first two pubs we visited, but I don't know where we went after closing. I walked home in that pouring rain. I remember that my coat was still wet when I left the house to come here."

"We'll talk to you again," said Keith Porter. "If we need the names of those drinking buddies, it won't be a problem, will it?"

"No, not a problem. What happens next?"

"We'll get our forensic people to go through everything in greater detail. We won't know for certain that we have a murder enquiry on our hands until we hear the post-mortem results. Only then will we have definitive proof of whether the fatal injuries were accidental. Did you touch anything inside the house while wandering around?"

"Several door handles," said Wes. "I poured myself a glass of water after I was sick in the kitchen sink. It was such a shock. Dad upset plenty of people, but he seemed indestructible."

"How long has he had the Bentley Continental?" asked Keith Porter.

"Less than a year," said Wes.

"A GPS tracking device would be standard on a car such as that," said Maxine Coleman.

"If it was, he didn't tell me about it," said Wes. "I doubt he would have bothered learning how to use it. He had a satnav, though. Why?"

"We could use that to learn where he went last night," said Maxine. "Perhaps he upset someone, and they followed him home, killed him, and took the watch and money to throw us off the scent."

"I know Dad disliked the idea of keyless entry," said Wes. "Even though car thieves found ways to activate fob keys even when locked inside someone's house. His car keys must be in one of his pockets. Do you honestly think a burglar could resist driving off in a two hundred grand motor?"

"They could never sell a supercar like that to a bloke down the pub," said Keith Porter. "If they knew the right people, they could either get it into a container bound for Africa or rip out half a dozen high-priced parts and sell them on eBay. It's looking less of a robbery every minute, Mr Guthrie. Ah, here come the forensic guys."

"We'll check for that location tracking device," said Maxine. "His satnav might give us details of trips he's made further back than yesterday evening. Our people will be here for several hours yet. You can get off home, Mr Guthrie. Better for you to inform family members before our significant presence alerts the local newshounds and the nosy neighbours. Can we hang on to that spare set of keys, please? When we're done, I'll get the uniformed officers to drop them into your farmhouse in Winterbourne Stoke. We can soon find your address."

Wes walked to his car and drove slowly down the lane to Netheravon Road. Then, turning left to head back to the A303, he saw Porter on his mobile phone. Coleman was speaking to a group of people in white suits.

"That was naughty, guv," said Maxine Coleman.

"Guthrie reckoned he got so drunk he couldn't recall specific details after around eleven o'clock. Winterbourne Stoke only has a couple of pubs. He walked home in the early hours. Where did he spend the missing hours?"

"If Traffic intercepts him on the main road, do you think he'll fail the breath test?"

"Finding his father dead could have caused him to throw up," said Keith Porter. "I have a hunch he was still hanging when he arrived here, and discovering the body was the final straw. He's hiding something, Max. I don't know what, but if he's done for drink driving, it might make him wake up his ideas and start telling the truth."

"With this family's money, he'll get a top-class brief. So traffic had better find a plausible reason to stop his car."

"They don't need a specific reason, Max," said Keith, "but I noticed his licence plate was muddied and suspicious. The five and nine on the number plate were further apart than they should be. Easy to read it as WES 9 RHM. I'd like to see a brief get around that. So, a legal stop, and then, have you had a drink today, sir? Piece of cake."

"What if he's under the thirty-five limit by this time?" asked Maxine.

DI Keith Porter shrugged.

"I suggested to Traffic that they do him for the number plate offences."

"Do you think he killed his father, guv?"

"How far is it from Winterbourne Stoke to this farm? Seven or eight miles. Thirty minutes by car in that storm. Don't forget to ask for the names of those mates he drank with in the village. He could have left them at eleven, driven here to lie in wait for his father, killed him, and then driven home. That story about getting soaked when he walked home could have been rubbish. Maybe he got soaked standing in the dark by the mudroom door."

"It was Wes who suggested the attacker took the watch and cash to throw us off the scent, guv. You said it was an interesting thought."

"Interesting and clever if he's our killer," said Keith Porter. "I don't know. We might be barking up the wrong tree. Did you hear the WPC when we asked if Kendal Guthrie had any enemies?"

"I spoke with her about that, guv," said Maxine. "Sarah Saunders reckoned the queue of people who hated Guthrie's guts would stretch down the lane and most of the way back to the Stonehenge Inn."

"Is it worth hanging around much longer?" asked Keith. "We could drive back to the station and salvage our Saturday afternoon. SOCO will be working here for hours. Who knows when the autopsy will get done? Where are those car keys, anyway?"

DS Coleman handed the keys to her DI. This was typical of Keith Porter. He had a sharp mind, and Maxine had to admit she hadn't spotted the number plate infringement, but his enthusiasm wore off too quickly. She wanted to chase up Kendal Guthrie's close contacts and start grilling them about where they were between eleven and one o'clock yesterday evening.

Keith Porter opened the driver's door of the Bentley Continental and whistled.

"How the other half lives," he said.

Maxine Coleman strolled across the yard to join him. She wasn't a petrol head. It was only a car and an obscene amount of money for a rich man's toy.

"Forensics haven't touched this yet, guv. Please don't sit in the driver's seat to see how it feels. Let SOCO retrieve the satnav data and anything from the GPS tracking system. It's their job. Let's get back to the station if you've had enough for this afternoon."

"Aren't you curious?" asked Keith. "Why have a double garage unless you've got something else to drive? I bet it's a Land Rover Discovery with a sticker on the rear window. My other car's a Bentley."

Keith Porter found the garage key fob on the same key ring, and they watched as the up-and-over electric doors slowly opened. The space on the left for the large supercar was empty, but a protective sheet covered a car on the right.

"What do you think?" asked Keith. "Something sporty? It's not a Discovery or anything too bulky."

He dragged the sheet over the bonnet to reveal a ten-year-old red Ford Focus.

"Put the sheet back, Keith," said Maxine. "Kendal Guthrie might have been a swine in his dealings with all and sundry, but he couldn't face getting rid of his wife's pride and joy."

"That's me told," said Keith, replacing the sheet and giving the bonnet a gentle tap. "I suppose a drink's out of the question after we finish at the station?"

"God loves a trier, guv," laughed Maxine.

Chapter Four

"HAVE YOU HEARD THE NEWS?"

"No, Alf," said Rosie, "I haven't been near a TV. I went shopping with my Mum this afternoon. Why, what's happened?"

"No, it's news closer to home. Doug Lawless rang half an hour ago to tell me the police have people at Kendal Guthrie's place over at Glenhead Farm."

"You've lost me," said Rosie. "I've never met Doug Lawless, have I?"

"Sorry, lass," said Alf, "Doug's Kendal Guthrie's neighbour. He farms the land closer to the village of Durrington. Harry Meaden's family has owned the farm on the other side of Glenhead for over a hundred years. I'm sure you'll guess from last night's performance that neither Doug nor Harry have a kind word to say about Guthrie."

"I wouldn't want that horrid man as my next-door neighbour," said Rosie.

Rosie had just walked through the side door, ready to start the evening shift. Alf had coped alone with the lunchtime trade, and as his wife, Joan wasn't prepared to work behind the bar these days. Alf asked Peggy Hollins, a widowed lady who lived two doors away, to work a couple of hours in the afternoon before Rosie arrived at seven o'clock.

Rosie took off her coat, removed her hat and scarf, and shook her head to encourage her hair into a semblance of order.

"At least now that storm has blown over, we should get more customers tonight," she said. "How was it earlier?"

"Pretty good," said Alf. "I was busy between twelve and two. Peggy tended the bar while I ate my lunch and had a nap. It's always quieter mid-afternoon, and if Peggy's a tad slower than most at serving people, they don't complain."

"That's because most drove here and aren't on a mission to get drunk," said Rosie. "The pub is a good place to spend two or three hours away from the wife and kids. You've got the TV for horse racing and football."

Alf watched as Rosie moved around the room, squaring up tables, tucking chairs underneath, and replacing soggy beermats. She returned to the counter and leaned against it.

"What did Mr Lawless think had happened at Guthrie's farm? Did someone steal his tractors? OMG, what if someone nicked that car of his? He'll be livid."

"Doug was driving past the farm on his way home from Andover. He'd watched the Town's football team winning another home match in the Wessex League. The farmhouse and the garage were lit up like a Christmas tree. He could see Guthrie's Bentley parked outside, surrounded by tape. Doug spotted several people in white coveralls moving here and there."

"If aliens were ever going to land here, the Plain would

be the perfect spot," said Rosie. "Was he sure the police were involved?"

"It's fifty years since the first UFO sightings near Warminster, lass," said Alf. "They haven't been back since the Seventies, as far as I know. If they were ever here."

"Warminster isn't much over twelve miles from here," said Rosie. "I was kidding. The men in white suits put the idea in my head. There *were* aliens on the Plain, then?"

"Maybe there were, maybe there weren't, lass. I reckon they took one look at Jim Thornton's monsters and tried elsewhere."

"I wish he hadn't told us that story," said Rosie. "I had nightmares."

The front door creaked regularly over the next hour as customers entered and left. When Jim Thornton came through the inner door by twenty past eight, Alf and Rosie had a decent crowd enjoying a drink and a chat. Alf's face wore a smile for the first time in weeks as the kerching from the till confirmed takings were back to normal.

Jim Thornton edged his way to the bar and found one empty stool. Rosie spotted him, smiled, and called out.

"I'll get your pint of bitter in two ticks, Mr Thornton."

"Thank you, Rosie," said Jim.

Rosie pulled Jim's first pint and set it in front of him. Jim handed her three one-pound coins.

"Have you heard about the excitement in Durrington?" said Rosie.

"Nothing exciting has happened there in my lifetime," said Jim.

"Alf said he heard the police were at Kendal Guthrie's farm," said Rosie.

"Nothing trivial, I hope," said Jim.

A young lad waiting to get served beside Jim turned around.

"He's dead, mate. My father drove past the farm at six o'clock. People were removing a body from the house and putting it in a van. Dad reckoned it headed for Salisbury."

"Mr Guthrie was here last night," said Rosie. "There was only a handful of us present. That man was rude to every one of us. I can't say I'm sad to hear he's gone. What was it? A heart attack, the same as his wife?"

"If he had a heart," said Jim.

"The police had set up a cordon," said the customer. "They weren't letting anyone get near the place. No idea whether he died from natural causes, an accident, or someone killed him. I don't suppose we'll hear for definite until Monday."

"That changes things for you, Jim," said Alf, "and Bob Ellison too. I wonder whether Wes Guthrie will be as vindictive as his father when he takes over the business?"

"Do you think the police will come here?" asked Rosie.

"You should call them," said the young lad. "You can tell them what time he left here. How long would it take him to drive home from this pub?"

"Twenty minutes, at least," said Alf. "Perhaps twenty-five. I closed early because of the weather. I was keen to let Rosie here drive home to Salisbury. Jim was making his way to the door. What do you reckon, Rosie? Five or ten minutes after ten?"

"It was soon after you told Mr Guthrie he was barred," said Rosie. "I remember that. Jim and Oscar must have followed Mr Guthrie to the car park. Dave was just leaving when I got back behind the bar. There was nobody outside a few minutes later when you let me out the side door, Alf. They had all gone."

"Did you pass Dave Vickers cycling home to Shrewton?" asked Alf.

"Yes," said Rosie. "He hadn't got very far. I expect it was hard work cycling in that wind."

"He might have stopped to talk with Guthrie," said Jim Thornton. "I didn't hang around once I got in the car. No way was I going to wait in the wind and rain to waste my breath on that devil."

"You told Kendal Guthrie he wasn't welcome here anymore?" asked the young lad. "There can't be many pubs where he's still allowed over the threshold. The police are going to be interested to hear that piece of news for sure."

"What did you want to drink?" said Alf.

He was keen to get the young lad away from the bar. He looked at the clock. Dave Vickers didn't always come in on Saturday nights, but Oscar Wallington might drop by in the next half hour. Alf decided he'd ask Oscar whether they should contact the police or wait until they knew how Guthrie died.

Oscar breezed through the door just after nine. Several customers recognised him, and it took him minutes to make it to the bar. Alf had his glass of whisky ready and waiting.

"Thanks, Alf," said Oscar. "I need that. What a day."

"I know," said Alf. "I didn't hear a thing until half-past six. A lad in the corner filled in a few details. I was wondering whether I should give the police a call."

"What are you on about, Alf?" said Oscar, picking up his double whisky.

"Didn't you hear? Guthrie's dead. Police and a forensic team have been at the farm throughout the afternoon."

"It never rains, but it pours," said Oscar. "I was supposed to have a day off today, but two emergencies cropped up on the estate. Instead of taking my good lady wife out for a meal tonight, I'm restricted to a swift one and then a quiet night at home."

"You said it never rains, Mr Wallington," said Rosie, as another happy customer eased past Oscar on their way to their table with a tray of drinks.

"I needed to go to Amesbury late this afternoon searching for a spare part. I overheard a conversation at the counter in the Home store. Kendal's son, Wes, got stopped on the A303 at around two o'clock. He must have blown over thirty-five on the breathalyser because the police took him away in the patrol car."

"Where does the son live then, Mr Wallington?" asked Rosie.

"Winterbourne Stoke," said Oscar. "He's a farmer, the same as his father."

"He must have had a skinful Friday night," said Alf. "Or he was dumb enough to drink at lunchtime."

"The guy in the Home store said Guthrie had just joined the A303 at the roundabout," said Oscar. "He came from somewhere such as Larkhill, Bulford, or Durrington."

"His father's farm is further on from Durrington village," said Jim. "Wesley was probably visiting his old home."

"Did Kendal speak with you or Dave when you left here?" said Alf.

"I didn't give him a chance," replied Oscar. "I drove towards Chitterne as soon as I could. Dave stayed in the hallway, putting on his helmet. He told me he had a pair of over-trousers in the pannier on his bicycle. I watched him struggling to get those on near the bike shelter as I drove away. Kendal would have used the same road as Dave and Jim towards Shrewton before taking the A303 and then the minor road to Durrington. Did you see him, Jim?"

Jim shook his head.

"I didn't see anyone on the road in both directions and was indoors within five minutes."

"Well, do you think I should give the police a call?" said Alf.

"Why?" asked Oscar. "Wes Guthrie could have reached the farm and discovered a burglary. What makes us certain someone died? The police would send SOCO for a robbery, especially if the victim were a prominent local citizen like Kendal Guthrie."

"That young lad with his girlfriend," said Alf nodding to the couple in the far corner. "His father told him he saw a body on a trolley. A van took the body towards Salisbury."

"I see," said Oscar. "Maybe his son found the body and had a stiff drink before dialling 999. It stinks, though, doesn't it?"

Alf's mind was on the same wavelength.

"I wouldn't put it past them," he said.

"You've lost me," said Rosie.

"Uniformed officers would be first on the scene," said Oscar, "along with paramedics, to see what's what. Once they knew what they were dealing with, they'd call for a detective team. Whoever was in charge smelt alcohol on Wes Guthrie's breath and stitched him up. They made a phone call, asking for a patrol car to find a reason to stop and breathalyse him."

"Why would they do that?" asked Rosie. "That's sneaky."

"Maybe they think Wes killed his father," said Alf.

"In which case, he deserves a medal," said Jim.

Rosie Ritchens decided it was time to do the rounds of the tables to collect empty glasses. It gave her time to think. There must be a pub in Salisbury in need of a barmaid.

Somewhere closer to home, that saved her the drive on filthy nights like last night.

The journey wasn't her primary concern. She wondered how long before the police learned about the ruckus Kendal Guthrie caused here. Rosie knew she had driven home alone and saw nobody until she got within two hundred yards of her parents' house.

What a pity she hadn't stopped to give the bloke a lift. He was soaked, but he could have given her an alibi for where she was at a quarter to eleven. Kendal Guthrie had pitched into Oscar, Dave, Jim, and Alf. Even she hadn't escaped the sharp edge of his tongue.

What if one of them followed Mr Guthrie home and killed him?

Rosie was confident it hadn't been Dave Vickers. He didn't drive, and it would have taken him an hour by bicycle if he hadn't got blown into a hedge halfway there. Rosie knew the building society manager had a soft spot for her. Dave was far too old for her, even if she fancied him, which she didn't. Rosie thought he was harmless, although she wouldn't miss Dave gazing at her with those puppy-dog eyes if she did find another job.

After that, Rosie thought things became more tricky. Mr Thornton had motive and opportunity. Because he left the pub car park before the others, he could have reached the farm before Guthrie. If Mr Ellison sold his farm to Guthrie, old Jim and his wife would get turfed out of house and home. Rosie had seen Jim's reaction when he heard that shocking news. Yes, Mr Thornton would have felt justified in ridding the world of Kendal Guthrie and his lust for money.

Rosie didn't always know what to make of Oscar Wallington. He'd been a soldier ever since leaving school until only recently. These days he was an estate manager. The two roles were different, yet Rosie suspected Mr Wallington had never adapted. His manner, and the way he spoke, retained an edge that implied authority and superiority. That was it. Rosie was proud of herself for that analysis. Mr Wallington always gave the impression that people like Alf and her should respect him.

Oscar didn't appreciate it when Guthrie teased him last night, calling him General and suggesting a car that cost a fraction of his Bentley Continental was good enough for the likes of Mr Wallington. Guthrie hinted Oscar was the sort of character who stole from his employers. Oscar wouldn't have enjoyed that. Rosie remembered when he'd tapped his nose, showing off about being skilled at avoiding the enemy and taking to fields and bridle paths to get home without detection.

No, telling Alf Collett she was looking for another job was best. After all, Alf had lingered by the door and watched her scurry to her car, then waited until she pulled away before waving. Did he wait until her rear lights disappeared from view and then leave the pub? Joan would have been none the wiser.

Alf could have driven after Kendal Guthrie and arrived at his farm in time to kill him, driven back here by a quarter past eleven, and gone upstairs to bed. If Joan woke up, it would be earlier than Alf got to bed most Friday nights. It wouldn't have seemed suspicious.

Alf's motive was less clear than Jim Thornton's. But suppose her boss wanted this pub to remain financially viable. What better way to secure its future than removing the man who hinted at opening a rival watering hole two miles away after Alf barred him? Then there was that accusation Mr Guthrie made concerning Imogen, the girl who worked behind the bar before she started here. So far, Alf had been the perfect gentleman, but what if he was waiting for the right opportunity to try something? It didn't bear thinking about. No, she would start looking for another job tomorrow. Somewhere with a younger crowd, where she might find a boyfriend nearer to her age.

Rosie returned to the bar to see Alf, Jim, and Oscar watching her.

"Everything okay, Rosie?" Alf asked.

"Daydreaming," she said.

Sunday, 15 February 2015

MAXINE COLEMAN WAS out on the streets bright and early. Physical exercise was something she hoped to have left behind her after her school days. Ten years later, much of which she spent at a desk or sat in a police car, had resulted in her weight creeping higher than she wished.

Why did it have to be so blessed cold in February? Maxine pounded the pavements close to her flat, hoping a three-mile run before breakfast helped shed a pound or two. Guys like Keith Porter kept mentioning her curves as if they were something to celebrate. Maxine wanted to lose the tummy she'd developed and not have a bottom that threatened to challenge the Kardashian clan at the rate it was growing. Or was it Klan?

Maxine had successfully avoided seeing Keith Porter at the station after they drove back from Glenhead Farm. His car had gone from the car park when she ventured outside. After picking up shopping on her way home, Maxine took a bath, wrapped herself in her onesie and fluffy dressing gown, and switched on Netflix.

Why did she prefer a bottle of Prosecco and 'Blood Ties' to going on a date on a Saturday night?

Maxine tried to push those thoughts from her mind. She planned to go into the office for a couple of hours this afternoon. Forensic results wouldn't be available just yet, and Keith had texted her late last night to say the autopsy was on Monday morning at nine o'clock. Her boss asked if she minded attending, as he had a meeting. That was bull. Nobody enjoyed autopsies, but Maxine had never had to run out of one yet, or vomited halfway through, unlike someone she could mention.

Keith had sent that text message as late as possible to annoy her. Maxine sent a terse reply, indicating she would be there on the dot. Timekeeping and DI Porter were strangers. When another message arrived on her phone, she feared the worst. Please, don't let there be any attachments to this text, she begged. It was okay. Keith had resisted the urge to send her a photograph.

In the second message, Keith told her Traffic had stopped Wes Guthrie, and he'd blown thirty-eight at the roadside. The traffic cops took him back to the station, and Guthrie had the nous to delay the test long enough to put him in the clear. Keith had told them to carry on with the number plate offence. It didn't carry a points penalty, but it could attract a thousand pounds fine depending on the judge.

Maxine hadn't bothered to reply. She could imagine Keith grinning like a Cheshire cat, thinking he'd got one over on the high and mighty Guthrie family. What a loser.

After she completed her run, Maxine showered and prepared a smoothie in place of the cooked breakfast she craved. It tasted marginally better than it looked. It was time to drive into the office to compile lists of people to interview. While there, Maxine thought she might drop by the forensic department to see the progress they'd made on the victim's satnav and mobile phone.

Maxine didn't think Wes Guthrie had killed his father. No, there was a killer among the dozens of people known to have hated Kendal Guthrie with a vengeance who was lying low today, thinking they had every chance of getting away with murder.

"Not on my watch," said Maxine Coleman. "Not if I can help it."

IN WINTERBOURNE STOKE, it was déjà vu all over again for Wes Guthrie as noon approached.

He remembered little of the French he learned at school, but the house had a certain froideur just like yesterday.

Wes wasn't worried about how hefty a fine he'd receive if the police carried out their threat to fine him for the rogue letter five. In the past six months, he'd seen a hundred vehicles with dodgy number plates on the roads, and the police didn't give a toss.

As soon as he spotted the blue lights in his rear-view mirror yesterday afternoon, he knew that Detective Inspector Porter had thought of a way to score a point. His father had warned him and Helen when they were teenagers that when you're successful, people are jealous, even if you've achieved success through hard graft.

They'll do whatever it takes to bring you down or find a way to let themselves feel they've got the better of you. It had become human nature. More so for people in this country than anywhere else, or so Wes Guthrie thought.

Millie had started into him as soon as he got home from the police station.

"An hour, you said. What sort of clock are you looking at?"

"Shut up, Millie, will you," he snapped. "My Dad's dead. Someone killed him last night. I found him lying in the mudroom."

"I'm sorry, Wes. How was I to know? Was it a break-in? What were they after?"

"It didn't appear to be a burglary, and until they do the autopsy, the police won't know how Dad died. His wallet was empty, and his Rolex was missing, but he still had his credit cards and mobile phone in his pockets. That doesn't seem right. He had his car keys in his coat pocket, too, so if it was a robbery, why didn't they drive away in his prized motor?"

"Kendal wasn't my favourite person in the world, but I've never wished him dead. Poor Helen, this will devastate her."

"I called Helen already. She and Guy had just arrived home from a night out at a restaurant. Not a great end to the day. She'll call in a day or two to find out when the police say I can arrange the funeral. Helen wants to fly home as she did for Mum."

"Will she be able to stay at the farmhouse?"

"I'm not sure she'd want to. We'll cross that bridge when we come to it. There's something else. I got stopped on the way home. I was still marginally over the limit after last night."

"You idiot, Wes. How could you run the farm if you lost your licence?"

"It won't come to that, Millie. I blew over on the preliminary breath test at the roadside. Both readings were under the limit when I used the machine at the station an hour later. They tested a blood sample too, so there's no reason to worry about getting an endorsement."

"You're still an idiot. If you hadn't got drunk with those mates of yours, you wouldn't have needed to wait until lunchtime to drive to your Dad's farm. What if he was still alive?"

"The paramedic said Dad died somewhen between eleven and one last night. Look, I may as well tell you. I escaped the points on my licence, but they stopped me because of my number plate. They reckoned it was filthy, and because I asked a guy at the garage to move the five and nine further apart, it broke the law."

"You're joking? There are hundreds of dodgy plates on the roads. Some make me laugh, and others make me cringe. No wonder the police get so much flak if they chase you for a trivial offence the same day someone murders your father. Well, that's it, Wes, you must change it. They've got you on their radar now."

Wes had to admit Millie was right. The trouble was, he knew that wasn't the worst of it. The police would soon ask for the names of the guys he was drinking with last night. As the evening wore on, Wes watched TV with Millie, but nothing sank in. He kept seeing his Dad's body on the floor in the mudroom and wondering who killed him and why.

News of his father's death had spread across Salisbury and the Plain by the morning. Wes knew that people would ring the house, passing on their condolences, expressing disbelief, or telling him what goes around comes around. It takes all sorts.

He'd taken a break from answering the house phone at

half-past ten and made himself a coffee. As he sat in the conservatory, staring into the garden, he heard the phone ring again. Mille answered. That was when the proverbial hit the fan.

His wife had stood in the doorway with her hands on her hips.

"So, where were you after eleven o'clock on Friday night, Wes?"

John Goodwin had just called to say how sorry he was to hear the news. He asked Millie to pass on a message that Chris Barton had taken a flight to Malta on Saturday evening and was unaware of what had happened. John had told Millie they had a great evening on Friday, but Chris had wanted to cut things short as he had a big day ahead.

"I carried on drinking on my own," said Wes.

"A likely story," said Millie. "Have the police asked where you were? We've watched enough cop shows to know they suspect a member of the family first."

"I told them I was out, drinking, until two o'clock. I said you'd remember me falling up the stairs when I got home. The senior detective asked if I could name the guys I was drinking with when they called me for an official interview. I said it wouldn't be a problem."

"What did you plan to do, Wes? Call John and Chris beforehand and ask them to lie?"

"Something like that. I didn't kill my father," said Wes.

"No, I don't believe you did, but you do have something to hide," said Millie. "I'm not stupid. The police might treat you as a genuine suspect if the tart you've been seeing doesn't give you an alibi."

Wes reckoned that was when the froideur set in, and he wondered how much worse things could get. He'd finished his cup of coffee ages ago. As Wes stood in the kitchen waiting for the kettle to boil, he learned the answer to his question.

Tamsin had rung his mobile phone ten times already that morning. Wes had enough things to cope with, so he ignored her. But as well as being insatiable in bed, Tamsin was persistent. The silly cow rang his home number. Wes was pouring the water into his mug when Millie's voice rose two octaves in the hallway, and the neighbour's dog pricked up its ears.

Wes closed his eyes and prayed.

"It's for you, Wes," spat Millie. She turned on her heel and stomped upstairs. The house shook as she slammed their bedroom door.

Wes wandered into the hallway and picked up the phone.

"Hello?" he said.

"Oh, darling. I'm so sorry. Your poor Dad. It must be dreadful for you."

Wes carried the phone through to the conservatory and closed the door.

"Why did you ring me at home?" said Wes. "I would have answered my mobile when I was good and ready. Do you have any idea what damage you've done?"

"Well, pardon me for breathing," said Tamsin. "I thought we had something special. All I said was that I was a friend and wanted to pay my respects. Your wife went through the roof."

"She hadn't suggested she suspected anything until yesterday morning," said Wes. "I got home later than I normally do when I have a drink with the lads, but Millie was straight in with the barbed comments. Then, one of my mates called this morning, and Millie answered. She now knows I wasn't with them after eleven o'clock. No big surprise, Millie wanted to know where I spent the next three hours. Come to that, so will the police."

"You can't tell them you were with me," said Tamsin.

"If I don't have an alibi, they'll start fitting me up for the murder. Why the hell can't I give them your name?"

"We've only known one another for three months," said Tamsin. "I thought it was going somewhere, and your marriage was over. Now, I feel you were using me to get what you weren't getting at home."

"That's not true, Tamsin," said Wes. "I do have feelings for you. This is important. I really need you to tell the police where I was on Friday night."

"I know you do, Wes. You know what you have to do to keep me sweet. Tomorrow night after work. Don't be late."

Tamsin ended the call. Wes looked at the handset. He had little choice, did he?

Chapter Five

Monday, 30 March 2015

KEITH PORTER SLOUCHED through the squad room door and slumped into his chair. Maxine Coleman feared the worst. Keith got their boss's call as soon as they'd arrived this morning. For six weeks, they had toiled over the Guthrie case. Six weeks of long hours, hundreds of interviews, and countless reviews of the evidence they had collected, searching for something to break the deadlock.

"What's the verdict, guv?" asked Maxine.

"The DS wants us to move on," said Keith. "We'll be working with different teams in the future. My team will tackle the significant increase in violence against the person, which has shot up by a quarter in the past twelve months. We can't argue with the facts, Max. Despite the resources we threw at the case, we've not identified Guthrie's killer, and this dramatic rise needs nipping in the bud. A large portion of these violent attacks had a sexual content. We'll make the streets safer rather than chasing around the Plain hunting for a ghost."

"Where will I be working?" asked Maxine.

"On another hot potato which the Police and Crime Commissioner dropped on the gaffer's desk. You'll be monitoring the incidence of Islamophobic hate crime."

"Wonderful," said Maxine. "How can less than half of one percent of the county's population generate a hot potato? It will be a public relations exercise and nothing more. The PCC wants the public to see we're ticking the boxes towards an inclusive society. So I'll spend a month helping to produce a report that tells him what we already know. Four people a week, on average, hear something that offends them, and one person gets physically attacked because of their race or religion. I know that's too many, Keith, but is it the most pressing thing on our agenda?"

"Ours is not to reason why, Max," said Keith. "Today's the last day we're paired together. It's been a pleasure. Even though you never succumbed to my subtly romantic advances."

"I've learned a lot from you, Keith," said Maxine. "I'm sure it will stand me in good stead in the future. By the way, subtlety isn't one of your strong points."

"I'll work on it," said Keith. "Don't take this the wrong way, Max, but are you eating and sleeping okay? Has this case got to you? You look thinner in the face."

"I'm eating and sleeping fine, Keith," groaned Maxine. "Whenever I found a spare hour over the past six weeks, I went running. For some unknown reason, although I've shed a few pounds and have blisters on every toe, the weight hasn't gone from the targeted areas."

DI Keith Porter looked puzzled, and then the penny dropped.

"The exercise won't harm you, Max," he said. "Just don't overdo it. I know we won't see as much of one another after today, but when our paths cross, I hope your best assets haven't disappeared altogether."

Maxine smiled. She hoped to find someone to appreciate the total package, not simply the assets Keith had admired every day he sat across the desk from her. He'd never change.

Keith Porter gathered a group of files from his desk, sighed, and looked around for a box to hold them. Once he'd located an empty box with a bottom he could rely on, Keith stowed the files, emptied his drawer of his bits and pieces, and with a nod, crossed the squad room to join his new colleagues.

Maxine knew she should have asked Keith whose team she was joining. She hoped it was a DI she could get along with. The other members of their old team would be scattered around the station by now, doing the same as Keith Porter. They would focus on a new set of problems, and most of them would already have consigned the Kendal Guthrie murder case to history.

That was the nature of modern policing. Results had to be immediate, if not sooner. The severity of the offence was less critical today in determining how to assign resources. As a result, killers and rapists went free because the volume of hours required to get a result wasn't cost-effective. The current thinking was that by tackling vehicle crime, there was added value from the number of drug offences identified.

Traffic cops termed it a 'double bubble' because as well as getting a driver for speeding, they could pile on charges for driving while disqualified or without a licence. The vast majority of drivers they stopped didn't have insurance either. As they sat in the car filling out yet another piece of paperwork, the officers slipped in the 'have you had a drink today' question. That was another tick in the box. But their best opportunity to get a full house was when they stood by the driver's window at the initial stop. They didn't need to concoct a reason to search the car. Almost every young driver they pulled over had a strong smell of cannabis inside their vehicle. So, even if the lad passed the breathalyser, there was a good chance the drug wipe would come up trumps with a fail, and then the search uncovered various amounts of weed.

Maxine ticked off the possible offences on her fingers. On a good day, traffic could get six 'results' from a stop that tied them up for a mere few hours. The courts let most offenders off with community service or a suspended sentence, so what was the point? Still, the 'results' counted towards an improving picture when compiling annual statistics that included every conceivable type of crime.

Meanwhile, Maxine had lost count of the hours she'd worked on the Guthrie case. Someone must have logged the whole team's hours somewhere, plus the input from forensics and the computer nerds. They must have been astronomic.

Maxine reflected on how Keith had run the investigation and whether she would have done things differently. She'd attended the autopsy first thing on Monday, just two days after the murder. The police surgeon confirmed the victim died from blunt force trauma. Kendal Guthrie received two severe blows to the top of his head from behind and one to the right-hand side just above the ear. They never identified the murder weapon, but the surgeon described it as likely to be a heavy, cylindrical instrument with no perceivable grooves or raised parts.

Maxine had never understood why he couldn't call it an iron bar and have done with it.

Kendal Guthrie suffered bruising to both sides of his torso. The bruising was consistent with Guthrie having fallen forwards following the initial blow to the top of his head and struck the corner of the chest freezer on the right of the mudroom. The police surgeon thought Guthrie could have regained his footing and been hit on the top and the left-hand side of the head.

As the attacker was now facing him, it opened up the possibility the attacker was left-handed. The bruising on the other side of his torso could have occurred when he fell for the last time and struck the metal workbench on the left-hand side of the mudroom.

Maxine was about to risk questioning that comment when the police surgeon added that the sequence of events could have been quite different. He couldn't say for definite whether the attacker was right-handed or left-handed.

Keith Porter always believed the attacker followed Guthrie through the mudroom door, whacked him three times over the head, and the bruising occurred as the big man hit both objects on his way to the ground. There was hardly room to move. Adding several other permutations was unhelpful. It would have been far more beneficial if they had found the weapon.

Keith's view was that there was no specific evidence of a struggle. There was nothing to prove Guthrie saw the face of his attacker before he died. Forensics found nothing clutched in his hands, no incriminating material under his fingernails. The only evidence that someone other than Kendal Guthrie was in the mudroom that night was the three wounds to his skull that resulted in his death.

Maxine flicked through the notes provided by WPC

Sarah Saunders and PC Zak Drake. Keith had looked at Zak's report and decided it supported his version of events.

"There you go, Max," he said. "When Drake looked inside the mudroom, he noticed the light wasn't on. Saunders missed that. It was broad daylight when they arrived at the farm. But when Guthrie got home the night before, the first thing he'd do as he walked into the mudroom would be to flick the light switch. It was pitch black and blowing a gale outside."

"The killer could have turned it off again as they left, Keith," Maxine had reasoned. "The security lighting would have stayed on long enough for Guthrie to get indoors. Once he'd locked the door behind him, surely, Guthrie would have been able to negotiate his way to the kitchen door, into the hallway, and upstairs? He'd lived there for donkey's years, and no doubt made it through the house in that fashion a hundred times before."

"My bet is he didn't turn it on, Max," Keith had argued. "Yes, I agree the security lighting allowed him to get the key in the lock and get inside, but those lights would have gone off during the attack. The way I see it, Guthrie got struck three times in the darkness. That's why the three blows weren't in roughly the same place. Guthrie was staggering or falling, and the attacker caught him on the side of the head. The surgeon couldn't prove the sequence of blows, anyway. Because it was dark, Guthrie couldn't avoid hitting something on the way down. The narrow gap between the freezer and bench would allow a fit person to walk to the inner door without mishap. But it would prove nigh on impossible for a tall, heavy, elderly man reeling from a sustained attack with an iron bar."

Maxine had conceded that Keith's version was the most plausible.

Results from forensics on items collected outside the mudroom were as useless as those gathered inside. The deluge on Friday night obliterated any footprints or tyre tracks left behind. They were long gone if there had been anything on the lane leading from Netheravon Road to the farmhouse. More than half a dozen vehicles had used it since Wes Guthrie arrived to check on his father.

Kendal Guthrie had lived in the area all his life, so the number of trips he had saved on his satnav was negligible. He knew his way around without a box on the dashboard. Forensics found nothing to tell them where he'd been on Friday night. Keith got a couple of Detective Constables trawling through CCTV footage. As Maxine predicted, the only cameras capturing the Bentley during the week before the murder were on major roads. There was little coverage on the wide-open areas of Salisbury Plain.

Keith produced a list of names he wanted to tackle while the trail was still warm.

"Wes Guthrie and his wife," he'd said. "Then the two farmers on either side of Guthrie's farm, Lawless and Meaden. That will be the schedule for tomorrow."

So, on Tuesday morning, Wes Guthrie arrived at the station for an interview.

Ten minutes in, Keith and Maxine had thought they saw a chance to solve the case. Wes Guthrie admitted lying to them, just as Keith suspected. He had left his drinking buddies at eleven o'clock. Maxine had asked him where he went after that. Wes gave the address and telephone number of a girlfriend, Tamsin Meredith. When Keith asked why he hadn't told the truth when they spoke to him on Saturday afternoon, Guthrie had said he didn't want his wife to find out he was playing away.

The surprise revelation interrupted the flow of Keith's

questioning. They needed to check Wes Guthrie was now telling the truth. The bright light they'd seen several minutes earlier was fading. Keith suspended the interview and decided to resume after they had spoken to the girlfriend. He talked to Millie Guthrie next and called Reception to bring her to the interview room.

Wes Guthrie wanted the final word before he returned to Reception to wait for his wife.

"You went to a lot of trouble for a dodgy number plate, DI Porter. Did it give you a buzz hearing your pals pulled me over less than two minutes after leaving the farm?"

"I don't know what you're on about, Mr Guthrie," Keith had replied.

Maxine had kept quiet. She thought what Keith had done was sneaky and vindictive.

Millie Guthrie had told them she suspected Wes was having an affair for weeks. She confirmed Wes got home at two o'clock in the morning. Wes had told Keith and Maxine on Saturday he and his father rarely socialized. Mille said they saw Kendal more when his wife, Poppy, was alive. Poppy doted on her two grandsons, as Helen and Guy didn't appear interested in starting a family.

Millie wanted to know when the police would release her father-in-law's body so the family could arrange the funeral. Helen was flying from Melbourne once they could confirm a date. Maxine told her it wouldn't be this week. It was more likely to be the following Monday or Tuesday.

"That tart Wes has been seeing had the nerve to call the house and say she was sorry for our loss," Millie had said. "If she turns up at the funeral, that will be it. I'll be walking out and taking the kids with me."

Maxine wondered how the marriage could survive, even if Ms Meredith stayed away.

Keith didn't think there was anything useful Millie Guthrie could add to the investigation at this stage, so he told her they would be in touch if they had further questions.

"Let's take a break, Max," he'd said. "Where's that phone number for the girlfriend?"

Keith had called Ms Meredith and invited her to attend the station first thing after lunch.

The second Tamsin Meredith entered the interview room, Maxine knew Keith Porter would be like putty in her hands. Tamsin had the lot. A great body and legs that went on forever. And although she wasn't a classically beautiful woman, Tamsin oozed sex appeal.

Maxine watched Keith change from a competent and responsible Detective Inspector into a puppy rolling on the floor in front of its mistress, begging to have its tummy rubbed.

"I have been seeing Wes for three months," said Tamsin. "It's not a casual fling. We're very much in love, and we'll be together when the funeral's over. We had arranged for him to drop by my place after saying goodbye to his old school friends. He arrived at ten past eleven and left my bed at twenty minutes to two. The poor dear walked home in that rain. Maybe I was silly to call him on Sunday morning, but he wasn't picking up his mobile phone. Why his wife got so stroppy with me, I don't know."

When Keith realised what a piece of work Ms Meredith was, he stopped drooling. After Tamsin left the room, Keith sighed.

"More negative results, Max. I don't see us shaking Wes Guthrie's alibi, and the wife and girlfriend didn't murder Kendal Guthrie. Let's hope we can get a lead to follow when we speak to Guthrie's neighbours."

Doug Lawless and Harry Meaden told much the same story. Maxine wondered whether they'd sat up last night running through it together. Kendal Guthrie was a tough, uncompromising business person who didn't let anyone get in his way. Both farmers were surprised it hadn't happened years ago.

After what seemed like a lifetime, they received a report on the contents of Guthrie's mobile phone. Their victim had many business and personal contacts, and Maxine had generated a list of interviewees, starting with those he'd spoken with most recently.

Lists were a constant thread in the method Keith adopted.

He and Maxine traced the contacts, crossed off any they had already seen, and one by one eliminated them from their enquiries. Once they had exhausted the frequent flyers, they passed the list of casual contacts to more junior team members. The minions had no better luck than their superiors.

Three weeks into the investigation, Keith called a halt while they undertook a review.

"What haven't we done?" he'd asked.

"We haven't asked the public for information, guv," one of the DCs had offered.

"What, and get swamped with calls from idiots who always confess to a killing? Or the time-wasters who will follow our cars on a wild goose chase and post the pictures on Instagram. No thanks."

"We just need someone to tell us they saw him Friday night," Maxine had said. "If we phrase the question correctly, we may get enough sensible responses to make it worthwhile."

Keith had reluctantly agreed to Maxine's idea.

The first person to call Maxine at the station was Wade Pinnock. He said he knew precisely where Kendal Guthrie was on Friday night. She invited him to drop in after work that day.

Keith wasn't expecting miracles when he saw the young lad. Maxine took the lead. She might get more out of him.

"So, Wade," she said. "How do you think you can assist us with our enquiries?"

"I took my girlfriend out for a drink on Saturday night, the day after the murder," said Wade. "We went to the Traveller's Rest out Tilshead way."

"Are you even eighteen?" asked Keith.

"Nineteen, actually," said Wade. "Do you want to hear this or not?"

"Just take your time, Wade," said Maxine, "and tell us in your own words."

"I found us a table in the corner and went to the bar to get the drinks. I heard the girl behind the bar ask an old chap sitting on a stool whether he'd heard about the excitement at Durrington. He said no, and the girl said the landlord had heard that you were at Kendal Guthrie's farm. The old chap made me sit up and take notice because he said he hoped it wasn't anything trivial. I thought that was disrespectful, as my Dad had seen a body coming out of the house on a trolley. That was at six o'clock when my Dad was driving home. Then the barmaid said Guthrie had been there last night and was rude to everyone. She wanted to know how he died. I said nobody knew for certain whether it was natural causes or something else. The landlord spoke to the old chap and said that Guthrie being dead changed things for him. He mentioned another bloke too, but I can't remember his name. When the barmaid asked whether the police would visit the pub, I told her they should call you. So you knew when Guthrie left, and you could work out what time he should have reached home. Oh, yeah, the landlord said he'd closed early because of the weather, and it was ten minutes after ten when everyone left. Then the barmaid reminded the landlord he'd told Kendal Guthrie he was barred. I told them again you would want to hear from them about that, but nobody noticed. The landlord suddenly realised I still wanted drinks and took my order."

"Do you know the names of the customers in the bar?" Maxine had asked.

"Alf is the landlord, but I don't use the pub often enough to know customers by name. Another bloke came in later on and was chatting to Alf. My girlfriend reckoned they were talking about me. They looked over to the corner where we sat. That's all I can tell you. We haven't been back since."

"You've been a great help, Wade," said Maxine. "Thank you for coming in."

"It was the right thing to do," said Wade.

When Wade left them, Keith hadn't seemed that interested in what they'd learned. Maxine thought it typical. As it wasn't Keith's idea to ask the public for help, he wouldn't accept it could be significant.

"Think about it, Max," he'd said. "Kendal Guthrie made enemies wherever he went. It stands to reason there would be similar conversations in every pub on the Plain that Saturday night."

"But Wade Pinnock heard that Kendal Guthrie was in the Traveller's Rest at around ten o'clock. We've been desperate to learn where he was, and now we know you dismiss it as irrelevant."

"It might be relevant, Max," Keith said, "but not

everyone who wanted the bloke dead was in the pub that night. His killer might have planned this for months. They could have driven from outside the county to Glenhead Farm and hung around for a couple of hours, waiting for Guthrie to get home. Don't build up your hopes. We'll visit the pub, speak to the landlord and get him to identify the others in the pub that night. Let's see where it leads."

Alf Collett, the landlord at the Traveller's Rest, had been surprised to see them. Yes, Kendal Guthrie had dropped by the pub that night for one drink. He wasn't a regular visitor. Kendal left the bar at around ten, along with the others. Alf told Keith and Maxine that he'd closed early to let poor Rosie get home to Salisbury.

"Rosie is your barmaid, is that right?" Keith had asked. "Why did you say poor Rosie?"

"Rosie Ritchens?" Alf Collett had replied. "Don't you recall the name?"

"The young girl who died in Majorca ten days ago," Maxine had said. "It was her first foreign holiday. She got hit by a car while walking along a road outside town in the early hours. Police believed Rosie staggered into the path of oncoming traffic because she was drunk."

Alf Collett told them Rosie stopped working at the pub two weeks after the murder. She had wanted to find a job closer to home to save the cost of driving backwards and forwards, and the murder had unsettled her. She didn't feel safe travelling home at night alone.

Alf had spoken to Rosie on the phone just before she flew out to Palma. Rosie had booked a fortnight's holiday to top up her tan, and relax, before starting work at a pub in Salisbury city centre. Alf said she was excited about the future.

Maxine had asked if Alf made a habit of making social

calls to staff after leaving his employment. He replied that he wanted to hear if she'd found a new job. He had been sorry to see her go. Rosie was a good worker, and they were thin on the ground.

Keith pressed Alf for the names of the other people drinking in the Traveller's Rest that Friday night. Alf said Dave Vickers had cycled over from Shrewton. Vickers was the manager of a building society branch in Amesbury. He was single and in his early fifties. He added that Jim Thornton and Oscar Wallington had also stopped by for a while.

Maxine made a note of the names and details of where they lived. She asked Alf Collett what they talked about that night. The landlord was vague about what people discussed. He said he wasn't always listening. Maxine asked what caused him to tell Kendal Guthrie he wasn't welcome in the pub in future just before everyone went home.

Alf told them he ran a happy pub where people knew there wouldn't be any trouble. However, he threw customers out at the first signs that they were looking to start a fight. He did the same if someone upset others with vulgar language or unwelcome comments. Zero tolerance was his motto, and Kendal Guthrie wasn't the type of customer the place needed.

"Who did Kendal upset that night?" she'd asked.

"Who didn't he upset, lass?" Alf had replied. "I can't remember what he said now, but Kendal wasn't fussy. He'd have a dig at everyone, hoping to get a reaction. It was his way. That Friday wasn't any different to any other day."

"Except Kendal Guthrie died shortly after walking out of that door behind us."

Keith had woken up.

Maxine knew Alf Collett had gone on the defensive at that point.

"Rosie stopped behind to help me wash the glasses and tidy the bar before she drove home. I went upstairs and watched TV for an hour before joining my wife in bed. I didn't hear Kendal had died until late on Saturday afternoon."

"Why didn't you volunteer this information as soon as you heard it was a murder enquiry?" Keith had asked.

"I had enough on my plate," said Alf Collett. "Joan hasn't been well, then Rosie upped and left. I had to scramble around for a new barmaid. Peggy Hollins, an elderly lady who lives just up the road, was my emergency standby, but she twisted her ankle going home from here on Saturday evening, the day after the murder. I thought you would learn where Kendal had been and drop in when you needed something. None of us liked Kendal that much, but whoever killed him must have had more of a reason than a few angry words."

"Do you own a car, Mr Collett?" Maxine had asked.

"I do. It's in the garage in the car park. Take a walk outside and check. It's right under our bedroom window. If I'd opened the garage door that night and driven the car out, my Joan would have woken up like a shot. She doesn't come down to the bar these days. She's too frail, but by all means, go up and ask her. Only an idiot would have gone out on a night like that. It was the worst storm of the winter."

Keith told the landlord they would continue with their enquiries, and if they needed to confirm his alibi, they would be back. They studied the garage when they walked outside. The heavy metal door looked old and not well-maintained. Maxine thought even a heavy sleeper would get disturbed when it screeched open.

Jim Thornton added nothing to what they'd learned from Alf Collett. The curtains were drawn in the middle of the day. A neighbour spotted them on the doorstep and told them Jim's wife had died in hospital at the weekend. When they finally got to speak to him, Jim said he visited the pub every night for two pints. He had reached home on the night of the murder ten minutes after leaving the Traveller's Rest. He had seen none of the others on the road because he'd been first to his car.

When Maxine asked why Alf had said Guthrie's death changed things for him, the older man thought for a while. Then he told them his former boss, Bob Ellison, had been approached by Guthrie, hoping to buy his farm. Bob had mentioned nothing to him, and although Guthrie mentioned it during their conversation at the pub, Jim hadn't paid it too much mind. He thought Guthrie was winding him up, as usual. Whether Bob Ellison would have sold to Guthrie if he kept on at him long enough was irrelevant now.

"Guthrie did love to stir the pot," he'd told Keith. "He'd say something he knew would likely get a particular person's back up. Nine times out of ten, it was rubbish, but many fell for it, and Kendal would laugh and walk away. Don't ask me to shed tears for the man. He got what he deserved if you ask me."

While they put their chat with Jim Thornton on hold, they visited Dave Vickers and Oscar Wallington. Maxine could tell Vickers must have had a soft spot for Rosie Ritchens. He said he was devastated by her death. As for Kendal Guthrie, Vickers added his name to the list of people who didn't have a good word to say about the man.

"It took me forty-five minutes to cycle home in the storm," he told them. "There were few cars on the roads, and because of the high winds, I had to dismount and push my bike in places. I was glad to get indoors, I can tell you. It was eleven o'clock when I eventually reached here."

When Keith asked how Kendal had upset him that night, Dave Vickers gave a wry smile.

"He had a dig at each of us," he said. "A sexist remark to Rosie, a malicious rumour about Alf and his last barmaid, which seemed more unlikely than snow in August. He bragged about his fancy car and suggested Oscar stole twenty grand from his employer to buy a new motor. He teased old Jim that Bob Ellison had had enough of farming and wanted to get out. As for me, it was my fault interest rates were so low on his savings. So he ran out of people to wind up in the end."

Keith and Maxine had interviewed Oscar Wallington at the Lodge House. The estate manager ushered his wife and children into the lounge and invited the detectives to sit with him around the large kitchen table. Keith asked Oscar to tell them about his visit to the pub on the night of the murder. He informed Oscar that they had spoken to Alf Collett and Dave Vickers.

"I arrived at the Traveller's Rest at nine o'clock and ordered a drink. The weather was lousy, and the pub was almost empty. I think Alf was chatting to Jim Thornton, and Rosie served me. Have you heard about Jim's wife?"

Keith said they had and asked him to continue.

"What about Rosie?" Oscar Wallington had asked. "That was terrible news."

"We know about Rosie," said Keith.

"I'm trying to remember what they were saying," said Oscar. "That's it. Rosie wanted to know when the MoD started using Salisbury Plain for training exercises. Jim Thornton explained how people used utensils in the fireplace in the past. You would have thought it was Halloween, not the middle of February. Jim warned Rosie there were ghosts and monsters on the Plain. As if there was a kind of Bermuda Triangle in those wide-open spaces. Guthrie arrived sometime later. He made a scene, flashing his wad of cash around for the entire bar to see. Guthrie reminded us to take great care when we left because we couldn't afford to pay for any repairs to his beloved Bentley. Then he laid into each of us, probing for a weak spot. He was an awful man who took great pleasure in hurting people."

"What time did you leave?" Maxine had asked.

"A minute or two after Alf had had enough of Guthrie. He barred him and said he was closing early to let poor Rosie drive home to Salisbury. Guthrie left first, and we waited for Dave Vickers to come out of the toilet and then went outside. The last time I saw Dave, I saw him struggling to get his wet weather clothes on in the bike shed. I arrived here twenty minutes after I left the pub."

"You didn't see any of the others?" asked Maxine.

"That was unlikely. I drove in the opposite direction towards Chitterne. Jim left before me, and Dave used the A360, as would Rosie when she finished. I can't imagine Guthrie risking the minor roads on a night like that. He wouldn't risk hitting a fallen tree as he rounded a tight bend in his Bentley. My guess is Guthrie followed Jim on the A360 until the A303. He'd leave at the next roundabout and take the Netheravon Road. That's where his farm was, I believe."

"You appear to know the area well," Keith said.

"I was stationed at Bulford Camp for several years," said Oscar. "Just a mile up the road. I served Queen and country for thirty years in different corners of the world. When I retired, the manor house needed an estate manager. My family loved the region, so we grabbed the opportunity."

"Can your wife confirm when you arrived home that Friday night?" Keith had asked.

"Sadly, no," replied Oscar. "The kids were on half-term from Monday the sixteenth of February. Corinne took them to stay with her mother and father on Friday evening."

Maxine sighed as she read the final pages of the murder file. No matter where they went with this case, they had hit a dead end. Keith had the last word over the public appeal. Wade Pinnock was the only genuine caller. Reception stopped logging the number of time-wasters when they reached twenty-nine.

It was time to move on. Maxine did the same as Keith Porter. She hunted for a sturdy box that nobody was using, put everything she needed to keep in it, and emptied her desk drawers. Then she sent a text to Keith's mobile.

"What am I supposed to do without you?"

She waited for the inevitable response. Her fingers poised to clarify the question.

"Sorry, I meant, who's leading the hate crime gig?"

Chapter Six

Monday, 27 August 2018

GUS HAD JUST SAT at his desk when the phone rang.

"Freeman? It's Kenneth Truelove here. DS Mercer notified me of the extraordinary matters you uncovered while solving the Reeves murder. You never cease to amaze me. I've set the wheels in motion to investigate the historical exploitation of underage girls by Street, Francis, and others. The enquiry will also look into the potential murder of Maureen Glendenning. I'm holding the first session of Operation Oakleaf at noon."

"A catchy title, sir," said Gus.

"Did you have a better idea?"

"I toyed with Figleaf considering most of those photos, sir, but you're much better at this than I am."

"You can't rest on your laurels, Freeman. Don't be late for our meeting."

Gus sighed.

"Did you have an exciting weekend, guv?" asked Neil Davis.

"It was too short. Neil," said Gus, "but exciting is being over-generous. What do we need to do to prepare our files for London Road on the Marion Reeves murder?"

"I've finished everything on my end," said Neil.

"We made sure we got everything done before we travelled to Scotland," said Lydia. "Perhaps we can give you the highlights at lunchtime if you're interested."

"They didn't turn you back at the border then, Alex?" said Neil.

"No, and Eleanor made us both very welcome. We had a terrific time."

"I didn't realise there *was* a border," said Blessing Umeh.

"There isn't," said Luke Sherman. "or at least, not yet. Blessing and I have thirty minutes of work on our files, guv. What time do you have to leave?"

"No panic just yet, Luke," said Gus. "The Chief Constable has turned our early morning meetings, which used to stretch to lunchtime, into brief conferences over a cold collation starting at noon."

"The Chief Constable doesn't think any less of us, though, does he, guv?" asked Neil.

"He just reminded me not to rest on my laurels, Neil. So make of that what you will."

"Got it, guv," said Neil.

"Right," said Gus. "Those who need to must put the finishing touches to your digital files. I'll leave the office at around half-past eleven. As for the rest of you, I hope to see clean desks and every scrap of material relating to the Reeves case removed. Then, we can make a fast start on our next case when I return this afternoon."

Neil, Alex, and Lydia began the deep clean.

Blessing turned her attention to the Freeman files and checked everything she had contributed was error-free. It wasn't easy to concentrate with the surrounding activity. Nobody had asked what a weekend she had.

Even though she tried to put it out of her mind, Blessing couldn't avoid thinking about the young man her father mentioned on Saturday afternoon when he'd rung her. She knew it had to be something unusual for her father to call. He left it to her mother and their regular Wednesday evening conversations to keep him updated.

Blessing knew that anything she told her mother about work or what she intended to do in her social life got relayed to her father as soon as she put down the phone. Then, the following Wednesday evening, her mother would tell her whether he approved or disapproved of her actions. It was just his way.

When Kelechi Umeh called her at the Ferris farm in Worton, Blessing had just eaten lunch with Jackie. John was working on the farm, and Jackie suggested she and Blessing spend the afternoon in the orchard. Blessing had a new book to read. The weather was beautiful, and the prospect of an afternoon relaxing in good company sounded idyllic.

When her father mentioned he had spoken with the family of Ekene Kanu, all Blessing's hopes and dreams for the future seemed to melt away. Kelechi wanted Blessing to come to dinner the following Sunday. On this occasion, she should arrive in time to attend church with him and Maryam. Ekene could see what a dutiful daughter they had raised.

Blessing had spent the afternoon with Jackie, mostly in tears, with her head on her landlady's shoulder. It was far from the idyllic afternoon she had planned.

When John Ferris returned to the farmhouse at the end of his working day, he listened to his wife relay the disturbing news.

"What would Gus think?" he said.

"He won't be happy," said Jackie. "Gus thinks a lot of Blessing. The poor girl doesn't want to marry a stranger. What can we do to help, John?"

"Not much, Jackie," said John. "It's not our business, even though Blessing sleeps under our roof. So call Suzie, sow the seeds, and perhaps before next weekend, our daughter can persuade Gus to intervene."

Blessing hoped the man sitting a few feet away from her would listen to his partner.

Meanwhile, Gus was deep in thought. As he had intimated to Neil, the weekend had flown past without him being able to achieve everything he'd hoped. He and Suzie had spent a quiet Friday evening at the allotment, followed by supper at home and an early night.

Now that Suzie wasn't rushing off to Worton for her weekly horse ride, they could enjoy a lazy morning at the bungalow. Suzie had other ideas, of course, and they spent the morning shopping in Devizes, fighting their way through the crowds.

As lunchtime approached, Gus thought he could salvage the day by suggesting a pub lunch in the country. Suzie decided it was high time Gus had a haircut.

"Have you exhausted your delaying tactics now?" he asked as they finally made it back to the car.

"I don't know what you mean," said Suzie. Gus could tell from the smile on her face she did.

"When we get home, I'll fix lunch," he said. "We'll sit on the patio in the back garden, and you can tell me about your meeting with Vicky Bennison."

Gus had first heard of the former Detective Sergeant when they reviewed the Gerry Hogan case. Vicky was teamed with DI John Kirkpatrick then and transferred sometime later to Oxford, working for Thames Valley. In June three years ago, she suffered serious injuries at an anti-austerity protest march in central London.

Gus used the fact Neil Davis and Vicky had gone through training together and took him to Abingdon when they needed her insight on the Hogan case. Vicky had spent the past three years working with a victim support charity. They only managed a fifteen-minute meeting in a garden away from her office, but Gus felt he'd convinced Vicky that not all police personnel would let her down when she needed them.

When Gus had discussed his ideas with Suzie, she agreed that working with Vicky Bennison would be beneficial, given the new role she had attracted. Geoff Mercer had a habit of choosing Suzie to front his fresh initiatives, and victim support had recently reached the top of the list.

After returning home on Saturday, Gus helped Suzie put away the shopping and prepared their lunch. Suzie went outside to move the patio furniture to give them shade while they ate. The afternoon looked set to be a scorcher. However, Suzie knew there was no point in taking any undue risks with her health, with her twelve-week scan due in a fortnight.

"Any preference for your soft drink?" Gus called through the open kitchen window.

"Surprise me," Suzie replied. "Just make sure you double-up on the ice cubes."

They ate their lunch, and after Gus cleared their plates and glasses, he settled in his chair.

"How did your meeting go at London Road?" he asked.

"Very cloak and dagger," said Suzie. "Vicky was bordering on paranoia about anyone seeing her arrive and leave the building. She's a damaged soul, and no mistake, Gus. The families the charity work with on domestic violence cases don't trust the police."

"Crime affects everyone differently," said Gus. "How people react depends on the nature of the crime, the sort of people they are, and the support they already have around them."

"Yes, and specially trained staff, like Vicky, spend hours listening to people learning what they need to help cope and recover from the impact of the crime. That support is always confidential and guided by the needs and wants of the victim. Vicky told me rebuilding self-confidence and trust in others is crucial. She and her colleagues help tackle the practical problems that families face."

"Did you find common ground?" asked Gus. "Somewhere that Geoff Mercer can see results are achievable through cooperation between you and the charity?"

"I told Vicky I was open to offering information on police and court procedures. What to expect and how to get the best from the system. Many of her clients could benefit from improving their personal safety. Not just techniques for defending themselves if attacked but for advice on fitting locks and alarms. I told Vicky I wanted to get to a point where victims see me as an ally, not another enemy."

"What did she say to that?" asked Gus.

"She said it wouldn't happen overnight. We're due to meet again in two weeks. On Wednesday, the thirteenth."

"A busy week," said Gus.

The pull of the allotment faded as the oppressive heat built, and their shaded nook became a far better option for the rest of the afternoon and early evening. After a refreshing shower, they'd changed, and Suzie drove them to the Fox and Hounds on the outskirts of Devizes for a meal.

"You didn't fancy eating in the Lamb tonight?" he'd asked.

"I thought I'd take advantage of one of the few remaining times when we could be alone," Suzie replied. "It won't be just the two of us for much longer."

The following day, brunch was very welcome and set them up nicely for a busy afternoon on the neglected allotment. Bert Penman's patch next door looked a picture by comparison. The Reverend had almost harvested her entire crop of salad plants, but Clemency Bentham wasn't present. She was probably resting after Holy Communion and Matins this morning and girding up her loins in anticipation of Evensong later.

"I wonder why the Church doesn't combine their services into one," said Suzie, leaning on her hoe. "They might get more people to attend if you could get everything out of the way in one go."

"Like a one-stop-shop, you mean?" said Gus. "For obvious reasons, you must realise I've never given the matter any thought."

"I know you're a non-believer, Gus," said Suzie. "I thought as Sunday was supposed to be a day of rest in the old days, parishioners had to be up early for the first service and couldn't go too far in the afternoon because they needed to get back for Evensong. My grandparents knew entire families who attended all three services. On top of that, the kids got packed off to bible classes in the afternoon."

"No rest for the wicked," said Gus.

"I wonder whether Irene will persuade Bert to go back

to church," said Suzie as she resumed ridding the earth around Gus's second crop of potatoes of weeds.

"Hang on," said Gus. "What's this fascination with the church today? Brett's lived in the area for months now. I don't recall the Reverend badgering him about sitting in the front row of the pews. It hasn't stopped Clemency from getting up close and personal with him."

Suzie didn't reply, so Gus kept wondering what he'd missed. They had discussed marriage and agreed it wasn't on the agenda in the foreseeable future. Gus eased his aching body upright and stared at the church. What else was there? The penny dropped.

An hour later, Gus sensed Suzie was growing tired. The weather was hot and sticky. The clouds above the hillside opposite suggested a looming thunderstorm. It was ever thus in this country. Three or four consecutive days with high temperatures, the only way it could break was with violence. There was never a gradual reduction in temperature to revert to a more moderate spell of summer weather.

"Let's call it a day, Suzie," he said. "Sit yourself down while I return our tools to the shed. Then, we'll walk home and freshen up."

They wandered up the lane as the church clock wound itself up to strike six o'clock.

"I've never seen many small kids near the allotment when I've worked on a Sunday afternoon," he said. "That means if they're christening a little one, they must do it in the morning."

"You're incorrigible, Gus Freeman," said Suzie, punching him hard on the arm.

"I prefer people to think of me as a lovable rogue," Gus replied.

Suzie suggested they prepared a salad when they reached the bungalow instead of going for another cooked meal in the Lamb. Much later, they sat under the stars on the rear garden patio with a cup of coffee and discussed the pros and cons of christenings.

"All done, guv," said Luke. "Everything's set for your trip to London Road."

Gus looked up from his blank computer screen and wondered how long he'd daydreamed.

"Coffees are in order," he said, jumping up from his chair.

Too much inactivity, and his team would catch him nodding off in the afternoons. That would never do. Only older people did that.

When Blessing saw Gus heading for the restroom, she seized her chance.

"I'll help with the coffees, guv," she said and hurried across the room before any of the others got in ahead of her.

Blessing closed the restroom door behind her and joined Gus by the Gaggia.

"Anything exciting happen this weekend, Blessing?" he asked.

"No, guv, something dreadful."

She told Gus about Ekene Kanu and getting summoned to appear in Englishcombe parish church next Sunday morning.

"What's the young man like?" asked Gus. "What does he do for a living?"

"I do not know, guv," said Blessing.

"So, your father has spoken with Ekene's father and agreed that a union between you is acceptable to both families. I wonder what Ekene thinks. Perhaps he's as keen to marry for love as you are. Could your mother give you his phone number on Wednesday evening? Why not grasp the nettle, and make the first contact, Blessing? If Ekene's of a similar mind to your father, a confident, modern young woman might scare him away. If not, you might be able to plot a way for both of you to escape."

"I knew you would think of something, Mr Freeman," said Blessing. "Did Mrs Ferris ring Suzie over the weekend?"

"Not as far as I'm aware, Blessing," said Gus. "Why?"

"Mr Ferris thought their daughter could stimulate your brain cells."

"Ah, I get your drift. John told Jackie to ask Suzie to work on me over the coming week. Why they think that would work is beyond me."

"So, you thought of this plan yourself, " Blessing said.

"It has one major flaw," said Gus.

He cursed himself for mentioning it when he saw her reaction. Blessings' shoulders slumped, and her bottom lip quivered.

"What is it?" she asked.

"You might have looked at Ekene next Sunday morning and fallen head over heels. If my ruse is successful, you could go your separate ways without realising you've missed your soul mate."

"If my mother has his number, I'll know as soon as I speak with him," said Blessing. "I'm a detective, after all, and I'll have a prepared list of questions."

"Make sure you compile that list on your own time, DC Umeh," said Gus with a grin. "Then let me have a quick look before you call."

"The others will wonder what we're up to," said Blessing. "We should get these cups of coffee back to them. I feel happier now, Mr Freeman. You are a wonderful boss."

Blessing and Gus carried three cups each into the main office and handed them around.

"I needed this," said Neil. "I've got a dry neck."

"Sorry for the delay. We had an extra cleaning job to do first, Neil," said Gus. "When was the last time you changed the filters on the Gaggia?"

The office was tidy when Gus gathered his files together and made for the lift. But, as he travelled to the ground floor, Gus wondered when Suzie's charm offensive would begin. It might be fun if he resisted for a while.

Upstairs in the office, Lydia Logan Barre thought it high time they told everyone about their weekend in Edinburgh. Gus wouldn't be back for a couple of hours, and they had nothing much to do, anyway.

Before she began, Lydia suspected Blessing had a secret.

"Tell me to mind my own business, Blessing," she said. "Were you and Gus talking about your father wanting to arrange a marriage for you in the restroom?"

"My father has found someone he thinks is suitable," said Blessing. "But Mr Freeman has given me an idea of how I might thwart my father's plans without cutting my ties with my family."

"That's great, Blessing," said Luke. "We know how important your family is to you. But, if Gus has come up with a winning idea, it might only be a temporary fix. The best way out is for you to find a steady boyfriend. Someone you fancy."

"I have been looking," said Blessing.

"Nobody you've seen matches PC Dave Smith, I suppose," said Alex Hardy.

Blessing sighed.

"Dave was tall and handsome and a great kisser. But he wasn't ready to settle down."

"Rick Chalmers is still available as far as I know," said Neil. "I have offered to fix you up before."

"Don't be gross, Neil," said Lydia. "Rick's a decent detective, but he's a typical middle-aged copper after a failed marriage. He drinks too much and survives on fast food."

"Charming," said Neil. "Rick's in his late twenties, the same as Luke and me."

"You can't argue he looks older than us," said Luke. "Several years of heavy drinking and an unhealthy diet are taking their toll."

"Come on, guys," said Alex. "Lydia is champing at the bit to tell you about our trip. We can put our heads together and think where Blessing might find Mr Right another time."

GUS EASED his Ford Focus into a vacant space outside the Wiltshire Police HQ main building, picked up his files, and trotted up the stairs to the front door.

The young lad in reception was new. Gus recognised the type; young, keen, over-zealous.

He tried to recall whether he'd ever been that keen to impress. The lad made Gus search through his pockets for the library card that announced him as a consultant attached to Wiltshire Police. Then he studied the photograph and compared it to the man standing before him.

"Are you sure you're Gus Freeman, sir?" he said.

"Positive," said Gus.

"I'd better check, sir. If you wouldn't mind waiting."

The youngster left reception and dashed upstairs to the first floor.

Gus looked at his watch. He was in luck. The traffic on the roads this morning had been lighter than usual, so he'd arrived with several minutes to spare—minutes which were ticking away at an alarming rate.

The sound of suppressed laughter came from the mezzanine. Gus realised someone was pulling his leg. He went upstairs to find the lad chatting with Vera and Kassie.

"Hilarious," said Gus.

"It's the haircut," the young lad said. "Vera says it's totally changed your appearance. I had to be sure. I didn't want to let a ringer into the building on my first day."

"Some people find their first day is also their last," said Gus, snatching his identity card from the wet-behind-the-ears PC.

"As for you two," he said, staring at Vera and Kassie. "You might have made me late for my meeting with the boss."

"Don't be daft, Mr Freeman," said Kassie Trotter, "you can make it across this floor in plenty of time."

"Ah, but this young man has to get me to sign in now he's verified my credentials. He just said it's his first day, and he must do everything by the book. What example would I be setting if I didn't follow the rules?"

"If you sign in and out when you have finished your meeting, I'm sure the books will be straight enough," said Vera. "Now stop winding everyone up and get to Kenneth's office."

"Will we see you later, Mr Freeman?" asked Kassie. "Or shall I throw your cream horn in the bin?"

"I wouldn't be too hasty, Kassie," said Gus. "After the trouble you went to baking in that heat over the weekend."

"I had to be careful, Mr Freeman," said Kassie. "I kept the curtains closed as I didn't have a stitch on when I prepared this week's batches of buns, horns, and muffins. It was hot work."

Gus spotted the lad from reception still lurking at the top of the stairs. The youngster swallowed hard, took one lingering look at Kassie, and bolted downstairs where he belonged.

"Kassie has an admirer," said Vera.

"Not before time," said Gus as he crossed the room to Kenneth Truelove's office.

"I need a man, not a boy," said Kassie.

Gus thought Kassie should ask Vera for Rick Chalmers's number but thought better of it.

"You made it at last then, Freeman?" said the Chief Constable. "Mercer has been here for two minutes. Time marches on."

"Sorry, sir. A case of mistaken identity," said Gus.

Kenneth Truelove wasn't listening. Instead, he stood up and walked to the window. That was a hangover from the days in his old room when he was still ACC. The view he had now was far less inspiring. Which meant there was trouble brewing.

Gus placed the files on Kenneth's desk without comment.

"Well done, Gus," said Geoff Mercer. "I know I've said it already, but the Police and Crime Commissioner had a smile a mile wide when he learned about Operation Oakleaf earlier this morning. You put a tick in the box by uncovering Marion Reeves's killer. The icing on the cake was us launching an investigation into historical offences that could provide the county force with positive headlines for years."

"There was something else behind that smile," said Kenneth. "At first, I worried it was relief at not finding his face among the guests at those parties. When I thought about it, he was too young, but his predecessor wasn't. The chap had a racy reputation, and I reckon the PCC was happy not to find the man's face among the partygoers. It wouldn't have put the role in a good light."

The Chief Constable moved away from the window and returned to his chair.

"Where are those ladies with our food?" he tutted. "No doubt they were chatting when you came up the stairs, Freeman?"

"I couldn't possibly comment, sir," said Gus.

A sharp knock on the door announced the arrival of the lunchtime tucker.

Vera and Kassie entered with their trolleys, transferred the contents to a side table, and left the room.

"Have you upset them, Gus?" asked Geoff. "I can't remember them not having something to say while they're here."

"Ms Packenham's regime must work, Geoff," said Gus. "You should be pleased."

"Right, let's have lunch," said Kenneth, "and then I'll run through your next case. It occurred three months before the Mark Malone murder out near Beckhampton."

"What part of the county?" asked Gus. "I was spending time on my allotment back in 2015. It may have escaped my notice."

"In the middle of Salisbury Plain," said Kenneth Truelove. "Are these two bacon buns yours, Mercer?"

"I wasn't taking any chances this week, sir," said Geoff. "Did the girls check what you wanted, Gus?"

"They were preoccupied," said Gus. "Looking at what's

left on the tray, they've decided I need to choose the healthier option. My wraps look positively vegan."

Gus took one for the team, and when everyone was ready, the Chief Constable produced a new murder file from his desk drawer.

"A wealthy landowner named Kendal Guthrie arrived home late at night in February 2015. I'm unsure whether it's relevant, but it was Friday, the thirteenth. No sooner had Guthrie let himself in via a side door when someone whacked him over the head with a blunt instrument. The police surgeon's best guess was it was an iron bar. The victim's son, Wesley, discovered the body early the following afternoon. The detectives had a multitude of potential suspects but nothing to link any of them to the attack."

"Who was in charge of the investigation?" asked Gus.

"DI Keith Porter," replied the Chief Constable.

"He was still a DS when I knew him," said Gus. "Keith had an eye for the ladies and a tendency to lose focus. Did he have a decent second-in-command?"

"DS Maxine Coleman."

"I remember her," said Gus. "Maxine was still a DC during my last six months at Bourne Hill. She showed promise. It's a pity they felt it right to pair her with Keith Porter. Chalk and cheese come to mind. You said they had a multitude of suspects. How come?"

"Kendal Guthrie made a lot of enemies," said Geoff Mercer.

"I'm assuming they couldn't see the wood for the trees," said Gus, eager to get his hands on the file.

"Porter and Coleman spoke to hundreds of people who did business with Guthrie. Nobody had a kind word to say about the fellow. The son, Wesley, looked a likely candidate for a while when they discovered he'd lied about his exact whereabouts on Friday night. A girlfriend came forward to provide an alibi. After the funeral, Wesley Guthrie's wife walked out of the marriage with their two sons. It's complicated, Freeman. I can't explain it in the time I have available. You need to tear this murder file apart to learn which witnesses or possible suspects are alive today or even still living in the UK."

"It doesn't sound like a typical case, sir," said Gus.

"The original investigation was typical," said the Chief Constable. "Porter and Coleman spent six weeks toiling away with no luck and then went their separate ways. DI Porter has progressed no further up the ladder, supporting your view t he doesn't have the necessary attributes. Maxine Coleman is on maternity leave. If she returns, it will be as a Detective Inspector."

"I won't take up any more of your time, sir," said Gus. "From what you've told me, we've got our work cut out."

Gus collected the murder file from Kenneth's desk and left the room.

"I thoroughly enjoyed my lunch, ladies," he said as he breezed past Vera and Kassie.

"Don't forget your cream horn, Mr Freeman," called Kassie.

"I'll undo the good work you did, Kassie," said Gus.

He stopped and turned back. Kassie Trotter approached him, holding a white paper bag in front of her. Grace Packenham and Rhys Evans arrived at the top of the stairs, returning from their thirty-minute lunch break. The look she gave Gus and Kassie could have curdled cream.

"I can't stop to chat, DI Packenham," said Gus. "I've got a murderer to catch. But at least you've caught the sun while outside this lunchtime. It's a start."

Gus disappeared down the stairs before Grace could

reply. He signed in and out at reception to keep the new boy's records straight and left the building.

No matter how tough this case would prove, he would tackle it with a spring in his step.

Chapter Seven

GUS TOSSED the murder file and the bag containing his cream horn onto the passenger seat.

Then he separated them, just in case.

The drive back to the Old Police Station office contained a series of stops and starts. On other occasions, it would have annoyed him. Today, Gus valued the time it allowed him to consider how to handle this new case.

When the Chief Constable said this case was recent, Gus imagined family members, witnesses, and potential suspects would be at hand. Ready, if not willing, to pick up the threads from 2015.

Often, when Kenneth Truelove tasked the Crime Review Team with solving a murder, the case had already had several reviews and reconstructions. Gus got the impression they were the first people to look at the murder of Kendal Guthrie since the original team disbanded.

That caused Gus to ask the inevitable question. Was it because the case was the stuff of nightmares?

With the time approaching half-past one, Gus rode to

the first floor to rejoin his team. The conversation was in full flow when he exited the lift but ceased at once.

"I come bearing gifts," said Gus.

"Is that what I think it is in the bag, guv?" asked Neil.

"It depends on what you think it is, Neil," said Gus.

"A sticky bun from Kassie Trotter?"

"Unlucky, Neil," said Gus. "My cream horn. Better luck next time."

Gus stowed the pastry delicacy in his desk drawer and opened the murder file.

He read from a detailed summary the Chief Constable had précised earlier. Kenneth Truelove was too busy these days to get mired in detail.

"Our murder occurred on Friday the thirteenth of February, three years ago. The victim was Kendal Guthrie, a wealthy farmer cum landowner. Guthrie was sixty-seven, a widower. His wife, Poppy, died from a heart attack two years earlier. They had two children. Wesley, thirty-eight, ran one of his father's five farms and lived in Winterbourne Stoke..."

"Do you want me to note the place names, guv?" asked Luke.

"Good idea, Luke," said Gus. "When we have our map of the Plain on the wall, we can see how everything relates. It could be beneficial in finding our killer."

Gus referred to the murder file again.

"Kendal had a daughter, Helen, thirty-six, married to Guy Stilwell. The couple lived in Melbourne, Australia. Don't build up your hopes, but make a note of the city, Luke. You'll see why later. Kendal lived alone at Glenhead Farm, Durrington, the family's original home, where they moved from Angus, Scotland, many moons ago. The weather on the night of his murder was dreadful. It was the worst winter storm, with trees uprooted by gale-force winds and swollen rivers bursting their banks. That worked both ways for our case. Only a fool had gone out on such a night, and the opportunity to find witnesses for people who did was limited."

"What is it you say, Neil?" said Alex. "Nobody said it was going to be easy."

"Is Glenhead Farm remote, guv?" asked Blessing.

"Not especially," said Gus. "There is a string of three farms on the right-hand side of Netheravon Road, Durrington. Glenhead Farm sits between farms owned by Doug Lawless and Harry Meaden. Both of their farms have been in their family for generations."

"Were there any issues between Kendal Guthrie and Lawless and Meaden?" asked Alex.

"They didn't always see eye to eye," said Gus. "Before you go too deep into that, let me tell you that Guthrie returned home between ten thirty-five and eleven."

"He was one idiot to venture out on a terrible night then, guv," said Neil.

"Farmers are used to inclement weather, Neil. Anyway, I told you he was wealthy. Kendal drove a Bentley Continental GT and wasn't shy about letting people know how successful he was."

"He sounds an unpleasant man, guv," said Lydia.

"The detectives in the original investigation arrived at the farm several minutes after two uniformed officers and an ambulance crew responded to a 999 call. Wes Guthrie had received a phone call from Helen, his sister, earlier in the day. She wanted to speak to their father because Kendal and Poppy would have celebrated their fortieth anniversary on the fourteenth. Helen wanted her father to know she was thinking of him ten thousand miles away.

Kendal hadn't answered the phone, and this seemed strange."

"Do we know where Guthrie went on Friday night, guv?" asked Neil.

"Yes, Neil," said Gus, "he drove from Durrington to a pub called the Traveller's Rest, just beyond the village of Tilshead on the A360. A distance of eleven and a half miles."

"I'm surprised the pub was worth a visit on such an awful night," said Luke.

"A public appeal was the only reason Porter and Coleman learned where Guthrie went for a late drink that night," said Gus. "They were three weeks into the investigation and had got nowhere."

"Why didn't the landlord, or landlady, come forward earlier?" asked Lydia.

"The landlord claimed he was busy. He blamed a staff shortage; his wife was ill, and he assumed the police would find out some other way."

"With a supercar like the Bentley, I'm surprised it didn't call in and volunteer the information itself," said Neil.

"Guthrie wasn't switched on to the technical advantages of owning such a car, Neil," said Gus.

Neil turned to grin at Luke. Gus was the ultimate technophobe.

"Anyway, the young man who called the police told Porter and Coleman in an interview he'd visited the Traveller's Rest on Saturday night after the storm abated. He heard Alf Collett, the landlord, say he closed early on Friday night to allow his barmaid to get home safely to Salisbury. Wade Pinnock, the witness, said he learned there were only four customers in the pub; besides the two people behind the bar. A man who lived near Chitterne, Jim

Thornton. A building society manager from Shrewton, Dave Vickers. An estate manager for a manor house on the Warminster side of Chitterne, Oscar Wallington, and Kendal Guthrie."

"Can you tell me the distances involved, guv?" asked Luke.

"Jim Thornton lived four miles away from the pub. Dave Vickers lived the same distance away on the A360 and cycled there. Jim and Oscar would have arrived via the B390, with Oscar having twice the distance to cover."

"Okay, I've got that, guv," said Luke.

"Pinnock got drawn into the conversation on Saturday because Alf Collett mentioned an incident at Glenhead Farm earlier in the day. He'd heard a rumour the police were there. Pinnock told him his father saw a body moved from the farmhouse at around six that evening. He said the farm was crawling with police and forensic people. That was when Pinnock learned Guthrie arrived at the pub at around half-past nine the night before. Guthrie bragged about his car, flashed his money around, and verbally abused each of the three customers and two staff. A few minutes after ten, Alf Collett had had enough and told Guthrie he was barred, asking everyone to leave and closing the pub. Guthrie had plenty to say about it, but the bar was empty by ten past ten, a quarter past at the latest. Rosie Ritchens, the barmaid, was last to leave. She stayed with Alf to tidy up, and then he watched her run across the car park in the pouring rain, get into her car, and drive home."

"So, Kendal Guthrie drove back to the farm in around twenty to twenty-five minutes, guv," said Alex. "If he left the pub car park straight after leaving the bar."

"If the landlord watched the barmaid leave, I reckon he would have spotted a Bentley," said Blessing. "If Guthrie didn't reach the farm until eleven, something delayed him. A fallen tree or a flooded road meant a detour."

"An excellent point, Blessing," said Gus. "I have the advantage over many of you. If I drove a Bentley, I would stick to the main roads. A car that size wouldn't suit the twists and turns, the hidden bends, and the potential obstructions of the minor roads covering the Plain."

"In that case, Kendal arrived closer to the earlier time, guv," said Alex. "Ten thirty-five to ten forty. That's a narrow window of opportunity."

"Kendal parked the Bentley outside a double garage at the head of the lane from Netheravon Road," said Gus. "He crossed the short distance to the farmhouse and entered through a side door."

"Did that take him straight into the kitchen, guv?" asked Lydia.

"No, a mudroom that served as a handy spot to stow muddy boots and clothing. Poppy Guthrie was house-proud and trained Kendal, and others, to keep the house's interior as clean as possible."

"Was his attacker already in the house, guv?" asked Neil.

Gus shook his head.

"Glenhead Farm didn't have CCTV cameras for security, but they had proximity security lighting. So, when Kendal stopped his car by the garage, the surrounding space was soon floodlit. He could cross the yard, unlock the door, and get inside before the timer switched off the lights."

"Wes Guthrie didn't find the body until the following afternoon, guv," said Neil. "If his sister was that worried, why didn't Wes drive over from Winterbourne Stoke earlier?"

"Eight miles, before you ask, Luke, door-to-door," said Gus. "Well, Neil, Wesley met with John Goodwin and Chris Barton, two school friends, on Friday night, and they visited pubs in the village. It was a regular get-together with significant quantities of alcohol involved."

"He was too hungover to drive," said Neil.

"When Wes Guthrie reached Glenhead Farm, he rang the doorbell at the front of the house. His father's car was outside, so he assumed he must be home. There was no reply, so Wes rang his father's mobile, thinking he could be occupied elsewhere on the farm. Instead, he heard his father's ringtone coming from inside the house. Wes let himself in with a spare set of keys and checked upstairs first, calling out his father's name. Then, Wes worked his way through the property, room by room, and found his father's body in the mudroom. Kendal Guthrie was face down on the floor in a pool of blood. Wes checked for a pulse but realised his father had been dead for hours. So he called the emergency services."

"So, it didn't matter that Wes hadn't reached the farmhouse earlier," said Lydia. "At least Wes didn't have that thought on his conscience."

"Why should he?" asked Neil. "The bloke's entitled to have a night out with his mates once in a while, surely? You can't go through life thinking you should sit by the phone in case one of the family has an accident or worse."

"If only it were that easy, Neil," said Gus. "The paramedics confirmed Kendal was dead. He'd suffered a series of blows to the head with a heavy object. The uniformed officers who attended the scene searched for a weapon in the mudroom without success. A more detailed search by other officers and forensics confirmed this was no burglary. Nothing had been disturbed within the house, garage, or outbuildings. While Wes Guthrie was still at the scene talking to DI Porter and DS Coleman, several facts came to light. First, a considerable sum of money was missing from Kendal's wallet. Wes told them it was normal for his father to carry a thousand pounds in cash. That had gone, but the killer hadn't touched the victim's bank cards or mobile phone. Second, they had removed a well-loved Rolex Submariner watch from his wrist, yet they had six gold rings valued at fifteen thousand pounds on his fingers."

"Alex said there was only a small window of opportunity, guv," said Luke. "Perhaps the killer was pushed for time. They could hang onto the cash and the watch until the dust settled, but the cards would get stopped quickly, and removing six rings from his fingers could prove tricky. Money doesn't feel the reason behind this attack."

"I agree, guv," said Alex. "The killer took the cash and wristwatch on the spur of the moment to disguise the attack as a robbery."

"Well done," said Gus. "That was the conclusion drawn by Porter and Coleman. One of the uniformed officers spotted something that could be important. I told you security lighting lit Kendal's way across the yard. Once inside the door, it might have been second nature to switch on the mudroom light. The light was off. Wes Guthrie confirmed the outside door was already open when he went to unlock it to allow the paramedics access."

"Guthrie unlocked the door, stepped inside, and someone hit him over the head," said Blessing. "Perhaps. he didn't have time to switch on the light, and it was so quick Kendal had no time to lock the door behind him. So why would the killer lock the door on their way out?"

"The security lighting wouldn't have stayed on long," said Lydia. "After the killer struck the three blows, the mudroom could have been in darkness. Wes found his father's body face down. Head wounds are notorious for the quantity of blood they cause. Which of us would fancy searching for a wallet or a watch in the dark, knowing you would get covered in blood?"

"You're suggesting Kendal unlocked the door, stepped inside, flicked the light switch, and was going to lock the door when the attacker burst in and struck him," said Blessing. "He would have seen his attacker."

"The autopsy suggested otherwise, Blessing," said Gus. "Two blows were to the top and back of the head. One was to the side, landing just above the victim's right ear. It proved impossible to determine the order in which the blows occurred. One theory was the first blow caused Kendal to fall to his knees, hitting his chest on the edge of a freezer on the way down. Bruising to the torso supported that theory. The blow to the side of the head could have occurred as he attempted to regain his feet, and he turned to face his attacker when they lashed out again. Kendal's body had bruising to the left-hand side, which was thought to have come when he fell towards a metal workbench on the opposite side of the mudroom to the freezer. After the third blow, whenever it occurred, the damage was fatal."

"Did they ever identify the type of weapon used, guv?" asked Neil.

"The best guess was an iron bar, Neil," said Gus.

"I'm lost, guv," said Blessing. "There are so many names, distances, and clues that might not be clues. So how do we even start?"

"If you think it's complicated now, wait until you hear the rest, Blessing," said Gus. "I reckon we need several maps of Salisbury Plain. They should cover Warminster in the west, Andover in the east, Upavon in the north, and a few miles south of Downton. Ask the Hub to blow them up to give us room to attach labels, stick pins, and make calculations. Whatever they do, they mustn't forget to tell us the new scale. We've got plenty of wall space."

"Are you going to tell us the additional complications, guv?" asked Lydia. "Or should we divide the murder file and pick it up as we go along?"

"Where do I start?" said Gus, puffing his cheeks. "Let's start with Wes Guthrie. Yes, he met John Goodwin and Chris Barton for drinks on Friday night. However, although his wife, Millie, told the police Wes stumbled upstairs at two o'clock, Wes had left his mates at eleven. For three months, Wes had been seeing Tamsin Meredith, thirty-one and single. He arrived at her house by a quarter past eleven and left to walk home in the rain after half-past one."

"Didn't that alibi seem dodgy to the detectives, guv?" asked Alex.

"There wasn't a way to disprove it, Alex," said Gus. "Porter and Coleman thought they were onto something when one of the drinking mates said they left Wes earlier than he'd told them in his first interview. But he was still in Winterbourne Stoke at eleven and eight miles from the farmhouse."

"And he was drunk," said Luke, "or well on his way."

"There couldn't have been any confusion about the timing of the attack, guv?" asked Neil.

"No," said Gus, "Death occurred no later than eleven, based on the paramedic's assessment. The pathologist confirmed the time of death after the autopsy."

"I have a feeling there's more to come," said Blessing.

"Millie Guthrie suspected her husband was having an affair," said Gus. "She told the detectives if Tamsin Meredith turned up at Kendal Guthrie's funeral, she would walk away from the marriage, taking their two boys with her."

"I can't blame her," said Lydia. "I'm guessing Tamsin attended the funeral?"

"That's in the past now," said Gus. "Wes and Millie divorced, and he married Tamsin Meredith a year after the funeral. So if we wish to speak to Millie, we only need to go to the Guthrie farm in Winterbourne Stoke. Kendal's considerable estate went in equal shares to Wesley and Helen. So Wes could afford to hand the farmhouse keys to his ex-wife."

"Of course," said Luke, "Wes returned home to Glenhead Farm. That's useful because we need to visit the crime scene."

"There won't be a problem with visiting the crime scene, Luke," said Gus. "I'm sure that Helen Guthrie will cooperate with our enquiries. She flew home for her father's funeral, spent a couple of days discussing her late father's business affairs with Wes and the family solicitors, and then flew home. She found her husband of twenty years, Guy Stilwell, in bed with an architect."

"Guy had been living a lie," said Luke.

"Exactly, Luke," said Gus. "The architect, Gavin Johnson, had been Guy's lover for a decade. The Guthrie family solicitors were busy in 2015 and 2016 sorting out Kendal's estate and two divorces for his children. Helen returned to the UK to live in the house where she was born. She employed a manager to help run the farms. The business's portfolio grew to seven during 2015 because Kendal's bids for two farms the MoD was putting back on the market were accepted."

"It's an empire, not a business," said Lydia. "What

happened to Wes, guv? Is he working on one of the other farms?"

"Wes is sheep farming," said Gus, "with Tamsin beside him. They live on North Island, New Zealand, at Taupaki, thirty minutes from Auckland. He copped flak in the village for cheating on his wife, and many locals feared he'd be as unpleasant and vindictive as his father. Finally, Wes decided enough was enough, and when Helen returned home, he talked her into employing Tom Dix, his second-in-command, as farm manager. Then he looked for a fresh challenge."

"You were right when you said it was complicated, guv," said Luke.

"Let me finish, Luke," said Gus. "We've only covered the Guthrie family so far. Hold on; I forgot one thing. Wes didn't go to Glenhead Farm on the fourteenth of February until he thought he was safe to drive, but Keith Porter suspected he was still borderline. So, when Wes left to return to Winterbourne Stoke to inform family and friends of the murder, Keith alerted traffic cops."

"Sneaky, guv," said Neil.

"Wes failed the roadside test but was okay when they tested him later at the police station. However, the courts fined him for an illegal number plate. That was another reason for emigrating to New Zealand. Wes Guthrie believed he was a marked man from that day, and police pulled him over every time they saw him on the road. It was as if they couldn't accept he wasn't involved in his father's death."

"It wasn't true, was it, guv?" asked Lydia.

"Of course not, Lydia," said Gus, "but that was his perception. Of course, Wes didn't help by driving his father's Bentley Continental for a while. My guess is Tamsin Meredith was behind that move."

"Just the thing to antagonise the locals and turn them against the couple even more," said Alex.

"What happened to the car, guv?" asked Neil.

"Wes sold it at auction before the move to New Zealand. It fetched close to a hundred grand, which he donated to animal charities. So that's it for the Guthrie clan. Now, let's move on to Jim Thornton. As you know, three weeks into the investigation, Wade Pinnock came forward in response to a public appeal for information. That call brought Porter and Coleman to Jim's door. Bob Ellison, a neighbour, told the detectives Jim's wife had died in hospital two or three days ago. After his wife's funeral, they spoke to Jim to check what he remembered of events in the Traveller's Rest on Friday, the thirteenth of February. Jim was in his seventies. And his wife's death hit him hard. He died eighteen months ago during a winter flu outbreak."

"That only leaves four people in the pub that night," said Lydia.

"Am I missing something?" asked Alex. "We heard little detail on Kendal Guthrie's character, but what we have heard paints him in an unpleasant light. It strikes me loads of people might have wanted him dead. You're concentrating on the handful of people he was with on Friday night, guv. Are you convinced one of them is the killer?"

"Far too soon to tell, Alex," said Gus. "I'm following the text from the murder file because it offers us the chance to create a picture of the main characters and where they were in relation to one another on the night of the murder. Of course, I'm getting ahead of myself. But in the file, you'll read that Porter and Coleman interviewed dozens of people who hated Kendal Guthrie with a vengeance. We can check their alibis, but three years ago, they passed every test."

"Porter and Coleman could have missed a suspect altogether, guv," said Neil.

"True, but my nose tells me whoever they are, they had to live near Glenhead Farm. Only a handful of hardy annuals were out on the roads that night. The furthest anyone we know about having to travel was a little over eleven miles. That was the victim himself. Therefore, it's unlikely our killer travelled from outside the confines of the area defined by my map specifications."

"How long is the lane from Netheravon Road to the farm, guv?" asked Blessing.

"I don't think anyone measured that, Blessing," said Gus. "What were you thinking?"

"Well, you know how far it is from the main road to the Ferris's farm, guv," she said.

"It has to be half a mile, but that's exceptional, surely?" said Gus.

"I'm checking online, guv," said Luke. "The map shows the lane as fairly straight and the farmhouse two hundred and fifty yards from the junction."

"I see what you're getting at, Blessing," said Gus. "Kendal Guthrie drove up the lane, and the lights on the garage and the farmhouse automatically came on. He turned off the engine, got out of the car, and hurried across the yard to the side door."

Gus stood up and mimicked the moves Kendal Guthrie would have made.

"Key in the door, step inside, flick the switch, and BANG, lights out. How much time elapsed between stopping the Bentley outside the garage and turning on the mudroom light?"

"Twelve to fifteen seconds, guv," said Luke.

"We need to check the lane when we speak to Helen Guthrie, guv," said Alex. "Verify what condition it was in at the time of the murder. Was it a tarmacked surface? Or was it full of potholes and pitted with ruts caused by heavy farm machinery? Twenty miles per hour could be pushing it if it was the latter. Thirty, if the surface was smooth and flat."

"I've done the maths," said Luke. "A vehicle travelling twenty miles per hour would cover one hundred and twenty yards in fifteen seconds. So even at thirty, they would still be short of where Kendal parked the car and wouldn't have enough time to get close enough to strike him over the head."

"If a vehicle was already on the lane when he got out of the Bentley, Kendal should have heard it or seen its head-lights," said Neil.

"It was blowing a gale and raining hard," said Luke. "Perhaps the driver killed his lights as soon as the security lighting switched on. It's still tight. I can't see how someone following Kendal could reach the mudroom door without being seen or heard."

"In that case, the killer was lying in wait," said Blessing. "Which throws the field wide open. Doug Lawless and Harry Meaden live on either side of Glenhead Farm. They fall well within the catchment area you described, guv. So if they saw Guthrie's car leave on Friday night on its way to the Traveller's Rest, they had plenty of time to get into posi-tion. Wind and rain wouldn't deter them if they hated the man that much."

"No, Blessing, I don't imagine it would," said Gus. "The worse the weather conditions were, the better it was for the killer. What chance was there of someone seeing them late at night? The dog walkers I rely on to see something useful were tucked up somewhere warm and dry."

"Is Alf Collett still the landlord at the pub, guv?" asked Neil.

"What pub, Neil?" asked Gus.

"The Traveller's Rest, guv. Don't tell me it's gone the way of so many others."

"Alf's wife, Joan, died in June last year, and Alf didn't have the heart to keep going. So most days, he hacks a small white ball around a golf course in Portugal. The Traveller's Rest was one of the eighteen pubs that closed every week in the UK during 2017."

"That leaves us with a barmaid and a building society manager," said Lydia.

"Careful, Neil," said Luke. "I know there's a joke somewhere, but please remember there are ladies present."

"It's not a joking matter," said Gus. "The barmaid, Rosie Ritchens, died in a traffic accident in Majorca only weeks after the murder. When Porter and Coleman spoke to Alf Collett, they learned Rosie had quit her job at the pub. She gave a variety of reasons. The altercation involving Kendal Guthrie upset her, and the drive backwards and forwards from Salisbury to the pub was taking its toll. Dave Vickers, the building society manager, fancied her, making her uncomfortable. He was in his early fifties, and Rosie wanted to work in a lively pub where she would meet blokes more her age. Alf Collett last spoke to Rosie when she got a job in a bar in Salisbury city centre and was off to Majorca for a two-week holiday. Rosie was walking back from town to her apartment block in the early hours and staggered into the road right in front of an oncoming vehicle. The driver didn't stop. The police found the burnt-out hire car on scrubland near the beach the following morning. They never identified the driver."

"That's terrible, guv," said Blessing, "the poor girl was a couple of years younger than me. Anyway, Lydia was wrong. You forgot the estate manager."

"Oscar Wallington," said Gus. "Yes. He's still working for the owners of the manor house. He will be available for an interview."

"Where are Keith Porter and Maxine Coleman these days, guv?" asked Luke.

"Keith Porter remains at Bourne Hill with his rank unchanged," said Gus. "Maxine Devereux, nee Coleman, is on maternity leave. Her promotion to Detective Inspector will follow if she returns to work."

"We have little to work with," said Blessing.

"Then we must make the most of what we have," said Gus.

Chapter Eight

"DIVYA WILL GET copies of the maps to us first thing in the morning, guv," said Luke.

"Thanks, Luke," said Gus. "Did you start a list of people we can interview?"

"I'd start with DI Porter and Maxine Devereux," said Luke.

"I prefer Dave Vickers and Oscar Wallington," said Alex. "They were in the pub on Friday night."

"Helen Guthrie might not have much to offer, guv," said Neil, "and the ex-wife, Millie, has an axe to grind. So I wouldn't rush to speak to them."

"Don't forget Wade Pinnock," said Blessing.

"Alf Collett's the only other person alive who was there on Friday," said Lydia. "Can you get clearance to fly to Portugal to interview him, guv?"

"I can get DS Mercer to ask the question," said Gus. "There's no mileage in ringing Collett. I need to conduct the interview face-to-face."

"Zoom's been available for three years now, guv," said Luke.

"That's an ice lolly, isn't it?" said Gus.

"No, a video call. You can see one another, guv," said Neil.

"The mind boggles," said Gus. "What will they think of next?"

"I still reckon Pinnock's your best bet," insisted Blessing. "He spoke to the landlord and the barmaid. Jim Thornton was in the pub on Saturday too, plus another customer Wade Pinnock couldn't name. That could have been Dave Vickers or Oscar Wallington."

"I like that idea, Blessing," said Gus. "We'll get an overview of events on Friday and Saturday night before we speak to the building society manager and the estate manager. I can't count on the Chief Constable sanctioning an overseas trip so soon after our recent flight to Spain. We'll need a solid reason to travel to Portugal to disturb Alf Collett as he's standing over a tricky six-foot putt."

"What about the two officers on duty on Saturday afternoon, guv?" asked Alex. "What were their names?"

"WPC Sarah Saunders," said Gus. "Her colleague, PC Zak Drake, was the one who queried the mudroom light. Of course, they wouldn't be at the top of my list, but add them to the mix, Luke, if you would."

"Okay, guv," said Luke. "I've got Doug Lawless and Harry Meaden on my list. Does that sound reasonable?"

"Of course," said Gus. "Add Bob Ellison's name while you're at it. Do you have anyone else you made a note of while I went through the text from the murder file?"

"Barton and Goodwin, the guys with Wes Guthrie on Friday night's pub crawl," said Luke.

Gus shook his head.

"Forget those two. Porter and Coleman found no evidence linking them to Kendal Guthrie. If they were as drunk as Wes Guthrie at eleven o'clock, they were too far from Glenhead Farm to play a part, just as he was."

"Tom Dix, now the manager at Glenhead Farm," said Luke. "He was Wes Guthrie's number two at the farm in Winterbourne Stoke three years ago."

"Check the murder file to see whether he's mentioned in connection with anything other than covering for Wes while he had a boozy weekend. It might be wise to dig into Dix's family background to learn whether they ever had a run-in with Kendal Guthrie. We don't want to miss the obvious."

"Got it, guv," said Luke. "If he's in the clear, we can scrub Tom Dix from our list."

"Get that list into a sensible order, Luke," said Gus. "We'll make a start tomorrow. We can't make much progress until the Hub provides our maps, so can everyone please delve into the murder file and get the crime scene photos onto a whiteboard? Prepare brief biographies for the names Luke itemised for the other board, and root around in the stationery cupboard for a dozen coloured drawing pins and a large ball of string."

Gus sat back and watched as the team got to work. He opened his desk drawer and checked the white paper bag. The cream horn looked too good to resist. If he left now, he could beat the rush, get home thirty minutes before Suzie, and make a pig of himself.

"I've just remembered a dental appointment," he said. "I'll see you first thing in the morning."

Gus covered the paper bag with his jacket and made for the lift. He heard a couple of voices wishing him luck as the lift doors closed.

Suzie found him in the kitchen at twenty to six.

"The roads were busy this evening," she sighed. "Did you get caught in that accident?"

"I must have missed it by minutes," said Gus. "I left work a few minutes early. We've got another tough nut to crack, and the Hub couldn't give us the tools we need until the morning. So I saw little point in staying to the bitter end."

"Where was the dirty deed done this time?" asked Suzie.

"Just up the road from the Stonehenge Inn in Durrington. Kendal Guthrie was the victim."

"I've only visited the pub once, a few years ago now."

"Did John and Jackie know the Guthrie family?" asked Gus.

"They knew Kendal and Poppy, yes," said Suzie. "She was a lovely lady. Her husband was arrogant, objectionable, sexist, and a dozen other names I could use. Dad wasn't surprised to hear someone murdered him. I suppose it was inevitable the Chief Constable would return to that case eventually."

"Kenneth Truelove wasn't involved in the investigation, was he? Surely, he was already in his ACC post?"

"He investigated a complaint against DI Keith Porter," said Suzie. "A female officer alleged he suggested they use the Bourne Hill photocopier for inappropriate images."

"DS Maxine Coleman?" asked Gus.

"No, a WPC called Sarah Saunders. Porter said it was a misunderstanding. There was no physical evidence, and the complaint died a death."

"He said, she said."

"Exactly," said Suzie. "Sarah Saunders thought the ACC should have accepted her word. Porter had a reputation for getting over-familiar with the ladies. Kenneth asked

Maxine whether he misbehaved when they worked on the same team. She said Keith got near the line on occasion but never crossed it. Maxine told the ACC a stern word worked wonders with children and suggested WPC Saunders took a leaf out of her book."

"It sounds as if Keith Porter escaped by the skin of his teeth," said Gus. "That explains why he hasn't moved up the ladder. We skipped through the murder file this afternoon. I hoped to find something concrete on which to base our review of the case. I've never come across anything like it. Five people were in a pub near Tilshead when Kendal Guthrie arrived. He ripped into each one of them, got thrown out, drove home, and as soon as he arrived, someone battered him over the head with an iron bar. Two of those five people are dead."

"Does anyone suspect those deaths are related?" asked Suzie.

"On the face of it, nothing supports that idea. A man in his seventies died of complications following winter flu, and a twenty-year-old girl died in a hit-and-run in Majorca. Her alcohol level at the time was off the scale. Spanish police have lost count of the number of British holidaymakers who come to grief after too much sun and sangria. They think she stepped off the grass verge, forgot which country she was in, looked right instead of left and got hit by a hire car. The driver was probably over the limit, ditched the car, and set it alight three miles along the road. I doubt whether they busted a gut looking for the driver."

"Kendal and Poppy Guthrie had children a few years older than me, didn't they?" said Suzie.

"Wesley and Helen," said Gus. "That's another complication we could have done without. Wes was playing away at the time of the murder. His girlfriend provided him with an alibi, which caused ructions with his wife, Millie. They divorced shortly after his father's funeral. As for the daughter, Helen, she caught her husband in bed with another man, gave him the elbow, and is now living at Glenhead Farm. Wes and his new wife are farming in New Zealand. A place called Taupaki."

"I know it," said Suzie. "My grandparents lived near Auckland for many years. There's a terrific farming community in the region with sheep, strawberries, all sorts."

"It sounds idyllic, but it doesn't help us much. I've emailed Geoff Mercer asking for clearance to fly to Portugal to interview the landlord of the pub where Kendal Guthrie spent his last evening. Fat chance the boss will sanction a flight Down Under. We're running on fumes, Suzie."

"Why don't we take a walk?" she said. "It's cooler this evening. The fresh air will clear your head—no allotment for you nor a trip to the Lamb Inn. We'll phone for a pizza later. Come on, let's shower and change first."

Gus perked up, but Suzie gave him a gentle nudge towards the bathroom and walked into the bedroom.

"Where are we going?" asked Gus as they left the bungalow. His watch read six-thirty. Suzie was right about the weather. The temperature had dropped several degrees since he left the Old Police Station Office.

"I've no idea," said Suzie. "I planned to walk for thirty minutes and then turn around and walk back. If we found an alternative route back, fine. Anyway, I thought you knew every nook and cranny in the village."

"I've lived here for four years," said Gus. "I know every inch between the bungalow and the allotment, plus parts of the village like Bert's house on the main road. Beyond that, it's a mystery. When I flipped through the Kendal Guthrie murder file this afternoon, I spotted a reference to myths and monsters. It was a topic of conversation in the pub on Friday the thirteenth, back in 2015. I could imagine the scene. A roaring fire inside the pub, while outside, the storm raged. I tried to explain to Blessing Umeh that Salisbury Plain is a vast expanse, and it's easy to get lost. People her age think they'll be fine with a smartphone to hand ready for any emergency. There are blind spots everywhere on the Plain. A hundred years ago, people living in remote villages and hamlets spent months never seeing another human being. The mind can play tricks, and trees blackened by lightning could become monsters when men returned from the pub on a dark, stormy night."

"I hope you didn't frighten the poor girl to death, Gus Freeman," said Suzie. "Ah, Oakfrith Wood, if I'm not mistaken. Don't you feel calmer already? Nest boxes everywhere, and plenty of ground cover for small birds and animals. I can imagine a carpet of bluebells being here in the Spring."

"Let's follow this path south," said Gus. "If it takes us past the cricket pitch, then we should see Urchfont Manor on our left."

"I didn't think you knew this part of the village?" said Suzie.

"Bert Penman mentioned it one day in the Lamb, ages ago," said Gus. "This path leads back to civilisation and the White Horse Trail. First, we can climb the hill and sit and enjoy the view. Then we can stroll back to the bungalow for that pizza."

"You knew what lay ahead of us if we'd kept going on this path, didn't you?" said Suzie. "Bert Penman told you about the field containing The Three Graves."

"He did tell me of a remote mound that lies in the

triangle formed by the villages of Urchfont, Easterton, and Potterne," said Gus.

"Back in 1644, three brothers died in that field from the plague. They were travellers from London who chose to die there rather than infect the villagers. As a result, Urchfont escaped the plague. Because of their selfless sacrifice, villagers buried the men on the hillside with an elm tree planted at the head of each grave."

"Bert reckoned they were Irish tinkers," said Gus. "It made for a delightful story on the last day of October."

"Ever the cynic," scoffed Suzie.

"I've lived on the edge of the Plain long enough to know ghost stories and mythical monsters abound. It's the same across the entire country, Suzie. They can't all be genuine. I could name a dozen towns that were major centres of wealth and affluence in the Middle Ages. As their influence waned, they had to develop a wizard wheeze that encouraged people to continue visiting their ancient backwater. What better way than to create a myth? It encouraged tourism if they had standing stones, a giant, or a white horse carved into the chalk hillside."

"Every native villager I know believes the brothers, Giddings, kept the plague from the village," said Suzie. "Not everyone has seen the headless horseman, though. So, that story's not in the same class."

"Go on," said Gus. "I'll fall for it."

"Seymour Wroughton owned Castle House at the end of the eighteenth century. The grand house bordered Folly Wood, and its reputation caused it to become Folly House to the locals. As he drove his coach and four horses on the approach to his home one night, it overturned, and Wroughton broke his neck."

"Where was Castle House? I've never seen it on any Ordnance Survey map," said Gus.

"Can't you guess? It stood on the steep ridge in the same field as The Three Graves. So, one hundred and fifty years after the brothers died on the hillside, Seymour Wroughton broke his neck. It makes you think the place is cursed, doesn't it?"

"Have you ever met a sober person who saw the ghost of this chap Wroughton?"

"I've heard that a few people have seen him," said Suzie. "But mostly they've heard the sound of horses hooves, the shouts of Wroughton as he struggled to keep the coach upright on the steep hillside and the agonies of doomed horses as they tumbled down the hillside."

They walked in silence for several minutes.

Suzie could see the path they were on would bring them back to the village by the housing estate where Irene North lived. Well, where Irene lived before she moved in with Bert Penman.

"What topping do you want on your pizza?" asked Gus.

"I thought you were thinking about the history lesson I gave you," said Suzie.

When they reached the bungalow, Gus entered the lounge while Suzie called for their large pizza. She was still considering which topping she wanted as they passed the Lamb and walked along the lane, so Gus decided to eat whatever she was having.

Suzie joined Gus in the lounge.

"Twenty-three minutes and counting until it's delivered," she said.

"Can you give me the benefit of your local knowledge?"

"If I can," said Suzie.

"As I read through the murder file this afternoon, I spotted the names of various unfamiliar establishments on the Plain. I've visited Porton Down recently, as you will remember, on the Dr Ian McGuire case. So what happens at Copehill Down?"

"I've ridden my horse out that way," said Suzie. "It's a training facility between Chitterne and Tilshead. They describe it as a FIBUA. That's fighting in built-up areas for the civilian. So, it's for urban warfare and close-quarters battle training scenarios."

"How long has the MoD had that facility available to them?"

"The best part of thirty years," said Suzie. "Dad said it started as a mock-up of a Bavarian village during the Cold War. They made minor adjustments to training for the Balkans, Iran, and Afghanistan. In recent years they've added a shanty town of cargo containers stacked and laid out in rows of tightly packed streets. It provides a training area closely resembling the Army's operational theatres in Iraq and Afghanistan. Restricted access is putting it mildly. You wouldn't want to wander into that area day or night."

"You said you rode past it?" asked Gus.

"The Plain is covered with lanes, byways, and bridle-paths, Gus. On foot or horseback, you could walk the perimeter of the facility. I've heard of people taking the odd photograph. I wouldn't recommend it, though, if you consider going there."

"No," said Gus. "I'm trying to understand where the farms are that border MoD land. Guthrie submitted bids for five farms the MoD released in 2015. His murder didn't affect the bids. Everything passed to Wes and Helen, and the solicitors holding the paperwork carried on working on their behalf. The upshot was that Guthrie Holdings, or whatever they call the family's empire, was successful in securing two farms."

"Do you have a map? Where are these farms?"

"We won't have anything until the morning," said Gus.

"Where will you put these maps?" asked Suzie.

"On the office wall, so we can see what we're looking at. They'll be around eight feet by ten feet."

"We can print something detailed enough from your computer right now. Let's make a start before the food arrives."

The front doorbell rang as the printer produced the map of the Plain. After they'd eaten, Gus wondered whether he'd ever have chosen a feta cheese, spinach, black olives, sundried tomatoes, and onion topping if left to his own devices. It was different, he had to admit.

"Can you tell me which farms we're interested in?" asked Suzie.

"Three were close together," said Gus. "They were at Enford, Lower Everleigh, and Collingbourne Ducis."

"So they would be sixteen to eighteen miles from Dad's farm."

"Half an hour on a tractor," said Gus.

"Quicker across the fields," said Suzie. "They're eight to ten miles from Glenhead Farm. I can see why Guthrie would want to add them to his portfolio."

"The more land he grabbed close to his centre of operations, the more it put the squeeze on farmers such as Doug Lawless and Harry Meaden. I wonder if he ever tried to buy them out?"

"You can ask when you interview them. Did Kendal Guthrie gain one of those three?"

"No, the two he secured were near Ablington and Larkhill."

"The first one was right on his doorstep, relatively speaking, and two miles further from Glenhead Farm on the Netheravon Road. I can't tell from this map, but it could be the farm next door to his neighbour."

"That would be Harry Meaden," said Gus. "The Lawless farm is closest to Durrington village."

"The Larkhill farm is interesting," said Suzie. "That must be on Durrington Down. While the first four farms the MoD selected for release were on the north-eastern edge of the Plain, Larkhill is more central. It's on the opposite side of the road to Glenhead Farm. Kendal Guthrie couldn't see it from his bedroom window, but it was just over the brow of the hill."

"Perhaps he got the best two of the five," said Gus. "Not that he lived to enjoy his success."

"Does it help you find his killer, Gus?" asked Suzie.

"We won't know that until we've interviewed the surviving characters in the drama, but this has given me a head start for tomorrow. What made you say the farm near Larkhill was interesting?"

"Well, think about it from the Army's point of view," said Suzie. "The MoD grabbed vast areas of the Plain in the years leading up to WWII. Those farms on the outer edge have become less important to them as Army numbers drop and training for modern warfare has evolved. I can understand them releasing those farms for sale to tenant farmers."

Suzie folded the map in half and pointed at Larkhill.

"Larkhill is still a garrison town," she said. "Two miles west of Durrington village by road. Stonehenge is not much more than a mile away to the south. Military camps have stood at Larkhill for over a century, and today it's the base for the Royal Artillery. They transferred from Woolwich ten years ago."

"We can ask Tom Dix how they can use the land they purchased," said Gus. "How many people are on-site?"

"Over two thousand," said Suzie. "Remember what I said about getting too close to these facilities, Gus Freeman. Larkhill is home to members of the Military Police Special Investigation Branch."

"That could prove useful," said Gus. "I'll ask Geoff Mercer to set up lines of communication. I draw the line at saluting, though."

"If they were on board, it might prevent you from getting arrested for trespassing," said Suzie.

"I'll hang onto this map," said Gus. "When I get into the office in the morning, we can label the restricted parts, like the live firing areas and the drop zones. We can highlight the military camps such as Larkhill, Bulford, and Tidworth. Warminster feels too far west to come into play. Thanks for your help, Suzie. I reckon we've got helpful information here."

"Glad I could help," said Suzie. "Will there be a reward?"

"I'll take you to dinner tomorrow evening," Gus said.

"You hated the pizza, didn't you?" said Suzie. "You'll have to get used to my random cravings for a while, I'm afraid."

"Let's hope the chef at the Lamb can cope," said Gus.

Tuesday, 28 August 2018

GUS WAS eager to get away on time this morning. He knew the Old Police Station office would be a hive of activity for the next few days. Suzie was dragging her heels this morning, spending far longer in the shower than usual. He listened to the sound of her singing and counted his blessings.

Somehow, they managed to get ready to leave the bungalow together at twenty-past-eight.

As they stood beside the doors of their respective cars, Gus called across to her.

"I love you, Suzie Ferris."

"That's good to know. Did you hear me singing in the shower?"

"I did. The radio in the kitchen muted the sound. Was there any particular reason for the serenade?"

"It wasn't for you," said Suzie. "I was just getting the little one's ears attuned to our kind of music."

"The earlier, the better, I suppose," said Gus. "Do you think they'll be an Eric Clapton fan?"

"It's not optional," said Suzie. "Will you be home early again this evening?"

"No guarantees," said Gus. "It depends on who Luke Sherman has on my interview schedule, when they're available, and how long it takes to get them to tell the truth."

"Do you think you've spotted someone who lied in the first investigation?" asked Suzie.

"I'm positive more than one person withheld vital information. Whether anyone told a blatant lie is another matter."

Suzie led the two-car convoy as they motored along the road towards the Lydeway junction. They joined the morning traffic on the A342 entering Devizes, and Suzie slowed to turn right into the London Road HQ car park. Gus flashed his lights as he drove past.

The only car in the car park reserved for Crime Review Team personnel belonged to Luke Sherman. Gus looked at the clock on the dashboard. Ten to nine. He remembered adjusting the clock at the weekend while he sat in the supermarket car park waiting for Suzie. He felt chuffed he'd remembered how to do it. The thing now was to remember to put the clock back an hour in the autumn.

When Gus arrived in the first-floor office, Luke looked up from his computer and grinned.

"I thought you would want to make an early start, guv," he said.

"You couldn't sleep either then, Luke?" said Gus.

"Nicky snores like you wouldn't believe, guv," said Luke. "Yet when I complain, he denies ever having snored. Nothing from the Hub yet, guv. Divya must have a reason for staying in bed until the last minute."

"I remember Blessing telling me about her on our recent night out at the Waggon & Horses," said Gus. "Divya's worked at the Hub ever since it opened. She used to work at a computer bureau near Tottenham Court Road, but Divya and her husband found it too expensive to live in London. So when an opportunity arose to move to Marlborough, it was a simple choice. Her husband is a junior doctor at the Great Western Hospital in Swindon. So they have a twenty-five-minute drive to work instead of over an hour and a half."

"Junior doctors are notorious for working longer hours than we do," said Luke. "It must be tough to sustain a relationship when one person works nine to five, and the other can do a week's worth in one shift."

"Maybe that's why so many people in our profession find partners doing a similar job," said Gus.

"I've had a thought, guv. What if Divya's husband had a colleague in Swindon?"

"Are you suggesting a subterfuge, Luke?" asked Gus.

"Either way could work, guv," said Luke. "One of her husband's mates could become Blessing's significant other to ward off the threatened marriage, or he might unearth a genuine prospect. Someone tall and handsome, who is a great kisser."

"Blessing could have competition," said Gus.

"If Nicky doesn't stop snoring, guv," laughed Luke.

They heard the lift descending to the ground floor.

Two minutes later, the office had a full house. Blessing and Neil rode up with Alex and Lydia.

"Any news from the Hub, Luke," asked Lydia.

"Nothing yet," replied Luke.

"Now everyone's here," said Gus. "Suzie and I went for a walk in the countryside last night. I learned a lot about the local area, and we filled in several details on a map of the plain. I'll point out the items you need to transfer to the large-scale maps if you gather around. Luke will highlight the relevant place names on one map. Then you will add the distances and who travelled, where and when. These five farms the MoD released in 2015 can go on a second map, along with the original five farms Kendal Guthrie controlled. There could be someone neighbouring those ten properties we haven't identified yet. We may only need to interview them for elimination purposes, but if we don't know who they are, we can't be sure we haven't excluded the killer from our case review."

"Yesterday, you thought the killer had to be local, guv," said Alex. "Isn't this widening the net?"

"When you study the map that includes the farms Guthrie bid for before he died, you'll see they lie within an eight-mile radius of Glenhead Farm."

"So at the furthest point, a killer could have been a mere fifteen minutes from his doorstep," said Lydia. "That feels local to me, guv."

Neil noticed movement on the security camera outside the building.

"We've got mail," he cried. "Divya is downstairs waving a large bundle of papers."

"Can I bring her to the office, guv," asked Blessing.

"Of course," said Gus, "get her to sign the Official Secrets Act first."

Blessing paused in her stride. Then she realised Gus was joking.

Two minutes later, the two friends emerged from the lift.

"You wanted large maps, Mr Freeman," said Divya. "You'll need more than Blu Tack to hold these on the walls."

"If they help us find our killer, Divya," said Gus. "I'm sure DS Mercer won't begrudge having to pay to give the walls a lick of paint."

"Would you like a coffee before you drive back to the Hub, Divya?" asked Luke.

"I wouldn't say no," said Divya.

Well done, Luke, subtle as ever, thought Gus.

As Luke and Divya disappeared into the restroom, Gus asked Alex and Lydia to put a map on the back wall. Neil and Gus placed a second map next to the whiteboard on the wall opposite the restroom. Gus stored the four spare maps at the bottom of the stationery cupboard.

Blessing stood by Gus's desk, studying the handheld map he'd referred to earlier.

"Where are the largest camps and barracks?" she asked.

"Larkhill, Bulford, and Tidworth," said Gus. "In the centre of that map."

"How often do they have live firing on the Plain?" asked Blessing

"Forty-eight weeks a year," said Gus.

"Gosh, it must be noisy," said Blessing.

"The sound carries over twenty miles when the wind's in the right direction," said Gus, "but the Plain covers an area of three hundred square miles. The MoD only occupies fifty per cent at present, and that percentage is dropping."

"It sounds like a dangerous place to go," said Blessing.

Lydia had joined Blessing at the desk and spotted something Suzie had highlighted last night.

"When was this place Imber evacuated?" asked Lydia.

"During WWII, two villages got evacuated," said Neil. "The inhabitants of Imber and Hinton Parva needed to move out to make way for training for Operation Overlord. After the war, the residents of Hinton Parva could return. However, Imber has remained closed except for an annual church service and an occasional Bank Holiday."

"What was Operation Overlord," asked Blessing.

"The D-Day landings in June 1944," said Alex. "We keep forgetting how young you are, Blessing."

"Didn't you study WWII at school, Blessing?" asked Gus.

"History wasn't my favourite subject, guv. We studied Joseph Lister and the American Plains Indians."

"I think I saw them at the Corn Exchange," said Neil. "Terrible name for a band."

Alex shook his head. Neil loved a joke.

"All roads around the deserted village are closed, I imagine, guv?" said Alex.

"Yes, because they lie within the Imber Range live firing area," said Gus.

"So you can't get near the village except on those special occasions?" asked Lydia.

"If you know the way, it's possible to cover the complete perimeter of the range on public footpaths," said Gus. "Suzie told me last night that she could ride on her horse around the Copehill Down facility. No doubt she could also find a way around Imber if the need arose."

Chapter Nine

LUKE AND DIVYA stood to one side with their cups of coffee while Gus and the others discussed the maps.

"So, you'll ask Arjun if he knows of any eligible bachelors seeking a cuddly, intelligent, and ambitious young Nigerian lady?"

"I will, Luke," said Divya, "but if he's as busy as my husband, Blessing might only see him once every couple of weeks."

"We do have a backup plan," said Luke.

"I haven't known Blessing for long," said Divya, "but she wouldn't agree with tricking her father with a pretend suitor."

"You're probably right," said Luke. "We need the genuine article or nothing."

"I'll ask Arjun when I see him next. He'll do his best, and I'll call you with an update. Thanks for the coffee, Luke; I'd better get back."

Divya handed Luke her empty cup and crossed the

room to the group of people huddled over the murder file and Suzie's handheld map.

"Thanks for inviting me up to your office. If you need anything more from the Hub to help with this case you're working on, you know where we are."

"These maps are superb, Divya," said Gus. "We're just finalising where everything needs to go. This office will resemble a Blue Peter challenge for the rest of the morning. Pins, rulers, and lengths of string. We can make inroads into the case now."

"No sticky back plastic then, Mr Freeman?" said Divya. "Gosh, that takes me back."

With that, Divya gave Blessing a smile and a wave and headed for the lift.

Lydia went to the stationery cupboard and retrieved the items Gus had mentioned.

"Right, guv," she said. "Where do you want to start?"

Luke fetched his notes from his desk. Alex and Neil prepared to help Lydia.

"What shall we do, guv?" asked Blessing as she and Gus appeared to be surplus to requirements.

"I haven't studied the interview schedule Luke prepared for me yet, Blessing. A quick check to ensure I'm happy with the order, and then you can call people to fix appointments."

"Got it, guv," said Blessing.

Gus noticed her envious glance towards the others standing by the map on the back wall.

"Don't worry, Blessing," he said, "you'll get your turn."

"It's okay, guv," said Blessing. "Andy Carlton, my old DI, told me when a team is successful, it's as much because of the efforts of those who handle the mundane tasks as the detective who makes the arrest. I just realised how much I would miss this if I were to marry Ekene Kanu."

"Tomorrow evening with soon be here," said Gus. "Don't forget to ask your mother for the young man's number. It can often help to get your retaliation in first."

Blessing wondered whether Gus would ever run out of proverbs or adages. She didn't always understand them, but this one felt appropriate.

Gus searched through the folders and papers on his desk.

"Here we are. Wade Pinnock, the young lad you thought was the place to start. Where did he live? Did it say in the murder file?"

"Netheravon, guv," said Blessing. "Wade still lived at home back then. His father witnessed the activity at Glenhead Farm on Saturday evening as he returned from watching football in Andover."

"That fits," said Gus. "He would have used the A303 as far as the Amesbury roundabout, then taken the third exit towards Durrington. Wade said his father drove past at around six o'clock. Find out whether Wade has moved out, fix a time, and we'll go from there to speak to the two detectives, Porter and Devereux."

"What if Wade Pinnock isn't immediately available, guv?" asked Blessing. "Do I threaten him with uniformed officers collecting him from home or his place of work?"

"Use your judgement, Blessing," said Gus. "I've got nothing to do except sit on my hands until you arrange my first interview. I'll use the time preparing the questions I want to ask each person on this list. Shout when you're ready to leave."

Blessing knew what she needed to do. A call to Wade's home address in 2015 revealed that he and his girlfriend, Hannah Rose, moved in together six months after the murder. They lived and worked in Salisbury, where Hannah was a reporter with the Salisbury Journal. Wade Pinnock worked for a car body repair firm. Wade's mother told Blessing the couple had at last fixed a date for the wedding next April.

Blessing rang the garage. The man who answered nearly deafened Blessing when he yelled for Wade Pinnock to come to the phone.

"Wade Pinnock speaking. Who is this?"

"Detective Constable Umeh, from Wiltshire Police Crime Review Team," said Blessing. "Can you ask your boss to let you use his office for an hour from half-past ten, please? We need to talk with you concerning the Kendal Guthrie murder."

"I'm busy working on a car. The customer's hoping to pick it up at lunchtime."

"I know what it's like to wait for a car to get returned to you in good working order," said Blessing. "If we have to send someone to fetch you and keep you hanging around at Bourne Hill police station for half a day, your customer's joy will get delayed even further. My boss and I will see you in one hour. Goodbye."

Gus carried on sketching out questions for later use and risked a smile.

"All set, guv," said Blessing, gathering her things and ready to accompany her boss on a trip to the cathedral city.

"That was lucky, Blessing," said Gus. "We're off far quicker than I thought."

"Luck had nothing to do with it, guv," she replied with a grin.

As Gus eased the Focus into Church Street, he asked Blessing where they were headed.

"It's on Churchfields Road, guv," she replied.

"Not the Industrial Estate again?" he asked.

"Not quite, guv," said Blessing, "four hundred yards past the entrance if I'm reading this map correctly. My sense of direction isn't great."

"It runs in the family," said Gus. "I remember."

Fifty minutes later, Gus turned off Churchfields Road into a small car park in front of a single-storey building. The dashboard clock read twenty-five past ten. The addition of office space to the original building looked to have taken place in the Sixties. The high-roofed black corrugated iron workshop behind it was where the hard work had happened since between the wars.

"Wade Pinnock should be in the offices somewhere," said Blessing.

Gus led them into the office building and, as expected, came face-to-face with a receptionist.

The young girl stopped filing her nails and sighed.

"Yes?"

"Wiltshire Police," said Gus. "We're here to see Wade Pinnock."

"He's in Mr Peter's office, over there," said the girl, nodding towards a large room in the building's corner.

"Don't get up," said Gus. "We'll find our way, I'm sure."

The receptionist went back to filing her nails. Gus and Blessing found a nervous-looking Wade Pinnock sitting on the window sill of his boss's office.

"You can sit in Mr Peter's chair if you wish, Wade," said Gus. "I'm sure he won't mind, I'm Mr Freeman, and you've already spoken to DC Umeh."

"I thought I'd put the Guthrie business behind me," said Wade. "What's happened for you to dig it up again?"

"The original enquiry didn't find the killer, Wade," said Gus. "No unsolved murder case is ever closed. We review cold cases, hoping to find answers to unanswered questions.

We've both read the interview you gave DI Porter and DS Coleman three years ago. Take us through it again, and we'll see whether you remember something new, or we can ask a question the detectives didn't think of at the time."

"What made you respond to the appeal the detectives issued, Wade?" asked Blessing.

"I thought it was the right thing to do," said Wade. "I was in the pub, listening to the landlord asking a customer if he'd heard about the incident at Glenhead Farm."

"Can we go back, Wade?" asked Gus. "How long had you been in the pub before you heard that conversation?"

"I picked up Hannah, my girlfriend, fiancée now, and we drove out to the Traveller's Rest. I suppose it was between eight o'clock and a quarter past when we arrived. The bar wasn't crowded, but there were enough people inside that you had to wait to get served. It was too small to have over two people serving anyhow. The Traveller's Rest has closed now, did you know?"

Gus nodded.

"Alf, the landlord, was serving a customer ahead of me, and he acknowledged an old bloke sat on a stool at the bar. He must have just walked in the door because Rosie, the barmaid, called out that she'd get his pint of bitter in two ticks. She called him Mr Thornton. Then Rosie asked if he'd heard about the excitement in Durrington. Mr Thornton said nothing exciting had happened there in his lifetime. Rosie explained Alf had heard the police were at Kendal Guthrie's farm. I was eager to get our drinks and return to Hannah, but something Mr Thornton said annoyed me."

"Can you remember what it was?" asked Gus.

"He said he hoped it wasn't something trivial," said Wade. "That's what made me butt in on their private conversation. I mean, someone had died; that's not trivial. I told him my Dad saw people carrying a body to a van, and police were at the farm gathering evidence. My Dad saw people dressed in those protective suits they wear, you know."

"As the afternoon progressed," said Gus, "the detectives realised they were dealing with a murder. Forensic evidence must get gathered as soon as possible at the crime scene. Carry on, Wade. You're doing well."

"Rosie carried on talking to Alf and this Jim Thornton. She spoke about Friday night and the storm. Only half a dozen people were in the bar, and one of them was Kendal Guthrie. He turned up at around half-past nine and spent every minute he was there slagging off the others one by one. The landlord said something to Jim Thornton that made no sense to me that Guthrie dying changed things for him, and a bloke called Bob too."

"Bob Ellison?" asked Blessing.

"Yeah, that could be the name," said Wade. "Alf wondered whether Wes Guthrie would follow in his father's footsteps. Rosie asked whether the police would visit the pub. I told them to call you and say what time he left. Alf said it would take Guthrie twenty to twenty-five minutes to drive home. That's when the three of them started discussing the last few minutes the pub was open the night before. I heard Rosie remind Alf that he'd told Guthrie to get out and banned him from returning. She mentioned several names and what they were doing at five to ten past ten. The names meant nothing to me, so they went in one ear and out the other. I commented on Alf banning Guthrie. Several places had done the same thing after they got fed up with his behaviour. I told them again to call you and tell you everything that went on that night. That's when Alf asked what I wanted to drink."

"What did you make of that?" asked Gus.

"It felt like he wanted to get rid of me," said Wade.

"Interesting," said Gus. "What happened next?"

"I took the drinks back to our table," said Wade. "Hannah and I got chatting to a couple sat next to us. It was good to talk about something else, to be honest."

"Did you stay for another drink?" asked Blessing.

"We made the ones we had last as long as possible. I told the other detectives that a chap came in thirty or forty minutes later who Alf and Jim Thornton knew. Several others in the bar knew him too, but I'd never seen him before. Hannah and I were too far from the bar to hear what they discussed, but it must have been the murder."

"What makes you say that?" asked Blessing.

"The new chap turned around and stared at us after Alf nodded his head in our direction. Jim looked our way, too. Hannah wanted to drink up and leave after that. She went to the loo, and I saw Rosie come from behind the bar to collect glasses, wipe over the tabletops, and put chairs and stools back where they belonged. While waiting for Hannah, I noticed the three men were watching Rosie. She seemed distracted, as if she had something on her mind. Perhaps, she was making her mind up about leaving. Only a few weeks later, she was dead. I suppose you know that too, don't you?"

"We do," said Gus. "You never returned to the pub after that night, did you?" asked Gus.

"We had a hundred bars to choose from," said Wade. "It wasn't the easiest pub to get to, and Hannah thought the place boring, and those three blokes spooked her."

"Did you hear anything else from other people not in the pub that night relating to the murder?" asked Gus.

"Not really," said Wade Pinnock. "The odd rumour that led to nothing. Somebody reckoned Wes Guthrie did it. Then they found out that he was in bed with another woman when his Dad died. The gossip mongers then switched their attention to a farmer near West Lavington who thought Guthrie cheated him over a business deal. That might have been the case, but half a dozen other names got thrown in the ring. Each man held a grievance against Guthrie for doing the same to them."

"Any of them might have wanted Guthrie dead," said Gus. "But the police checked their alibis and found they were nowhere near Glenhead Farm in the tiny time frame that defined the fatal attack."

"That's right, and two months later, everything went quiet. Life went on. The only excitement was hearing of Wes Guthrie's divorce, then that of his sister, and the fuss made when Wes married his girlfriend."

"It wasn't popular," said Gus.

"You can say that again," said Wade. "I can't remember people getting so animated on the Plain as when we heard they planned to marry and emigrate to New Zealand."

"What did it have to do with people who live in the region?" asked Blessing. "It's a free country. Wes and Tamsin were free to marry and go wherever they wished."

"People in the countryside don't think that way," said Wade. "They're concerned for the environment, conservation, protecting rare species of birds, butterflies, and moths. We must reserve the land for agricultural use at all costs. Where will youngsters who live in the middle of the Plain work if people like Guthrie continue to buy up farm after farm? His family had farmed there for generations. Wes could have carried on the traditions and helped to protect the future, but Helen was never interested right from the start. She didn't even get a pony when she was five years old. That's not natural around here. Why do you think she disappeared to Australia as soon as she married? She hated farming. Now she's overseeing the whole business. Any chance Helen Guthrie gets to sell to a developer will be it. She will take the money and run. One of the world's last semi-natural dry grassland and scrubland areas will get bulldozed into the ground."

"Conservation is a subject close to your heart then, Wade," said Gus.

"Not really," he replied. "Hannah writes nature and wildlife features for the newspaper. I get what we're doing to the planet drummed into me daily at home. The part about a lack of jobs and homes for local young people was me. A cottage up the road from my Dad would have suited us, but we're paying through the nose for a box on a soulless housing estate. The places my grandparents would have moved into are selling for silly money and are second homes for Londoners who only come here at weekends."

Gus knew the truth of that. He didn't know whether someone would kill Kendal Guthrie to prevent the lands his forefathers had farmed for generations from getting sold to a developer. The case was suddenly heading opposite the direction he'd thought.

"Thanks for your time, Wade," said Gus. "Thank your boss, too. Please get in touch with us if you remember anything you think could help us with our investigation. You can get back to fixing that car now."

"The boss put someone else on it," said Wade. "I hope you find whoever did it. Nobody had a kind word to say about Guthrie, but what happened wasn't right."

"My thoughts exactly," said Gus.

They left the office together. Wade Pinnock turned left and headed through a door into the main garage. Noise levels in the office increased significantly until the door closed. Gus and Blessing turned right and passed the girl in reception on their way to the front door. She was touching up her make-up.

"It must be lunchtime," said Gus as they reached the Ford Focus. "I reckon she'll follow us outside in a minute."

"I'll make the calls for your next appointment, guv," said Blessing.

They sat in the car, and Blessing called Bourne Hill to speak to DI Keith Porter.

The office door opened, and the receptionist came out. She didn't spot Gus and Blessing, the blue sky, or the car park's rough surface because her smartphone was more interesting than the world surrounding her.

"Keith Porter's in court today, guv," said Blessing.

"They caught up with him at last," said Gus.

"Not yet. Keith's giving evidence, guv," said Blessing. "I'll try Maxine Devereux."

Gus switched on the engine and drove toward the car park entrance. He passed the receptionist, holding a shoe with a broken heel. His window was closed, but he could tell whoever she spoke to on the phone was getting an education in Anglo-Saxon swearwords.

"Maxine Devereux will see you now, guv," said Blessing.

BACK IN THE Old Police Station office, the rest of the team was floundering.

"Jim Thornton," said Luke. "He lived four miles from the pub. Jim drove there on both Friday and Saturday nights using the B390. When did he arrive? Do we know?"

"Based on the interviews in the murder file, he was a regular," said Neil.

"When Wade Pinnock heard the people at the bar discussing the incident at Glenhead Farm, Jim Thornton was there, waiting to get served," said Alex. "That had to be somewhen between eight-fifteen and eight-thirty."

"Jim Thornton was already there when Dave Vickers arrived on Friday night," said Lydia. "He passed him cycling through Tilshead."

"Dave Vickers lived in Shrewton and cycled four miles to the pub along the A360," said Luke. "I can see no mention of him being there on Saturday."

"Oscar Wallington lived eight miles from the pub," said Neil. "He drove there on the B390, the same as Jim. Dave Vickers said they discussed the MoD presence on the Plain when Wallington arrived. So, that must have been closer to nine o'clock."

"Kendal Guthrie drove the eleven and a half miles from Glenhead Farm in his flash Bentley arriving at half-past nine," said Neil.

"How do we know?" asked Lydia.

"I remember somewhere Wes Guthrie saying it was common for his father to carry loads of cash because he incorporated a spot of business with a night out," said Alex.

"Have we missed something?" asked Luke. "Could Kendal have met someone earlier that evening? Did forensics prove where the car had been that night? What about the mobile phone? Did neighbours see him leave home at around nine to drive directly to the Traveller's Rest?"

"Let's get the locations, journeys, and distances Gus is so keen on onto the maps," said Neil. "We'll note any questions that arise and he can deal with them when he returns."

"Wes Guthrie drove eight miles from his farm in Winterbourne Stoke to Glenhead Farm on Saturday afternoon," said Alex.

"When did he leave home?" asked Lydia.

"Early afternoon," said Luke. "That's easy to check by asking Millie."

"That's a fifteen-minute drive," said Neil. "The paramedics and the uniformed police will confirm when the emergency call came in and what time they arrived at the scene. So it will be simple to check what time Porter and Coleman arrived."

"Why bother?" asked Neil. "We know Wes was too drunk to drive there on Friday night. Anyway, he had other things on his mind."

"Maybe Wes met someone after he left his wife," said Lydia.

"The person who killed Kendal," said Luke.

"We need to get a tighter definition of these timings," said Alex. "At the moment, Wes has enough time to meet someone, get to the farm, double-check every clue had been removed, and then make the emergency call."

"Wes told the police he searched the whole house and found the body in the mudroom," said Lydia. "The last room on the ground floor. Wes had a spare set of keys. With a storm raging outside, it was more likely his father would use the side door to get in, surely? So why didn't Wes go there first?"

"He was hungover," said Alex, "concerned for his father but expecting him to answer the doorbell when he arrived. He didn't think he'd find a body."

"We do the same again," said Neil. "Get the detail onto

the maps and add it to the list of queries for Gus. If we run out of pins and string before they get back, we'll start checking those timings. They could be key."

"MAXINE DEVEREUX and her husband chose a pretty spot to live, guv," said Blessing. "What a charming village. Since I moved south from the Midlands, that's one thing I've noticed about Wiltshire. There's no shortage of beautiful places on the outskirts of the towns."

"I never visited Winterslow on police business, Blessing," said Gus. "It's right on the border with Hampshire and home to two thousand people, give or take. I hope they realise how lucky they are."

Gus revised his opinion on the population as they found a modern housing estate around the corner. At least the developer attempted to blend in with properties that had stood in the village for centuries.

"That's it, guv," said Blessing, "number seventeen."

Gus parked the Focus on the road, and they prepared to walk up the short pathway to the front door.

"This road is quite narrow, isn't it, guv," said Blessing. "Several cars are parked half-on, half-off the pavement."

"It's a sign of the times, Blessing," said Gus. "Each house has a garage at the side. Many couples can't exist without two cars. The front garden is so tiny there's not enough room for a second vehicle."

"It could be tricky for an ambulance or a fire engine to negotiate the narrow road, guv," said Blessing.

"I appreciate that," said Gus, "but the pavement isn't the place to park. How does a person on a mobility scooter get past? What about a young mother like Maxine Devereux, who has a buggy for her infant child to manoeuvre? I feel sorry for anyone who has twins on this estate."

Blessing wondered why her boss suddenly seemed concerned with the welfare of children. She stretched out an arm and rang the doorbell at number seventeen.

An attractive dark-haired woman opened the bright blue door.

"Good morning," said Maxine. "You must be DC Umeh and the gentleman with you I've met already. How are you, Mr Freeman? I'd ask you how retirement was going, but it appears you're back in harness."

"Hello, Maxine," said Gus. "I didn't think you would remember me. Yes, I'm back as a consultant for the time being. The temptation was too hard to resist."

"He was a legend, DC Umeh," said Maxine. "Come through to the kitchen. I'll get the kettle on. Oliver was asleep in the conservatory but stirred just before you pulled up outside. So he'll be ready for a feed in a few minutes."

"How old is Oliver?" asked Blessing.

"Four and a half months," said Maxine. "He's a little poppet. Of course, we have his bedroom upstairs, but on these hot summer mornings, the conservatory is the coolest room in the house."

"The Chief Constable mentioned you were on leave for another few weeks," said Gus. "Will you return to take the Detective Inspector position you've earned?"

"Gary and I are still undecided," said Maxine. "My husband is a professional rugby player in the English Premiership. His salary is currently more than enough to allow us to live comfortably. Gary's career will be over five years from now, and he'll be coaching or managing. It's a tough sport, so there's always the risk of serious injury bringing things to a halt earlier. I want to wait until Olly goes to school before returning to work. Don't get me wrong, I loved my job, but sometimes the people at the top made things less enjoyable. I don't need to tell you that, Mr Freeman."

"Please call me Gus," said Gus. "Blessing, and I have come to talk about Kendal Guthrie."

The kettle had boiled, and Maxine soon brought three cups of coffee to the kitchen table. In the conservatory, Blessing heard a sneeze and a snuffle.

"Is the baby awake?" she asked.

"He can hang on for a few more minutes," said Maxine. "You learn to decipher which sounds are urgent. Otherwise, you would never have a minute to yourself."

"I'll bear it in mind," said Blessing.

"Have you spoken to Keith Porter yet?" asked Maxine.

"He's giving evidence in a court case this morning," said Gus. "The only person we've spoken with during this review is Wade Pinnock. The upright citizen who responded to your appeal to the public."

"I wish there were more like him," said Maxine. "Did you get anything new?"

"You know how it goes, Maxine," said Gus. "Three years on, and either he has embellished the story after telling his mates how he helped on a murder case, or he's genuinely remembered something important."

"Try me," said Maxine. "I remember most of that interview. It was a case we didn't solve. Keith didn't fret over it long, but it always annoyed me. I vowed whoever was responsible wouldn't get away with it on my watch."

Gus took Maxine through the conversation they had with Wade Pinnock earlier.

"There are two things that differ from the statement he gave us, Gus," said Maxine. "Wade didn't suggest Alf

Collett was rushing to serve him. I felt it was a case of being so involved in discussions over the previous night's events he hadn't spotted Wade was waiting to get served."

"Alf Collett retired to the Algarve after his wife died," said Gus. "I'll ask what it was he didn't want Wade to overhear, provided I can get clearance from my immediate superior to fly over. What was the second thing?"

"Wade did mention another man coming into the pub later that evening. He did not know who he was; we assumed it was Vickers or Wallington. There was no mention of the three men at the bar staring at Rosie Ritchens, although Wade said they appeared to be talking about him at one point. What do you think it could mean?"

"Perhaps we still haven't heard the entire story of what happened in the pub on Friday night," said Gus. "You and Keith might not have learned where Guthrie was if it hadn't been for Wade Pinnock coming forward. None of the people there that night contacted the police of their own volition. Does that mean they had something to hide?"

"Guthrie had a go at each of them," said Blessing. "Jim Thornton said it was typical of the man. He'd say something to provoke an argument. It didn't have to be the truth, just plausible enough to get a reaction from his target."

"Something Kendal Guthrie said hit home," said Maxine. "His killer was in the bar that night."

"We've started looking at where everybody was when Alf Collett closed the pub," said Gus.

"We could never get around the fact Alf threw Guthrie out, and Guthrie left the pub before any of the others," said Maxine. "Jim Thornton was on his way to the door when Guthrie picked on him, hinting Jim and his wife could be on the streets if Bob Ellison sold up. Jim stayed behind to wait for Oscar Wallington. Dave Vickers would have to cycle faster than Chris Hoy to get to Glenhead Farm to commit the murder. Rosie was last to leave after she and Alf washed their glasses and tidied the bar. We wondered whether Alf used his car that night, but it wasn't possible with his sick wife in a bedroom overlooking the garage."

"What did you make of the second change to Wade's version of events?" asked Gus.

"You would be guessing, Gus," cautioned Maxine. "Wade suggested Alf was keen to get him away from the bar. But, if Alf was thinking of the murder and forgot he was supposed to be serving pints, everything else falls apart. Wade's fresh memory comes into play when you take the other option and say they had something to hide. As you said, perhaps he embellished his story in the past three years, and that incident with Rosie didn't happen that way. There could be a dozen reasons for her to appear distracted, and the three men could have been looking towards several people in the bar. Wade said the pub was quite busy. Who knows, they could have seen someone they knew walk through the door?"

"It wasn't Vickers," said Gus. "He didn't cycle to the Traveller's Rest on Saturday nights."

"The pieces we have for our jigsaw don't fit, guv," said Blessing.

"We haven't found the missing pieces yet, Blessing," said Gus.

"We lost count of the number of people we interviewed," said Maxine. "Many of them danced on Kendal Guthrie's grave, but none were near Glenhead Farm between ten-thirty and eleven o'clock on the thirteenth of February."

Chapter Ten

"WHAT HAVE we got left to cover?" asked Lydia.

"We've labelled every farm controlled by the Guthrie family on the second map," said Neil. "Luke added any farm that belonged to a person interviewed during the first investigation."

"Doug Lawless and Harry Meaden's farms made sense," said Alex. "I'm not so sure whether we needed those on the northern and western edges of the Plain. Porter and Coleman confirmed their owner's alibi three years ago. How does any of this help us?"

"The farm near Larkhill sticks out from the rest," said Luke. "We must remember to add that query to our growing list. Only time will tell, Alex."

"We might not see Gus and Blessing again today," said Neil. "Is there someone we could interview from your schedule, Luke?"

"OK, why not try Millie Guthrie, or whatever her name is these days," said Luke. "She can confirm the time her ex-husband left home."

"Let's think what else we can ask," said Alex. "If that's all Millie can offer, then a phone call will suffice."

"If Gus has a question for Wes's ex-wife resulting from this morning's interviews, he'll need to make a follow-up call," said Luke. "I can think of several names on my list who might get irritated by that."

"Tough," said Neil. "This is a murder enquiry. Can anyone think of what else Millie could help with?"

Alex and Lydia shook their heads.

Luke called the farm in Winterbourne Stoke, and after putting a finger to his lips, he switched to speakerphone. A female voice answered.

"Millie Newsom speaking. How can I help you today?"

"Ms Newsom," said Luke. "I'm Detective Sergeant Luke Sherman from Wiltshire Police. We're taking a fresh look into the death of your father-in-law Kendal Guthrie."

"Why now, after three years? You didn't find whoever did it then. What makes you think you'll do it now?"

"We can but try, Ms Newsom. It's what the public expects. We're interested in the afternoon of Saturday, the fourteenth of February, in 2015. Wes Guthrie had spent the morning at home…"

"Drunk as a lord," said Millie, "after crawling back here from that woman's bed. I'm not likely to forget, am I?"

"I understand the memory must be painful, Ms Newsom," said Luke. "Can you confirm when Wes left you to drive over to Glenhead Farm to check on his father?"

"It was gone noon," said Millie. "I can't be certain, but it must have been before one o'clock because the boys came back in time for lunch for a change. Wes had left before they went to wash their hands. I reckon it was between half-past twelve and a quarter to one."

"When was the last time you visited the farm, Ms Newsom?" asked Luke.

"Not in the last three years, that's for sure. Before that, I guess Wes and I went there the summer before Kendal died. Why?"

"What was the lane like between the Netheravon Road and the farmhouse?"

"The same as it had been for a year," said Millie. "Full of potholes and deep ruts where the tractors churn up the ground in the winter. The surface was bone dry and similar to driving over a cattle grid for two hundred yards that day. Mud and muck made it impossible to do over five to ten miles an hour in the winter. Kendal had money to burn, but he wouldn't spend a penny repairing what had turned into a dirt track. Poppy would have had a fit."

"One last question, and we'll let you get on with your day, Ms Newsom," said Luke. "We may get back to you if our ongoing enquiries raise further questions. Who did you think killed your father-in-law?"

"That's easy," said Millie. "I thought Wes did it for a long time. The police swallowed the alibi that woman gave him, but I couldn't explain how he got to the farm in time. His mates said they left him at eleven o'clock, and I thought they also lied. When I was in the pub in the village celebrating the divorce, I asked the landlord if he remembered that night. He said he was on the verge of asking Wes and the others to leave because they were noisy and getting drunk. He called last orders at ten to eleven. Wes told Chris Barton he didn't want another drink, and all three left a minute before he called time at eleven. Wes didn't do it, so I tried to think about who hated Kendal enough to kill him. Money had to be involved somewhere. It was always money with Kendal. He fleeced someone or used his wealth to ruin somebody's life. I could never settle on a name. There were loads of people he'd screwed one way or another."

"That's very interesting," said Luke. "Thanks again for your cooperation. Good afternoon."

"Will that timing be accurate enough for what we need?" asked Alex.

"I doubt it," said Neil. "Nice touch querying the lane surface Blessing was interested in. You'll need to recalculate your sums, Luke."

"The fact that anyone following Guthrie up the lane might only travel at five to ten miles per hour makes it even less likely they arrived after him," said Lydia.

"We've got further confirmation Wes Guthrie didn't travel to Glenhead Farm on Friday night," said Alex. "However, when Mille Newsom made a new list of potential killers, she focused on money as the prime cause."

"At no point did Porter and Coleman discover a business transaction between Kendal Guthrie and either of the people in the Traveller's Rest," said Neil. "Surely, that would have come to light during the first investigation?"

"Dave Vickers said Guthrie's attack centred on the ease with which people borrowed money and the pathetic return savers got on their hard-earned cash," said Lydia.

"What are you thinking, Lydia?" asked Luke.

"We know how wealthy Guthrie was, but where did he keep his savings? Would it have a detrimental effect on Vickers if Guthrie moved his account elsewhere?"

"A rural branch might close if it lost a major account, I suppose," said Neil. "Banks, post offices and building societies close branches every week. The aim is to force everyone online. So, in his early fifties and single, Dave Vickers had a motive. Guthrie could cost him his job."

"Set aside the fact he couldn't have reached the farm

before midnight," said Lydia. "What did the other comment mean? Who did Vickers loan money to that caused a problem for Guthrie?"

"Gus can ask Vickers that question when he sees him," said Luke. "I've done the maths, Neil. A vehicle would cover sixty yards in fifteen seconds at ten miles an hour. So it was one minute from the junction to the garage in those conditions. As Lydia said, we need to find someone who could have been close to the mudroom door at ten thirty-five."

"That rules out everyone Porter and Coleman interviewed," said Alex, "unless Guthrie arrived later."

"The autopsy confirmed the provisional time of death given by the paramedic. Kendal Guthrie died no later than eleven o'clock," said Luke. "The window of opportunity was twenty-five minutes and no more."

IN WINTERSLOW, Blessing and Gus prepared to leave Maxine and little Olly. The snuffles had become more frequent and turned to plaintive cries. Olly was hungry.

"Do you want to meet him?" asked Maxine.

"Yes, please," said Blessing.

Gus studied the scene as Blessing oohed and aahed at the infant when Maxine carried him through to the kitchen from the conservatory. One minute, Olly was desperate for his mother's breast; now, he was content to allow a stranger to fuss over him. It felt strange to Gus. If Tess had ever been like Blessing, it must have happened when he wasn't around. Still, it was something to look forward to, and no doubt it would be different when it was his child.

"Where are you off to next, Gus?" asked Maxine.

"We hoped to speak to Keith Porter, but he's giving evidence in court."

"He'll be at the Law Courts on Wilton Road," said Maxine. "If you drive there now, there's a good chance you'll catch him in the lunchtime recess. Even if he's given his evidence this morning, the Keith I worked with will stay until he's filled his face. He likes to make a day of things to reduce the time he has to work."

Blessing dragged herself away from Olly and tried Keith Porter's mobile. Gus made his way to the front door as Maxine prepared to feed her son.

"Just close the door behind you on the way out," she called. "Good luck."

"Good to see you again, Maxine," said Gus. "Many thanks for your help."

Gus stepped outside the house and closed the front door.

"DI Porter will wait for us at the Law Courts, guv," said Blessing.

"I was more familiar with the old courts," said Gus. "This combined building opened ten years ago and saw the closure of smaller buildings in the county. Such as the one in Devizes, around the corner from the brewery. We'll be there in fifteen minutes."

They found Keith Porter lounging in the sunshine outside the modern building.

"How's the case going, Keith?" asked Gus.

"Oh, it *is* you, Gus," said Keith. "I wasn't sure when your sergeant called. I can't think what possessed you to come out of retirement. The sooner I can hand in my warrant card, the better. The evidence we put together for the CPS should have guaranteed a positive result, but you know how these things go. That judge hasn't given anyone a custodial sentence in three years. We're pushing the proverbial uphill. What did you need me for?"

"Kendal Guthrie?" said Gus. "We've spoken to Wade Pinnock, and he made two observations we can't see in the murder file. Maybe he forgot to mention it at the time, or he could have polished the story to make it appear more exciting than it was."

"I wasn't happy making a public appeal in the first place," moaned Keith. "Wade was the only sensible reply we got. What did he say that was different to the tale he told Maxine and me?"

Gus took Keith Porter through the same process as he'd done with Maxine Devereux.

Keith made the same comments as his former colleague. However, when they spoke, Wade made it sound as if Alf Collett had just realised he was waiting for a drink and stopped chatting to serve him. As for Rosie Ritchens, Keith was unaware why Collett, Thornton, and Wallington should have had an issue with the young barmaid and vice versa.

"Do you ever see Maxine these days, Keith?" asked Gus.

"I've not seen Max for a couple of years. Why?" replied Keith.

"We just came from her house. You both remember Wade's story the same way."

"We were an excellent team," said Keith.

"Have you had any thoughts in the past three years on the Guthrie case?" asked Gus.

"Despite the rumours, I care about the ones that get away," said Keith. "I put those cases in a box and close the lid to clear my mind for the next case that drops in my lap. What people at work don't realise is that lid doesn't prevent the victims from coming back to haunt me."

"What made you call Traffic that afternoon to get Wes Guthrie stopped on his way home?"

"The family name, his attitude when we arrived. I was

hoping for a quiet afternoon; take your pick. But, if I'm honest, the main reason was I wanted it to be him, but the longer we were there, the less likely it became."

"Did you ever have a gut feeling for who it was later, sir?" asked Blessing.

"We couldn't see the wood for the trees," said Keith. "There was a mile-long queue of people glad to see Kendal Guthrie dead. Could we put any of them at the murder scene? Could we heck. It would be great to put possible names in a hat and draw out the unlucky winner. Knowing my luck, we would have had this judge on the bench when it got to court, and the killer would have got community service."

Gus decided he shouldn't expose Blessing to any more of Keith Porter's cynical view of life as a modern detective. It was bad, but it wasn't all bad.

"Do you think something we learned this morning will prove vital in solving the case, guv," said Blessing as they drove away from the Law Courts.

"The case pulls you one way, then another piece of the jigsaw pulls you in the opposite direction," said Gus. "Let's see what the rest of the team achieved in our absence."

An hour later, they were in the lift heading for the first floor of the Old Police Station office.

"Welcome back, guv," said Neil. "Get a load of our wall art. We have several questions for you."

"Or did you solve the case already?" asked Lydia.

"Coffee, black without," said Gus, "and whatever Blessing's having."

"Leave it to me, guv," said Neil.

"A tough morning, guv?" asked Alex.

"A frustrating one, Alex. I thought I had something yesterday, but it's gone again today."

Gus walked to the back of the room, studied the first map, and then switched to the second map with the high-lighted farms.

"Good work," he said. "Now, I need to find out how to use these maps to solve this case. What else did you do?"

"We phoned Millie Guthrie," said Luke. "Millie reverted to her maiden name of Newsom after the divorce. She confirmed Wes left home between twelve-thirty and twelve-forty-five on Saturday afternoon. Wes would have reached Glenhead Farm fifteen minutes later. We know he tried the front door, called his father's mobile, and searched the house. Wes found his father in the last room he looked in, the mudroom. A 999 emergency operator logged his call at one fourteen. The same operator received a message informing them the paramedics arrived at Glenhead Farm at one twenty-eight. The uniformed officers had come up the lane one minute earlier. DI Porter and DS Coleman arrived at five minutes to two."

"We discussed various scenarios," said Neil. "Such as whether Wes had time to tidy the scene, removing any evidence of a contract killing. Although the timings aren't a perfect fit, they don't give enough scope for Wes to have been involved."

"Millie Newsom confirmed the lane from the road to the farm was full of potholes and ruts," said Luke. "Kendal stopped maintaining it after his wife died."

"The chances of someone driving up the lane unnoticed behind Kendal Guthrie get slimmer by the minute," said Gus.

"Yes, guv," said Neil.

"Millie spoke to the landlord of the pub in Winter-bourne Stoke village, guv," said Luke. "He remembered Wes leaving at one minute before eleven on Friday night.

Wes and his mates were noisy and well on the way to getting drunk. He was on the verge of chucking them out."

"When did this conversation take place?" asked Gus.

"Millie had a party to celebrate the divorce, guv. So, after the time Porter and Coleman spoke to her."

"I found a note in the murder file saying they couldn't interview the landlord in February, guv," said Lydia. "He was on holiday in Tenerife, and they'd already spoken with John Goodwin and Chris Barton to check Wes's alibi."

"The most interesting comment came from Millie when we asked who she thought killed her father-in-law and why, guv," said Alex. "Millie said it had to be money. Everything was about money in Kendal's life, but there were too many to choose from."

"What did Sarah Saunders and Zak Drake say?" asked Gus.

"I haven't got hold of them yet, guv," said Luke. "We know the time each emergency service arrived on Saturday afternoon from the 999 emergency logs. Did you have other questions for them?"

"Nothing that comes to mind at present, Luke," said Gus. "How's my schedule looking for tomorrow?"

"Helen Guthrie, first thing, guv, at half-past nine, followed by Dave Vickers at eleven. After lunch, Oscar Wallington's free to speak to you. I haven't heard from London Road yet regarding the Algarve trip."

"Thanks, Luke. I suggest we spend what's left of the afternoon updating our digital files and come back in the morning bright-eyed and bushy-tailed."

"Highlights, guv?" asked Neil.

"Ah, Wade Pinnock and the detective team. Blessing can run through the highlights with you while I chase Geoff

Mercer at London Road. Like you, we uncovered the odd fresh fact, but heaven knows what they mean."

Blessing did the honours, and everyone kept their heads down for the next two hours. Gus left the office at five o'clock and made his way home. Suzie stood by her Golf when Gus swung the Focus through the gateway.

"Why so glum, chum?" she asked. "Tough day?"

"It had its moments," he said. "What are your thoughts on breastfeeding?"

"I'm all for it," said Suzie. "Although, of the things I thought you would say, that was way down the list."

"We interviewed Maxine Devereux this morning," said Gus, "and met Oliver, who's four and a half months old. Blessing fell in love with him, and I doubt whether Maxine will return to work after her maternity leave. However, she would make an excellent DI."

"Did you get to hold the baby?" asked Suzie as they walked into the bungalow together.

"Heavens, no," said Gus. "I want our child to be the first."

Suzie stopped in the hallway and kissed him.

"We'll make an old romantic out of you yet, Gus Freeman."

"Not so much of the old, young lady," he replied.

"We can't stand here all evening. Shower and change, then we'll visit the allotment for an hour. I called the Lamb before I left work, and we've got a table in the beer garden with our name on it for half-past seven."

Suzie sat and watched Gus potter on his vegetable patch for an hour. She could tell his heart wasn't in it.

"Come on, spill the beans," she said. "What is it about this case that's bothering you?"

"My gut instinct told me from the outset that times,

distances, and locations were vital elements in finding Guthrie's killer," said Gus. "The team completed the maps we discussed last night while Blessing and I were in Salisbury this morning. When I looked at them this afternoon, I couldn't fathom how they helped. Based on the reports in the murder file, everyone tagged Kendal Guthrie as a man obsessed with money. Someone who flaunted his wealth, antagonised everyone he met, and used the money he'd earned to the detriment of many. The word charitable wasn't in his vocabulary. Even Millie Newsom, that's Wes Guthrie's ex-wife, by the way, was adamant the motive had to be money. Millie believed we should search for someone Guthrie did business with that cost them a fortune, their livelihood, and even their home. Porter and Coleman interviewed every farmer my team included on their map. Some suffered financial hardship because of Guthrie, but there wasn't one person who could have been at Glenhead Farm on the night of the murder. We seem to be hunting a ghost."

"Who else did you see today?" asked Suzie.

"Keith Porter, who was negative and cynical, as always. He can't wait to retire. He's got a decade to go before he qualifies. Do we want him moping around at Bourne Hill for that length of time? Wade Pinnock, the public-spirited young man who responded to the public appeal, gave us the few scraps of information that might point us in the right direction."

"Did he offer something new?"

"Hard to tell after three years," said Gus. "He was nineteen when he called in with his evidence. He's still wet behind the ears, but this morning he added two insights that could blow the case wide open. Can we believe him without hearing the same thing from someone else who was there on Saturday night?"

"What did he say?" asked Suzie.

"He hinted Alf Collett and maybe others had something to hide. Did Alf genuinely miss the fact a customer was waiting to get served? Or did he want to be rid of Wade in case he heard too much of the previous night's events?"

"What could that mean?" asked Suzie.

"Who knows?" said Gus. "You'll understand the difficulty when you hear the second thing. Wade reckoned Rosie, the barmaid, looked distracted when clearing tables later in the evening. Wade said she appeared troubled, and three men at the bar were staring in her direction. They were the landlord, Jim Thornton, and probably Oscar Wallington. That same group had stared at Wade and his girlfriend earlier, making them uncomfortable. The couple never returned to the Traveller's Rest."

"The difficulty is that Rosie and Jim are dead," said Suzie. "The landlord is in Portugal, and if those three men had a secret, they're unlikely to corroborate anything Wade said."

"Exactly," said Gus. "Plus, if money was the motivator, how could either of those men have had dealings with Guthrie that didn't come to light in the first investigation?"

"Who's next on your list?" asked Suzie.

"Helen Guthrie, Dave Vickers, and Oscar Wallington," said Gus.

"If Vickers wasn't in the pub on Saturday night, he's the one I would target for details of the conversations between the others and Kendal Guthrie. How did Keith and Maxine tackle this issue on the first occasion?"

"You might be onto something there, Suzie," said Gus. "Vickers said that Kendal had a dig at each of them. He made sexist remarks to Rosie and accused Alf of having an affair with his last barmaid. Kendal suggested Oscar Wallington should steal from his employer as if Kendal knew Oscar was capable. He told Jim Thornton he could be out of house and home in months. Kendal blamed Vickers for low savings rates on his money. It was superficial, but Porter and Coleman didn't delve deeper."

"Vickers cycled to and from the pub," said Suzie. "He wasn't the killer. The other three could have had something to hide. Dave Vickers is perhaps the only person still around who can unlock that secret."

"You realise what you're saying?" said Gus.

"One of those three men killed Guthrie," said Suzie.

"If Wade Pinnock's insight concerning Rosie was right, she could have suspected that was the case as early as Saturday evening."

"Wade said all three were staring at her, Gus," said Suzie. "Does that mean they were in it together?"

"Let's not jump to that conclusion until I've spoken to Dave Vickers. Based on the evidence uncovered, neither man had enough motive to kill Kendal Guthrie. Porter and Coleman didn't get the opportunity to check what time Jim Thornton arrived home. The Traveller's Rest wasn't on their radar until Wade Pinnock called three weeks after the murder. Jim's wife had been buried before they got to speak to him. Wallington's interview was also delayed; his wife and children were on a half-term holiday from the thirteenth of February. So nobody could check what time he got home. With Alf Collett's wife confined to her bed, he maintained she would have known if he'd gone out that night. His garage was right below the bedroom window. Even if all three men had a reason to lie to the police, we've got a map on the wall in the office that shows none of them could get to Glenhead Farm and kill Guthrie. Millie Newsom told Luke this afternoon that the lane was passable with care, especially on a night such as that. No way could anyone have reached the farmhouse without alerting the victim."

"The killer got there earlier and lay in wait," said Suzie. "A killer with a solid motive for wanting Guthrie dead. Unless Dave Vickers blows that theory out of the water, it means you've not got a single name in the frame."

"It's not very often you're wrong, but you're right again," said Gus. "Let's wrap this up and get into the Lamb for a bite to eat."

Wednesday, 29 August 2018

GUS AND SUZIE left the bungalow at eight-thirty. Gus had kept tossing and turning last night, trying to think what they were missing. Suzie's sleep suffered as a result, but she knew Gus would get there in the end.

"Are you driving direct to Durrington?"

"Yes, Helen's 'first thing' was half-past nine. If she were a true farmer's daughter, I would have had to catch her at six, no doubt."

"Cheeky," said Suzie. "Dad still gets up at silly o'clock, and Mum's not far behind him. Helen never struck me as wanting to follow her brother into the business."

"Millie Newson told Luke that Helen hated farming and couldn't wait to get away to Australia."

"That didn't end well," said Suzie.

"No, and Wade Pinnock echoed Millie's view. His fiancée is a local reporter, and she believes Helen Guthrie aims to sell the business to developers. She's not concerned with the damage it would do to the environment."

"If that's true, then she inherited some genes from her father."

"I'll see you tonight, sweetheart," said Gus.

"Keep smiling," she replied with a grin.

Gus followed Suzie to the gateway and gave her a wave as she turned right to drive along the lane, heading for London Road. He turned left to make his way to Upavon and then took the road south across the Plain to Glenhead Farm. This way would get him there in thirty minutes. He could use the spare time to check out the farms on either side, and the one on Durrington Down Kendal Guthrie had wanted to gain. You never knew what you would find when you went for a wander.

A few minutes before nine-thirty, Gus negotiated the lane from the road without incident and parked beside the double garage. The dry August weather hadn't turned the surface into a dust bowl. The tarmac looked to have some wear. Maybe it was one of Helen's first jobs when she arrived home for good. He wondered what car Helen drove. The murder file mentioned Poppy's ten-year-old red Focus. Gus assumed Wes got rid of that at the same time as he auctioned the Bentley.

Helen Guthrie answered the doorbell within seconds. Gus knew she was only a handful of years older than Suzie, but they looked light-years apart. Helen had lost both parents in her thirties and discovered her husband in bed with another man. How could anyone keep cheerful through that?

"Mr Freeman," she said without the hint of a smile. "Please come in. I took the precaution of asking Tom Dix, my manager, to join us and Mitchell Underwood, the family solicitor. Unfortunately, he hasn't arrived yet, so we'll have to wait."

Gus followed Helen Guthrie into the lounge/diner. The décor was much as he expected, as was the layout of the ground floor. He'd seen the crime scene photos in the murder file. However, Helen had opted to keep many of her father's fixtures and fittings. A new widescreen TV was the only visible change. Tom Dix, who had worked with Wes Guthrie for several years, stood by the fireplace, looking very much at home.

"This is an informal meeting, Ms Guthrie," said Gus. "We need clarification on several items. First, we have never considered you played any part in your father's death. The presence of a solicitor isn't a problem, but I can't see what Mr Underwood can offer this get-together."

"Guthrie Holdings is a business, Mr Freeman," said Tom Dix. "We employ many people. Mr Underwood will advise us on any matter which might bring the company name into disrepute. Please, take a seat."

As Gus sat down and prepared to await the arrival of Mr Underwood, he heard a car pull up outside. Tom Dix answered the door while Helen Guthrie stared at her lap. Gus did a quick rejig of his list of questions. If they wanted formal, they could have it.

Mitchell Underwood strode into the room, his briefcase under his arm. Whatever was inside didn't spoil the cut of his expensive suit.

"Good morning Mitchell," said Helen. "Right, Mr Freeman, you may begin."

"Who do you think killed your father, Ms Guthrie?" asked Gus.

"I've said all along that a wife, girlfriend, or someone close to them, is protecting my father's killer," said Helen

Guthrie. "They will unlikely come forward after three years, but I live in hope."

"Why do you think they killed him?"

"Envy; vengeance, who knows? I know many people who live on the Plain hated my father. He made money through hard work and astute business deals. There are always winners and losers in that world. My father was a winner."

"How much did your father tell you about the business while you lived in Melbourne?"

"Nothing, Mr Freeman. I didn't want to know. I had a business to run."

"What was your impression of the last business deal he entered into with the MoD?"

"He knew the Mod wouldn't allow him to buy all five farms due for release," said Helen. "Thanks to Mitchell's diligent research, we weighted our quotes in favour of us gaining the two we needed."

"Interesting," said Gus. "Us and we, although you insisted you weren't interested while you lived in Australia. We have no reason to connect his murder with the two farms Guthrie Holdings purchased months after his death. How would you respond to that?"

"No comment," said Mitchell Underwood.

"I've interviewed a thousand criminals who have chosen that line of defence, Mr Underwood," said Gus. "The fact you supplied the comment and not your employer suggests someone has briefed you well. I won't waste any more of your time. I'll look for someone who does want to help find Kendal Guthrie's killer."

Chapter Eleven

GUS HADN'T FOUND out what car Helen Guthrie drove or any other inconsequential things he'd planned to ask as he lay awake last night. As he left Glenhead Farm, Gus was fuming.

The drive from Durrington to Shrewton only took fifteen minutes, so he had an hour, at least, before Dave Vickers could see him. Gus stopped for coffee at a shop near the Methodist Church. He needed to regroup, get his temper under control, and make sense of what just happened.

"Coffee, black, without sugar, please," he said. The older woman at the counter smiled.

"Find yourself a seat," she said. "I'll bring it over in a tick."

Gus found a seat by the window and pretended to people watch.

"We haven't seen you in here before, have we?"

His new friend had arrived with the coffee.

"My appointment in Durrington ended earlier than expected," said Gus.

"People don't have time to chat these days, do they? It's all business. We get passing trade from younger folk in the village. They take their coffee with them on the way to work. You've just missed that crowd. The next rush will be when the school run ends and young mums drop by. Some stay and sit like you. Most have a standing order they can collect before getting home."

"Your cafe must experience traffic peaks and troughs, " Gus said. "I suppose the afternoon school run creates another one?"

"Not so much, because they can't afford to buy the kids drinks and cake. When we were their age, we had a proper breakfast, made coffee or tea at home, and chatted to our neighbour over the garden fence after dropping the kids at school. I don't know what the world's coming to."

"I enjoy a proper breakfast," said Gus.

"Well, I can whip you up sausage, egg, and bacon if you like, dear. Kathleen's my name. I expect you guessed with Kath's over the front door."

"I already ate," said Gus, "but thanks for the offer. My partner and I had cereals and yoghurt this morning."

Gus noticed Kathleen's frown.

"I know," he said, "Not a proper breakfast, but Suzie's expecting our first child, and a fried breakfast is off the menu for a while."

Gus wondered why he was sharing his innermost secrets with a stranger. It was just as well that he came alone this morning. They only had another two weeks to wait before telling the team and their friends the news.

Kathleen was one of those people with whom you instantly relaxed.

"I'm glad I came here," said Gus. "I was ready to punch someone when I left Durrington."

"What is it you do, dear?" asked Kathleen.

"I'm a retired Detective Inspector who came out of retirement to help a young team of detectives solve what they call cold cases."

"Oh, I know what they are, dear. I've seen it on TV."

"Did you ever meet Kendal Guthrie?" asked Gus.

"I remember how glad people in the village were when they heard he was dead," said Kathleen. "Poppy, his wife, came here, now and then. A lovely lady. Too good for him, but it takes all sorts, doesn't it? Kendal and I never spoke, but I didn't hold with the ill-feeling people stirred up against him and his children. The father was a hard business person, that's all; the son and daughter came from the same mould. My Fred, before he died, used to say, it's just business, Kath. No point in getting riled up when someone gets on in life and you get left behind. They've got the knack of lying in muck and getting up smelling of roses. It's not personal, just business."

Gus finished his second coffee, which Kath had poured without Gus asking, and checked his watch. Time to go. He said goodbye to Kath and headed outside. Luke had given him Dave Vickers's address, and Gus had raised an eyebrow when he noticed the appointment wasn't taking place at a building society branch. Gus parked the Focus and approached the front door of the village's modest two-up, two-down cottage. He quickly tapped the ornate knocker and listened as the sound echoed along the hallway.

"You must be Mr Freeman."

Dave Vickers was tall and, by some standards, over-weight. But Gus thought with his height; Dave could carry it off.

"That's me," said Gus. "How are things?"

"Mustn't grumble; come in," said Dave, leading Gus into the tiny front room. "I soon came to terms with the firm closing our minor branch in Amesbury. I got over that quicker than I did young Rosie's death."

"Are you working again?" asked Gus.

"Part-time, Mr Freeman," said Dave. "Three hours every afternoon in a convenience store at a garage. I use my financial background to beneficial effect in the evenings with an online service sorting out people's tax affairs and providing investment advice. You don't need much to get by when it's just one of you."

"My colleague, DS Sherman, told you why I was calling on you this morning, Dave. I was hoping you could tell me everything you remember from the Friday night Kendal Guthrie died. When the detectives spoke with you three years ago, they didn't give you a chance to dig deep into the detail, did they? Don't worry; I'll give you a lift to the garage if time gets tight."

"The detective in charge wasn't happy we didn't come forward straightaway," said Dave. "Rosie thought we should. Bless her, but Alf wasn't keen at first."

"Let me stop you there, Dave," said Gus. "Start at the very beginning. Tell me who said what to who while you were in the bar that night. Take your time."

"I cycled to the Traveller's Rest every Friday night without fail," said Dave. "I admit I went more during the week than I used to once Rosie started working there. When I left here, it was blowing a gale, but the rain hadn't started. So I thought I could get there in the dry. You don't worry as much if you get soaked on the way home, do you? The rain had started as I approached the village, but I had put on my wet weather gear to be prepared. Jim Thornton passed me in Tilshead. If I hadn't stopped at the traffic lights for the roadworks, I would have been at the pub before him for a change. Rosie and Alf were behind the bar when I arrived, and Jim sat on his usual stool with a pint. It did not surprise me there were no other customers because of the weather."

"What were the roadworks for, Dave? Do you remember?" asked Gus.

"Wessex Water were replacing piping that had been in the main street since Victorian times."

"Interesting," said Gus, "carry on."

"I bought a drink and stood by the bar while Jim gave us a lesson on decimalisation and how the brewers used it as an excuse to raise prices. He had a few pet grievances, and that was one. I'd just sat next to the log fire to get warm when Oscar Wallington walked in."

"What time was this?" asked Gus.

"Jim must have arrived by twenty past eight. I was only minutes behind him. I reckon Oscar arrived at a quarter to nine. Oscar ordered a double scotch and soda, as usual. Rosie came closer to the fire and sat opposite me. I suggested I put another log on to keep the cold out. Alf said not to bother. He was already thinking of closing early. Alf reminded us Rosie had a longer drive home than the rest of us, and the storm was getting worse. Roads could get blocked. As Rosie used the poker on the fire to get life into it, Jim told a story about the old days. His grandfather drank in the pub when men heated their beer with the tools hanging in the fireplace."

"A long-standing tradition," said Gus, "supposed to ward off coughs, colds, and all manner of ailments. Doctors today would say it was rubbish. What happened next?"

"Jim and Alf must have been talking with Rosie before I arrived about the MoD and how long they'd been using the

Plain. Jim suggested Rosie ask Oscar, as he'd spent thirty years in the Army and much of that time at Bulford camp. Oscar explained how the Plain was dotted with restricted areas, which necessitated longer journeys for people like Rosie approaching the village from Salisbury. Oscar asked Rosie where she lived. He knew where Jim's cottage was; he passed it on his way to the pub. Oscar drove everywhere in an old Defender, a four-wheel drive. I suppose it suited the job he'd had for the past four years. An estate manager has plenty of ground to cover."

"Oscar lives in the Lodge House," said Gus. "Have you ever met his wife and two children?"

"No, they never came with him to the pub. Oscar wasn't as regular a customer as Jim and me. It seemed there wouldn't be more people daft enough to come in for a drink, and the conversation got random over the next half hour. We discussed the perils of drink-driving. Jim told Rosie to take care driving home, not to stray into lanes and tracks she didn't know. He tried to scare her with ghost stories,"

"The headless coach driver myth has reached this far, has it?" said Gus.

"I don't recall that one, no," said Dave. "Not long after Jim's story, Oscar bought another drink, and Kendal Guthrie walked in. I heard Alf groan. Kendal didn't visit the pub often, but he was straight into his favourite subject, himself. There was nowhere for him to hang his camelhair coat. He made sure everyone knew it cost twelve hundred quid. His suit was tailor-made and would have cost me a month's wages. When he finally reached the bar, he ordered a gin and tonic. The usual pantomime followed as he took his wallet out of his jacket pocket. He ensured everyone in the room could see the banknotes stashed on either side. His first target was Oscar. He called him a squaddie masquerading as a gentleman farmer. Then he bragged about his posh car and laughed at Oscar's battered Defender. Oscar was on the defensive from the start. Kendal Guthrie had got to him. Oscar resented the squaddie reference, as he'd started at the bottom and worked his way up as far as an NCO could go in the Army. Fair play to the chap. After that, Guthrie started calling him General, trying to provoke a further reaction. It was common knowledge the previous estate manager had embezzled a sizeable amount of money from the manor's owners. Still, they retrieved most of it through the Proceeds of Crime Act, and Oscar's reputation since he'd worked for them was flawless. Nevertheless, Guthrie hinted Oscar could help himself to twenty grand to buy a decent car. Of course, nothing as grand as Guthrie's, but something matching where Guthrie considered the likes of us stood in the world. He was a rotten individual."

"What did you make of Oscar Wallington?" asked Gus.

"Oscar wasn't a regular, but although he could be pompous and imply he was better than the rest of us because he was ex-military, we never fell out. Perhaps if I'd seen him somewhere other than in the Traveller's Rest, we might not have had much to say to one another. Guthrie briefly switched his attention to Rosie and warned her that Alf had wandering hands. He suggested Alf and the previous barmaid, Imogen, had something going. Every week, I was there while she worked in the pub; I saw nothing to support that. What I did notice was Imogen overcharged strangers that came in. Alf had to let Imogen go after discovering she pocketed ten quid a week on top of her wages. When I spoke up and told Guthrie he was talking out of the top of his head, he had a go at me."

"Lending too much money to people who couldn't afford to pay it back if there was a downturn in the economy," said Gus.

"We tried to avoid that, Mr Freeman," said Dave. "Guthrie seemed more concerned with low-interest rates on his savings."

"Did Guthrie Holdings have accounts at your branch?" asked Gus.

"I'm not at liberty to say too much," said Dave. "Kendal had several personal ISAs with us, yes, but the company banked elsewhere."

"So, your branch wouldn't have closed because Guthrie moved his savings?"

"They moved after he died, anyway," said Dave. "The rumour was that Helen Guthrie merged the company and family assets overseas, but I'm unaware of where."

"Where did Guthrie switch his attention next?" asked Gus.

Dave thought for a while.

"He returned to Oscar and spoke about when he was in the Army. Guthrie said the men in the trenches took the blame when things went wrong. It was never the top brass who suffered. Oscar looked flustered. It was only a second before his usual impassive look returned, and Jim broke the spell by getting up to leave. Guthrie pretended not to have spotted him before, but that was rubbish. He tried to convince Jim that Bob Ellison was selling his farm. Bob's father had employed Jim his whole working life and promised Jim that he and his wife could see out their days in the tied cottage they occupied. Jim thought Bob Ellison would have mentioned it, but Guthrie told Jim he could get forced out of his home, especially as he was in line to buy it. I told Jim to contact a solicitor."

"Was there any truth in it?" asked Gus.

"No idea. You would have to ask Bob Ellison," said Dave. "The next day, I heard Guthrie was dead. I didn't go to the pub on Saturday or Sunday. My next visits were Monday and Wednesday night."

"Let's get back to Friday night, Dave. What did Guthrie say after Jim queried the fact Ellison was selling up?"

"Guthrie told us he'd submitted bids for five farms the MoD no longer needed. He named them and admitted he wouldn't get all five. Then he switched back to the Ellison farm. Guthrie already controlled the farms on either side. Even if he only got two of the five that the MoD were keen to shift, Bob's farm interested him most. Alf had enough by then and asked Kendal to leave. He told him he never wanted him back in the pub. Alf called time. Guthrie was still shouting the odds. He warned Alf he'd turn Jim's cottage into a pub if he bought Bob Ellison's farm. Guthrie had the money to run it in such a way it would force Alf out of business. Guthrie reckoned two farms he hoped to buy would be perfectly placed for housing estates. The Army was pulling out of Germany, and the troops and their families needed married quarters for people stationed at Larkhill, Tilshead and Bulford camps. Guthrie left us in the pub and went outside laughing."

"This was between five and ten past ten, wasn't it?" said Gus.

"That's right. We discussed what Guthrie said for maybe five minutes. Jim was ready to go but hung around for Oscar and me. He didn't want to bump into Guthrie in the car park."

"I imagine Guthrie and his Bentley were long gone?"

"After I took my empty glass to the bar, I needed the loo, and Rosie went into the Ladies ahead of me. When I came out, she was washing up with Alf behind the bar. Jim and Oscar had waited for me. Guthrie had waited for us when we got outside, and he sat in his car with the engine idling. He gave us the finger, laughed, and then drove away. Jim and Oscar dashed to their cars in the rain while I donned my wet weather gear and started the long cycle ride home. Rosie passed me just beyond Tilshead village."

"Did you catch Jim or Oscar?" asked Gus.

"Not likely, was it? It was tough work cycling in the wind."

"Perhaps they weren't delayed by the traffic lights," said Gus.

"They were green when I cycled through," said Dave.

"Any idea what timing delay they had? Where were they situated?"

"The streets are windy through the village, Mr Freeman. Wessex Water had dug up the left-hand side of the street for two hundred yards. You couldn't see the other traffic light around the corner. I reckon it must have been forty-five seconds at least that I waited for them to change from red when I was cycling to the pub earlier. Why?"

"Timings, locations, and distances felt important to me when I started reading the background to this case, Dave. Just a gut feeling we coppers get. Before I spoke with you, I thought I was on the wrong track. Now I'm not so sure. Always go with your gut, Dave."

"Is that everything?" asked Dave. "I made it home that night in the end, but it was one of the last times I made the trip. Rosie decided to quit, and you know what happened next. My heart wasn't in it anymore. I still cycle everywhere, but if I want a drink, I can pick up a few cans at the garage and bring them home."

"Do you want a lift, Dave?" asked Gus, looking at the time.

"Thanks for the offer, but no thanks. It's a tidy walk, and I can cycle it in ten minutes."

"Well, best of luck, Dave," said Gus. "Thanks for your help. My next appointment is in just over an hour, with no chance of driving back to the office. I'll grab a bite to eat in the village."

"Kath's place is warm and friendly," said Dave.

"I had coffee and a chat with Kath before I came here," said Gus. "Time to taste her snacks."

Dave showed Gus to the door, and they said their good-byes. Gus drove the Focus back towards the café and wondered whether he had time to update the team on what he'd learned.

IN THE OLD Police Station office, Alex took charge when they arrived at nine o'clock.

Neil got tasked with speaking to WPC Sarah Saunders and PC Zak Drake. Alex thought it essential to confirm the timings the emergency services people provided.

Luke agreed to revisit interviews with farmers from the original investigation. Alex wanted to be sure they weren't overlooking someone who could have been gunning for Guthrie. Luke needed help from the forensic accountants at the Hub. He left for Devizes at a quarter past nine.

At half-past nine, Geoff Mercer called Gus. Alex answered and told Geoff that Gus was in Durrington. Geoff wanted to pass on the message that a trip to Portugal didn't appear justified. Alf Collett's wife would have known if he wasn't in bed next to her. Furthermore, the original reports in the murder file didn't point to Alf Collett as a suspect.

"That doesn't stop you from calling him if you think he can add fresh evidence, DS Hardy," said Geoff.

Alex looked at Lydia and Blessing. They were playing with numbers. Blessing had a bee in her bonnet over something. Alex made the call himself.

"Take me through it again, Blessing," said Lydia.

"I read Maxine's report on the interview with Alf Collett again," she said. "It was something Maxine said about Rosie Ritchens. The murder took place on the thirteenth of February, right? Maxine persuaded Keith Porter to go for the public appeal after they'd worked the case for three weeks. By my reckoning, they issued the appeal over the weekend of the sixth to the ninth of March. Wade Pinnock came back to them straightaway. They interviewed him on Tuesday the tenth. The date and time are recorded at the top of the sheet. This text is from the recording made at the time. They drove to the Traveller's Rest and spoke to Alf Collett the same day. They wanted to know who else had been in the bar that night."

"What did Maxine say about Rosie?" asked Lydia.

"Let me find it," said Blessing, "here we are. Alf told Keith and Maxine he'd closed early to let poor Rosie get home to Salisbury. Keith asked him why he said poor Rosie. Maxine said she was the young girl who died in Majorca ten days ago, on her first foreign holiday. Police believed Rosie was drunk and walked in front of a car."

Lydia picked up Blessing's train of thought and continued:

"Alf Collett told them Rosie stopped working at the pub two weeks after the murder. Hang on. That can't be right. If Rosie died ten days before Alf's interview, she would be in

Majorca on the last day of February. What does that mean?"

Blessing saw Alex was on the phone. He saw her waving her arm and put his hand over the mouthpiece.

"I'm trying to get hold of Alf Collett," he said, "but he must have booked an early round of golf."

"Leave a message and ask him to ring back," said Blessing.

They took Alex through the logic.

"I wonder if I can get hold of Gus," he said. "He's seeing Dave Vickers later and Oscar Wallington this afternoon. We need to check whether Rosie left her job at the pub earlier than Alf told the police. Why would he lie?"

"I've checked the report of her death in Majorca on the internet," said Lydia. "Rosie got knocked down at twelve thirty-eight. Technically, it was the first of March. Rosie landed in Palma at lunchtime on the twenty-eighth of February. Alf spoke to Rosie just before she flew out to Palma. Rosie had booked a fortnight's holiday before starting work in a Salisbury pub."

"When Alf Collett spoke to the detectives, they queried why he rang an ex-employee, didn't they?" said Alex. "He said he hadn't wanted her to leave. She was a good worker."

"The distracted look Wade Pinnock mentioned to Gus yesterday becomes more telling now," said Lydia. "Was Alf concerned Rosie might say something from Friday night that could point the finger at the killer?"

"We don't believe Alf was responsible for the murder. Who could Alf be shielding? Jim Thornton, who might have been facing eviction? Guthrie didn't have as much to say to Vickers and Wallington. It was unpleasant, perhaps, but hardly grounds for either of them to commit murder."

Alex checked his watch. Gus would be at Durrington

now with Helen Guthrie. Gus would turn off his phone until he returned to the car. Their best bet was to catch him between ten forty-five and eleven o'clock when he wasn't driving. Gus didn't understand Bluetooth.

"Can we do something else?" asked Blessing.

"What did you have in mind?" asked Alex.

"Gus was adamant times, places, and distances were important," said Blessing. "Can we make the adjustments we know of to re-calculate how long it would take for Kendal Guthrie to drive from the pub to Glenhead Farm?"

Lydia sighed.

"What if Gus brings back more minor alterations from Vickers and Wallington? It will be a waste of time. We could get a different lead to follow when Alf Collett calls back."

"You're probably right," said Blessing. "Alex, can you ask Gus if it would help to make those journeys ourselves?"

"That is the thing Gus loves," said Neil. "He walks around the murder scene to get a feel for the area, doesn't he? He took me to the nature reserve a few weeks back. Lydia went with him to Churchfields Industrial Estate. We could do worse than drive to Tilshead and spend half a day checking the layout. It's not the same looking on Google Maps."

"You and Luke have got enough to keep you busy today," said Alex. "When Gus updates us on his meeting, I'll tell him of the discrepancy Blessing found. He'll be back in the office mid-afternoon at the earliest. He'll certainly want to be there when we venture onto the Plain."

That sounds as if we're waiting until tomorrow, thought Blessing. She knew something tied the map Gus was keen on with a fact they'd learned in the past twenty-four hours. Blessing's gut instinct told her it would lead to the name of the person who murdered Kendal Guthrie. What she needed to do was prove it. She couldn't do that sitting at her desk.

GUS LEFT the café at a quarter to two. He'd enjoyed a pleasant lunch and was ready for his interview with Oscar Wallington.

Kath was right. The foot traffic ebbed and flowed, but everyone who visited Kath's went away with a smile. Of course, the food and drink played their part, but the owner provided the magic.

As Gus reached the Focus in the car park, he could hear the faint sound of his phone ringing. He sat in the driver's seat, rescued the phone from the glove compartment, and looked to see who was calling.

"Alex, how can I help?"

Alex told Gus what Blessing and Lydia had found. Alex added that Alf Collett hadn't returned their call, and Geoff Mercer wouldn't sanction a flight to the Algarve.

"Phone Geoff," said Gus. "Ask him to contact the Portuguese police, get Collett in custody, and you can arrange one of these Magnum calls, or whatever they are. Tell the girls it was good work."

"Zoom, guv," said Alex. "Leave that to us. What did you learn this morning?"

Gus told Alex about the frosty reception chez Helen Guthrie. He added that Dave Vickers believed Guthrie Holdings now banked overseas.

"I didn't get to ask whether they intended selling out to developers or venture capitalists. Dave Vickers changed the timings for our journeys, with roadworks in Tilshead and Kendal Guthrie not leaving the pub car park until he had a final opportunity to take the rise out of the others. One comment Guthrie made seemed to fluster Wallington. Neither Alf Collett nor Wallington mentioned that when interviewed. I'm ten minutes from the Lodge House; thanks for the update. I hope to be back by four. When I return, it will take me the rest of the afternoon to get my files in order. First thing tomorrow, we'll review where we are and decide on a course of action. Bye for now."

No sooner had Alex started looking at the next job on his list than his phone rang.

"Alex, it's me again," said Gus. "Do me a favour. Call Geoff Mercer and ask whether he's got a name for us to contact in SIB. If we decide to explore in the morning, I don't want someone getting shot at."

"I'll get on to that straight away, guv. Anything else?"

"Bob Ellison?" said Gus. "Has anyone spoken to him yet? If not, get Luke or Neil to find out whether Guthrie was pulling Jim Thornton's leg. I can't recall in the murder file when Keith Porter spoke to Ellison, except when the farmer told him Jim's wife had died."

"We'll find out, guv," said Alex. "I'll double-check the murder file first."

Gus was gone. Alex sensed the pace of this investigation was quickening, and it was only day three.

"Do either of you remember reading a report of an interview with Bob Ellison?" he asked.

"Ellison wasn't one of the farmers on the list of people with an axe to grind with Kendal Guthrie," said Neil. "Why would they have interviewed him at all?"

"Bob Ellison was Jim Thornton's landlord," said Alex. "His late father was Jim's boss for decades. Fred and Jim were friends rather than employer and employee. Guthrie's attack on Jim Thornton centred on the sale of the farm. Was Guthrie winding him up?"

"When they interviewed Alf Collett three weeks into the investigation, he was vague about what Guthrie said to Jim Thornton and the others," said Neil. "Porter didn't press him for details. Instead, he was interested in the names of the other customers."

"Remind me what Dave Vickers said," said Alex.

"He reckoned Guthrie teased Jim over the potential farm sale," said Neil. "Vickers advised Jim to get a solicitor in case there was a threat of eviction in the offing."

"I've found those reports in the murder file," said Lydia. "Wallington was vague about what was said. As for Jim Thornton, he dismissed the notion Ellison was keen to sell. He believed Bob Ellison would keep him in the loop. Jim said it was irrelevant anyway now that Guthrie was dead."

"That wasn't the case, was it?" said Alex. "The firm's solicitors continued with the submissions for the MoD package of farm releases. The business didn't close because Kendal Guthrie died, so if Kendal had approached Ellison, there would be a record of that meeting and any progress noted in a company document. Can you talk to Bob Ellison, Neil? Let's fill in the blanks. Guthrie Holdings don't own Ellison's farm today, but was there ever a time when they could have struck a deal?"

"On it, Alex," said Neil.

"If you need to call Geoff Mercer," asked Lydia. "Do you want me to try Alf Collett again?"

Alex gave her a thumbs up and rang London Road. Geoff Mercer was in a meeting, but Vera Butler was preparing to call Gus to pass on the information.

"Geoff spoke to the senior officer at Campion Lines, Bulford Camp," said Vera. "Second Lieutenant Jamie

Barnes-Trewick is the man you want. I'll e-mail you his contact details."

"Many thanks, Vera," said Alex. "It will be my first time liaising with the Royal Military Police. I assume they have Scene of Crime Officers the same as we do in their SIB?"

"The set-up is much the same," said Vera. "I don't know whether you know, but retired CID officers are used to investigate Territorial Army cases handled by SIB."

"Gus could have got himself a job with them," said Alex. "I'm glad he didn't."

Vera laughed and ended the call.

Alex looked over his shoulder and spotted Lydia deep in conversation. With luck, Alf Collett was back from the golf course. Beside Lydia, Blessing Umeh had a frown on her face. Alex hoped her father's threats weren't affecting her ability to do her job. Neil was still talking on the phone, and Luke wouldn't return from the Hub for several hours. What else could they push ahead with until Gus returned from seeing Oscar Wallington?

"Another concern to scratch from the list," said Neil after he ended his call. "Bob Ellison just confirmed he never spoke to the police after seeing them on Jim's doorstep. Yes, Kendal Guthrie wanted to buy the farm, but Bob refused to sell it. His family has been there as long as a Guthrie had farmed at Glenhead. Bob still has no plans to get out. He told me if there had been anything that affected Jim Thornton and his wife, they would have been the first to know."

"Thanks, Neil," said Alex.

"Alf Collett's a miserable so-and-so," said Lydia. "We won't get to speak with him face-to-face, so I fired a list of questions at him. I thought just querying when Rosie left might put him on his guard."

"Good thinking, Lydia," said Neil. "You hid the question we needed to answer among standard questions relating to his original statement."

"I'm learning from the best, Neil," said Lydia.

"You're very kind," said Neil.

"I meant Gus," said Lydia. "Anyhow, Alf Collett said the story about the barmaid, Imogen, was a total fabrication. He fired her for petty theft. Guthrie might have overheard Imogen saying something else lay behind it, and Kendal twisted the story to suit his ends. Alf's version of what was said to Dave Vickers and Jim Thornton didn't differ from what they told the police. He never believed Guthrie would follow through with the threat to open a pub in competition with the Traveller's Rest. Alf's wife, Joan, was fading away, as was the passing trade for the pub. Alf said he would have gone out of business before the ink was dry on any contract signed between Bob Ellison and Kendal Guthrie, anyway. He sounded an unhappy man. I asked about the days following the murder. He told me Rosie rang him on Sunday to tell him she was thinking of leaving. Alf tried to get her to change her mind. He suggested she had a few days off. Rosie didn't work again until Thursday evening. That was the nineteenth of February. She told him she'd decided not to return. Alf called her on Friday, the twenty-seventh, for one last attempt to get her to change her mind. Rosie told him she was off on holiday and she'd found a job in Salisbury."

"Was that it?" asked Alex. "Didn't you ask why he told the police she'd quit two weeks after the murder?"

"Of course I did," said Lydia. "The twenty-seventh *was* two weeks after the murder. Alf always wanted to believe Rosie would come back if he gave her time. But, once he heard she was off to Majorca and returning to a new job, he had to accept she'd quit for good."

"Fair enough," said Alex, "but there's still one thing that bugs me. Alf didn't mention Oscar Wallington during your conversation, did he?"

"Well, he did, but he didn't elaborate on what Guthrie said to Wallington, except to mention the sarcastic way he used the term, General, every time he spoke to him. There was no substance to the verbal attack. We can always go back to Alf, depending on what Gus learns this afternoon."

"You're probably right," said Alex. "It's tough to see why Alf Collett should cover for Oscar Wallington. He wasn't a regular like Vickers and Thornton."

"Alf mentioned him and Dave Vickers when I asked what happened in the days following the murder," said Lydia. "We knew Oscar was in the pub on Saturday night. Vickers wasn't there, but he cycled from Shrewton on Monday and Wednesday night and sat with Jim Thornton for a natter. Vickers was disappointed to learn Rosie was taking time out. Alf said he hadn't told him she was looking for another job. Wallington came into the pub on Thursday night. Alf told me he didn't see Wallington again until the following Friday. Jim was in every night as usual until his wife went into the hospital. Vickers cycled there on Monday, Wednesday, and Friday."

"So, all three men were in the bar on the twenty-seventh of February?"

"Yes, I suppose they were," said Lydia.

Chapter Twelve

GUS PARKED the Focus alongside a battered Land Rover Defender. He thought he must be at the correct address, and Oscar Wallington still hadn't found a way to finance a new car in the past three years. The Lodge House was an impressive building standing to the right of the estate entrance. Unfortunately, Gus couldn't see the manor house from the gateway. Oak trees flanked the tarmacked road that stretched away into the distance.

Gus looked for a doorbell, but true to form, the building sported a wrought-iron bell pull with a weathered look suggesting it had belonged to the Lodge for a century.

Oscar Wallington answered the door in seconds. If Gus knew nothing of the man before he met him, he would still have guessed ex-military. Gus remembered the wording from the murder file; a squaddie masquerading as a gentleman farmer.

"Good afternoon, Mr Freeman," said Oscar. "Do come in."

Oscar took Gus through the hallway into the estate

office. Floor-to-ceiling shelving covered two walls, and the antique pedestal desk looked as if it had come straight from Gus's bank manager's office when he lived in Downton. At one time, a predecessor had used it as a library. A large sash window looked out over rolling fields.

"A pleasant spot to work," said Gus.

"It is," said Oscar. He sat behind the large desk and pointed to an uncomfortable-looking chair next to the window.

"My colleague has told you why we wanted to speak with you again, Mr Wallington," said Gus. "The Kendal Guthrie murder file remains open. Three years have passed, and it's my job to review the case and uncover the truth."

"I'll do whatever I can to help, Mr Freeman," said Oscar. "Fire away."

"We understand you spent most of your working life as a career soldier."

"I entered the Army from school as a raw recruit and worked my way up to WO first class. The country was at war with Argentina in my last year at school. That lit a fire in my belly to do my bit. I never visited the Falklands after the conflict ended, but I served in Kosovo and Afghanistan. My career also saw me posted for spells in Germany and Northern Ireland. The latter was where I met Corinne, my wife. After I got posted to Bulford Camp, we felt settled enough to start a family. My time in Wiltshire has been a happy one, Mr Freeman. We didn't want to move away when the army decided the time had come for me to retire. The manor house owners had just parted company with their previous estate manager, and I applied for the post. The last seven years have been successful for the estate and us as a family."

"Interesting," said Gus. "Let me remind you of the

night of the thirteenth of February, 2015. A dreadful night in more ways than one. What possessed you to drive from this lovely property to the Traveller's Rest in the middle of the Plain?"

"It was a stressful day on the estate, and I needed to unwind," said Oscar. "I was alone in the house as it was half-term, and Corinne and the boys were away. I was to go with them, but a series of unexpected crises kept me at home. Corinne was not amused. I went to Alf Collett's pub now and then, and I believed I could rely on my trusty Defender to get me there and back."

"You can recall the start of that evening well. What about while you were in the bar?"

"Can I remember it word-for-word? I doubt it. Rosie had asked Jim Thornton how long we'd had soldiers on the plain. I could tell her that. Let me see, Jim told tall tales of ghosts and monsters, frightening the young girl to death. Sorry, poor choice of phrase. When Guthrie arrived, he had something nasty to say to everyone. I copped it at first. Jim bore the brunt when Guthrie reckoned he was buying Ellison's farm. That could have put Jim out of his tied cottage. I'd crossed swords with Guthrie before in other bars. He had a talent for upsetting people. Nine times out of ten, what he said wasn't genuine. If his target showed any weakness, Guthrie kept sticking the knife in. If you stood your ground and showed him you knew what he was saying was rubbish, he moved on to someone else."

"Guthrie intimated you were capable of embezzlement," said Gus. "Was that genuine?"

"Of course not," said Oscar. "That was the chap who sat in this chair before me. Guthrie seemed to think estate managers, per se, were untrustworthy. It was water off a duck's back to me."

"What did you make of his comment that generals never accept responsibility for something which goes wrong in the heat of battle? It's the lower ranks that usually carry the can?"

"Did he say that? I can't recall what that might have meant. Dave Vickers had been under fire for offering low-interest rates on savings. Then Guthrie switched his attention to Alf and Jim. I supported Alf's action to ban the fellow. Guthrie was running out of places to get a drink. His behaviour that night was typical. He didn't pick anyone out for special treatment, Mr Freeman. If you'd pitched up at the Traveller's Rest, he would have found a way to get under your skin."

"I've no doubt he would, Mr Wallington," said Gus. "However, if someone had murdered Guthrie within hours of his talking to me, I would have contacted the police as a matter of course. As a man who served his country for thirty years, I'm surprised you didn't come forward. In fact, none of you offered information on where Kendal Guthrie had been that night, who he had spoken to, and what time he left the pub. I understand why you might not wish his accusations to get a public airing, but your silence suggested you had something to hide."

"We discussed things on Saturday evening after we heard the news," said Oscar. "Dave Vickers wasn't there, so we didn't think we could decide unless everyone agreed. I went back on Thursday evening, but Alf had forgotten to ask Dave for his opinion. Alf was more concerned about Joan's deteriorating health and Rosie taking time off to decide whether or not she wanted to keep working there."

This was news to Gus.

"I thought it was two weeks before Rosie left the pub?"

"I heard Rosie tell Alf she wasn't returning to the pub

after that night. On my next visit the following Friday, Dave, Jim, and I chatted to Alf at the end of the night, and we agreed we should contact the police. Dave asked what Rosie thought we should do, and Alf said he'd spoken to her earlier in the day. She was flying to Majorca from Bristol in the morning and starting a new job on her return. I don't know why Alf didn't call the police on Saturday morning. We four heard the news from Majorca at different times and places on Sunday evening or Monday. I can't remember when I went to the Traveller's Rest next. I only visited the pub on around thirty occasions during the year anyway, but when I spoke to Alf next, it was after your colleagues had met us and taken our statements."

"When I spoke to Dave Vickers earlier today, he said you and Jim Thornton waited for him to join you by the pub door on Friday night."

"We did. Dave needed the loo before cycling four miles home. When we got outside, it was raining and blowing a gale. I watched Dave struggling into his wet weather gear in the lean-to where he kept his bicycle. Jim left, I followed him, and Dave would have started cycling a minute later. Why?"

"Did you see Kendal Guthrie?" asked Gus.

Oscar laughed.

"Cheeky devil couldn't resist letting us glimpse his fancy motor. He left thirty seconds ahead of Jim, give or take."

"What were conditions like in the village?" asked Gus.

"The roadworks traffic light turned red as I approached the 'Wait Here' sign in the road. I switched off my head-lights, and as I couldn't see anyone driving towards me, I must admit I carried on—mea culpa. When driving to the pub earlier, I hung around for two minutes for the blessed green light. There was next to zero chance of meeting anyone on such a filthy night. So I took the B390 back here. Jim's cottage was in darkness when I drove past. His car was on the grass verge. Tied cottages are basic; they don't tend to have a garage."

"I think that's it for now, Mr Wallington," said Gus. "If we have further questions, we'll get in touch."

"You know where I am, Mr Freeman," said Oscar.

"Is your wife here this afternoon?" asked Gus.

"Corinne was in the kitchen when you arrived. Unfortunately, I must drive to the manor house, so I'll have to leave you. If you want a word with her, just turn left as we leave the office and follow your nose. The smell of baking will tell you when you're there. Our eldest boy takes his finals next May, and his younger brother goes to Durham at the end of September. The poor woman has so much to do without needing to dash off for the school run and other activities. I'm sure you know what it's like."

Gus didn't, but he wanted a quick word with Corinne Wallington.

"WAS THAT THE LIFT?" asked Neil. "The boss is back."

Gus exited the lift and dropped his folder onto his desk.

"What a day," he said. "It started badly at Glenhead Farm, improved significantly in Shrewton, and slowed to a snail's pace after I reached the Lodge House. On the plus side, if someone has a minute to make coffee, I've brought baked goods from Corinne Wallington. So we can have a civilized break while we review what we've achieved."

Lydia and Blessing walked to the restroom.

"Where's Luke?" asked Gus.

"On his way back from the Hub, guv," said Alex. "Ten minutes, and we should have a full complement."

Luke found a cup of coffee and a madeleine on his desk when he returned to the office.

"What have I done to deserve this?" he asked. "Or have you solved the case in my absence?"

"I take it you didn't find the magic bullet at the Hub?" said Neil.

Luke shook his head.

"A waste of time."

"Rather like my meeting with Helen Guthrie," said Gus. "She had her manager and solicitor riding shotgun. I didn't learn whether she was in the farm business for the long haul or looking to make a sharp exit with a fortune. I don't believe anyone in the room was involved in Kendal's murder, so I decided I was wasting my time. Dave Vickers was a pleasant chap and very helpful. Wessex Water was replacing old pipework in the village, which didn't come to light in the original investigation. Dave reckoned he stopped at the lights for almost a minute. When I asked about the conversations in the pub early that night, there was nothing unusual. It matched what we'd heard before. When Guthrie arrived, he asked who got the blame when something went wrong in the heat of battle, and Dave thought that fazed Oscar for a second. No idea what that meant. Oscar and Jim hung around for Dave when Alf called time, so they left the pub together. That was different to what we thought because Guthrie was in his Bentley with the engine running, waiting to flip the middle finger as he drove away. That alters his leaving time. If they were against him, the lights could add additional time to his journey. I'll jump ahead a second because Oscar told me he ignored the red light, checked for oncoming headlights around the corner, and then took a calculated risk."

"That could bring him two minutes closer to Kendal's car, guv," said Neil.

"First, if he'd chased after Kendal, would he tell the police he'd ignored a traffic light? Second, even if he was five yards behind Kendal, we've repeatedly shown that none of them could reach the farm ahead of him."

"OK, guv. What else did Dave Vickers have to offer?" said Luke.

"Hang on, Rosie told Alf she was leaving, looking for another job," said Alex. "Lydia got through to him. He tried to persuade Rosie to stay. Alf let her have three days off to think things over. The confusion arose because Alf always believed he could persuade Rosie to return. We already knew he called her on Friday the twenty-seventh before she went on holiday."

"That matches what Oscar Wallington told me," said Gus. "Oscar went to the pub on Thursday the nineteenth, and Alf had forgotten to ask Dave on Monday and Wednesday what he thought they should do. Rosie worked Thursday night and told Alf it was her last night. On the twenty-seventh, the four men were in the bar after closing time. Alf told them he'd spoken to Rosie on the phone earlier, and she confirmed she wasn't returning to the pub after her holiday. Alf was supposed to call the police the next day. Oscar didn't know why Alf delayed. Maybe he thought they didn't work weekends. Rosie died in a hit-and-run twenty-four hours later, and Keith and Maxine started chasing the people in the bar on Friday night on Monday the ninth of March."

"Where do we go from here, guv?" asked Luke.

"Each of us has files to update," said Gus. "Get everything you've worked on today recorded as soon as possible. Tomorrow, I want Alex and Lydia to recalculate Kendal's journey time based on the new information. It needs to be as exact as we can make it, even if it's irrelevant. Another team of detectives will look into this case in the future if we can't solve it. I don't want them to point the finger at us and say we left a stone unturned. We follow every lead, no matter how tenuous."

Gus and the team left the office at five o'clock. Tomorrow was another day. The mood was downbeat. No matter what they did, specific facts kept blocking their progress.

AS BLESSING DROVE TO WORTON, she imagined the evening ahead. First, her mother would ring at seven o'clock for their weekly chat, and she had to ask for Ekene Kanu's phone number. Then, after Gus returned from meeting Dave Vickers and Oscar Wallington, the numbers she had wrestled with throughout the day changed again. The final straw was Gus giving Alex and Lydia the task of recalculating the numbers.

How could she resolve the niggle she'd felt for the past two days? Were they missing something? Why not phone her mother as soon as she reached the farm, eat the meal Jackie Ferris prepared, and drive to the Plain to check for herself?

Blessing parked her Nissan Micra by the kitchen door and ran inside.

"You're in a rush tonight? Do you have a date?" asked Jackie.

"I wish," said Blessing. "I want to go for a drive in the countryside later. There's something I need to check."

"You've got a splendid evening for it," said Jackie. "Be careful, though. It will get dark by half-past eight. The

Plain isn't friendly at night if you don't know the area well."

"Tilshead is only eight miles away," said Blessing, "My destination is ten miles further on, towards Salisbury. So I should be there and back in a couple of hours."

Blessing ran upstairs to her room. She showered and changed, then called her mother. It was tough to get a word in edge-wise, as usual. Maryam wanted to know everything that had been going on at work. Blessing kept glancing at her watch.

"Can you give me Ekene's number, please?" she said. "I wish to speak with him before Sunday."

Blessing kept her fingers crossed that her mother saw this as a positive move. Then, after they said their goodbyes, her father would hear the news. She was in luck. Maryam gave her the phone number and didn't query why she needed it.

"Sorry to cut things short this week," she told Maryam. "I'm doing a spot of homework later."

"Don't work too hard, Blessing," said Maryam. "We'll see you on Sunday. Don't be late."

Blessing put Ekene's number into her phone and ran downstairs. John and Jackie were chatting in the kitchen.

"Are you hungry?" asked Jackie.

"Always," said Blessing.

"Do you want me to come with you this evening, Blessing," asked John Ferris.

"I'll be fine," said Blessing. "I'll call you when I leave Durrington on my way back."

Blessing set off at seven o'clock for Tilshead. She passed the boarded-up Traveller's Rest on the outskirts of the village. The clock on the dashboard read seven twenty. Blessing stopped the car, got out, and walked back to the pub car park. A six-foot chain-link fence surrounded the plot, but it was possible to see Alf Collett's garage and the tiny bicycle shed Dave Vickers used.

When she set off towards the village, Blessing started the stopwatch on her phone. She knew the route they believed Kendal Guthrie took by heart. Blessing drove at a steady thirty miles an hour along the A360 for three-quarters of a mile and stopped on the grass verge. She paused the stopwatch.

What did these grey posts with yellow-painted tops mean at this crossroads? There were no directional signs, just signs indicating yet another bend for traffic approaching from Shrewton. Blessing got out of her car to read an official-looking notice. Ah, this was a spot where military vehicles crossed the public road. Blessing could see at least a dozen wooden huts on the brow of the hill. The entrance marked one of the many restricted areas on the Plain mentioned by Gus and the others.

Blessing returned to her car and studied a copy of the map Suzie Ferris had prepared. If she drove one mile straight ahead, she should be able to turn right and head for the Bustard Inn Tea Rooms. If the track was in as good a state as it appeared from here, it shouldn't be a problem.

Blessing looked in both directions. She could explore if she let this car drive past on the way towards Tilshead before moving. Her warrant card was in her handbag if she had to talk herself out of trouble. The climb to the top of the hill went without incident. Blessing sang to herself to counter the butterflies in her stomach. She wasn't used to being reckless, but Blessing believed the situation demanded it.

The Tea Rooms were four hundred yards ahead of her when her heart sank. A car was heading towards her, and whoever was driving wasn't sticking to the speed limit she'd spotted as she left the A360 ten minutes ago. The driver flashed his lights and swung his car across the track. Blessing braked hard and stopped.

Blessing shivered despite the warm sunshine. A tall, dark-skinned man in uniform got out of the car and walked towards her little Micra. She couldn't see his face because of the aviator sunglasses he wore. What was that on his hip? Was he armed?

Blessing grabbed her handbag, searched for her warrant card, and got out. She drew herself to her full height but still had to look up.

"Where do you think you're going? This area is restricted. You must have seen the signs."

"My name is Detective Constable Umeh from Wiltshire Police. We're investigating a murder that took place in 2015. I'm testing a theory."

"Well, DC Umeh, warrant card or not, you can't wander on the Plain without permission. It can be a dangerous place. We have live firing exercises almost daily, and an armoured vehicle would soon make a mess of your car."

"You haven't identified yourself," said Blessing. "How do I know you're in a position to tell me where I can or cannot pursue my enquiries?"

"Your DS Mercer contacted us asking for a liaison officer a couple of days ago, DC Umeh. I'm Jamie Banks-Trewick with the Royal Military Police Special Investigation Branch. I thought your Mr Freeman would contact us before sending Dora the Explorer on a mission."

Blessing realised the Second Lieutenant was teasing her.

"My name is not Dora. It's Blessing," she said.

"Well, Blessing," said Jamie. "It's best if you come with

me. Lock your car, jump in beside me, and I'll escort you to the Tea Rooms. I'll bring you back, don't worry."

"That's not where I need to go," said Blessing as she slid into the passenger seat of his car. "I want the quickest route from here to Glenhead Farm, Durrington. Do you know it?"

Jamie nodded, swung the car around and headed towards the Tea Rooms.

"What are you doing?" he asked as Blessing checked her phone.

"I want to know how long it takes. Slow down. You're going too fast."

Jamie grinned and eased off the accelerator.

"I'll scoot around to the north of Larkhill Camp," he said, "and approach the farm on the A345 Netheravon Road into Durrington. It won't take long."

"That was what I was hoping," said Blessing.

"There we are, Blessing," said Jamie as they stopped at the end of the lane. "Do you want me to drive to the front door?"

"Heavens, no. They've tarmacked the drive, but that doesn't matter. I can work out how long it took."

"Can I take you back to your car now?" he asked. "With luck, it will still be in one piece."

"Yes, please," said Blessing. "That's it, I've done it. I know how the killer got to the farm ahead of Mr Guthrie."

"I've no idea who that is, Blessing. I've only been at Bulford Camp for eighteen months."

"Mr Guthrie drove a Bentley Continental," said Blessing. Jamie whistled.

"Exactly, a fancy motor, not designed for the terrain we crossed just now. We believe Guthrie stayed on the main roads and covered twelve miles between the pub and the farm. We now know he left the pub close to a quarter past ten."

"Twenty-five minutes, give or take," said Jamie.

"The weather was awful that February night," said Blessing, "and roadworks could have delayed him further. Either way, it was still twelve miles. The distance you and I covered this evening was eight and a quarter miles by cutting across the countryside using tank tracks and trails."

"Public roads on the Plain never take the direct route," said Jamie. "Since the Army arrived here, crows have been out of work."

Jamie could see Blessing hadn't got the reference.

"There's no such thing as eight and a quarter miles as the crow flies, not out here. Whoever your killer was, he found the closest equivalent to the phrase. He must have local knowledge."

Jamie and Blessing reached her car.

"It's safe," she said. "That's a relief."

"Do you want me to escort you to the exit, Blessing?" said Jamie.

"That won't be necessary," she replied. "I'm sorry for being a nuisance. It was worth it."

"Yes, it was, wasn't it? I hope I see you again."

Blessing got out of the car and walked to her Micra. The sun disappeared behind the hills in the distance, and the temperature dropped.

"It's so peaceful here, isn't it?" she said.

"I recommend you get off home, Blessing," said Jamie. "Tomorrow morning at 0900 hours, a major exercise gets underway. The ground on either side of the valley beyond this hill will swarm with men and armoured vehicles. Over at Copehill Down, they're running sessions on close-quarters fighting techniques with live ammo."

"I read about that in our files," said Blessing. "They call that fighting in built-up areas, don't they?"

"The top brass uses that phrase," said Jamie. "The lads on the ground use the term FISH. Fighting in someone's house."

"What do you look like without your sunglasses?" asked Blessing.

Jamie whipped off his aviator shades and struck a pose.

"What do you think?"

"I think I'd better go," she said, giving Jamie the biggest smile she possessed. "Yes, I hope we meet again too."

Blessing hoped Jamie wouldn't watch her negotiate a three-point turn on this single-lane track; it could be embarrassing. But she needn't have worried. The radio in his car squawked, and he gave her a wave as he dashed to answer it. As he sped away towards the Tea Rooms, Blessing started her car and eventually had it facing the right way. She remembered having one thing to do before driving back to Worton. Blessing called Jackie Ferris and told her she would be back in half an hour.

As she eased the car along the tracks to the junction leading back to the A360, she spotted a vehicle coming from Shrewton. Blessing waited for the Land Rover to disappear around the bend and towards Tilshead village. She quickly returned to the main road and set off for Worton.

There were no roadworks tonight, but the odd car was on the road. When she reached the other side of the village, she relaxed. If only the driver behind would dip his headlights. Why was he driving so close? Blessing felt her Micra jump forward. Had the car behind her hit her bumper? She pulled into the side of the road, grabbed her handbag, and got out. It was that Land Rover again. It looked to be an old Defender.

"What are you playing at?" she asked, waving her warrant card. "DC Umeh, Wiltshire Police. You were driving far too close to my car."

"I know," said the driver. "I wanted you to stop."

"You're Oscar Wallington," said Blessing, suddenly feeling very alone. "I know what you did."

Oscar was out of his vehicle and stood on the grass, away from traffic. Blessing followed him.

"As soon as I saw your car at the top of the hill, I knew what you were up to," said Oscar. "It's such a shame. I can't let you take your information back to your colleagues. I've lived and worked on the Plain for years and know every inch. It was simple to work out how to get to the farm before Kendal Guthrie. He made it easier by hanging around until we came out of the pub. I knew nobody would patrol the hillside and beyond. They were tucked up in their barracks, listening to the wind and rain. As for Larkhill, my Defender was well known there. If someone looked out of a window as I passed, it wouldn't have registered as something strange."

Blessing looked around her. Why weren't there any cars around when you needed them? Before she could react, Oscar grabbed her arms, bound them behind her back with a zip tie, and bustled her into the passenger seat of the Land Rover.

"Where are you taking me?" asked Blessing. "You won't get away with this. I called my landlady before I started back."

"The Plain covers a vast expanse," said Oscar. "It will take them hours to find you, even though we're only driving three miles."

Blessing could see buildings ahead but no lights anywhere to be seen.

"Where is this," she asked, afraid to hear the answer.

"The end of the line," said Oscar.

He pulled up next to a two-storey building and got out of the Land Rover. Blessing tried to kick him as he opened the passenger door, but he was too quick for her. Oscar grabbed her left shoulder, dragged her out of the vehicle, and pinned her to the ground. He stuffed a rag into her mouth and wrapped duct tape around the lower half of her face to secure it. Seconds later, he had wrestled the frightened young woman through a doorway, up a flight of stairs, and into a bedroom. Oscar used more duct tape to secure her ankles, and Blessing found herself propped in the corner of the room under a window. Oscar left the room and returned, carrying a cardboard figure.

"It will be quick," he said. "I've trained hundreds of men in this makeshift town. A group of young recruits will descend on Copehill Down at dawn. They'll sweep through the buildings looking for the enemy."

He placed the cardboard figure on Blessing's lap.

"Say hello to an ISIS zealot."

Oscar disappeared again, and Blessing struggled against her bonds and tried to shift her companion.

"You look tired," said Oscar when he returned and bent over her. Blessing felt a scratch on her neck. Her eyes dropped a minute later, and Oscar Wallington stood up from where he was sitting on a mattress.

"Sweet dreams," he said. "I need to leave, I'm afraid."

Blessing was out cold before Oscar Wallington reached the top of the stairs.

Chapter Thirteen

JACKIE FERRIS LOOKED at the clock in the kitchen yet again. Blessing should have reached the farm ages ago. John was in the yard checking the outbuildings and paying one last visit to his precious horses. As soon as he came indoors, they needed to call Gus.

"Still no sign of her, love?" asked John as he walked through the kitchen door. "Perhaps she stopped in a pub for a drink."

"Please get in the Land Rover and drive out there, John. Blessing inherited her sense of direction from her father. She could have had an accident or got lost in the dark. I'll phone Gus and put him in the picture. I'm worried."

John Ferris turned on his heel and returned to the yard. It wouldn't be any hardship driving to Tilshead and back, but if Blessing went off-piste, it would be like looking for a needle in a haystack.

Jackie called Gus in Urchfont. Her daughter answered.

"Suzie, it's Mum. Can I speak to Gus, please?"

"What's the matter, Mum?" asked Suzie. "We were on our way to bed."

"Blessing's late. She phoned from the middle of the Plain and should have arrived hours ago."

"Sit tight," said Suzie. "We're on our way. What's Dad doing?"

"He just left in the Land Rover, heading for Tilshead. We're not sure where she was going after that."

"Gus will know," said Suzie. "We'll see you in fifteen minutes. Quicker if I drive."

Suzie pulled up outside the farmhouse kitchen door twelve minutes later.

Gus wondered how many more grey hairs he had amassed on that trip. But at least it was for a good cause.

"Any news from John, Jackie?" he asked as they walked indoors.

"Nothing so far," said Jackie. "Where would she have gone?"

"Durrington, possibly. You say she drove to Tilshead first?"

"She was in a rush as soon as she got home, Gus," said Jackie. "Blessing called her mother instead of waiting for her to ring. Then she drove onto the Plain at seven."

"What time did she ring to say she was leaving?" asked Gus.

"Around half-past eight. I'm worried Blessing's lost and is going around in circles on those crazy lanes and tracks. You know what they're like, Suzie."

"I don't suppose Blessing mentioned where she was when she rang?" asked Suzie.

"Didn't think to ask," said Jackie. "What can we do?"

"I'll call Geoff Mercer," said Gus. "Maybe he can scramble a helicopter to circle the most likely areas looking for her car. Boots on the ground are what we need. I asked for a liaison officer from the SIB, but unless Alex heard something today, Geoff might not have anyone organised yet."

Jackie's phone rang. It was John, so she handed the phone to Gus.

"I've found Blessing's car abandoned on the side of the road half a mile out of Tilshead. She was a little over ten minutes from home. The driver's door was unlocked, and the keys were still in the ignition. Her handbag's missing too."

"Right, thanks, John," said Gus. "Don't go any further onto the Plain. Have a look around Tilshead village. Hunt for any CCTV we might check."

"Do you think someone's taken her?" said John.

"It's likely," said Gus. "Blessing must have found the answer to a problem that's bothered us since Monday. I know who we're after now, and the man is dangerous."

"I'll see what I can dig up, Gus," said John. "Will you be coming out here soon?"

"Give me a few minutes to speak to Geoff Mercer, and Suzie and I will be on our way."

"Who do you think it was, Gus?" asked Suzie.

"Wallington," said Gus. "If someone's taken Blessing, it can only be him. Alf Collett's in Portugal, Dave Vickers doesn't drive, and Jim Thornton is dead. So Blessing worked out how Wallington reached Glenhead Farm ahead of Kendal Guthrie."

Gus called Geoff Mercer. His boss didn't complain about the lateness of the hour or waste time asking what had happened. He recognised the urgency in Gus's voice.

"Whatever you need will be available, Gus. Vera sent contact details for your liaison man from the RMP to Alex

Hardy. I assume you were out of the office if you didn't get them. You want Second Lieutenant Jamie Banks-Trewick."

Geoff rattled off Jamie's phone number and told Gus to join the search.

"I'll get the chopper in the air if practical," said Geoff. "and get as many uniformed officers as we have available on standby to assist in the search. Anything you can do to narrow the search area, the better."

"Thanks, Geoff," said Gus. He nodded to Suzie. They were off to Tilshead. As they dashed outside to the car, Gus called the SIB officer. The call went to voice mail.

"Damn," said Gus. "It seems as if our SIB contact has gone to bed."

Gus left a message. He and Suzie raced towards Tilshead.

"There's Blessing's car," said Suzie. "I can't see Dad anywhere."

"Carry on into the village. John's looking for CCTV coverage of the A360."

"There's his Land Rover on the garage forecourt," said Suzie. "I almost missed it behind the fuel pumps."

John Ferris was inside the twenty-four-hour shop attached to the garage. He spotted Gus and beckoned him inside.

"The lad on the till doesn't understand the system, but I've used one similar at the farm. I think I've captured the two vehicles coming through the village."

Gus studied the grainy footage.

"This was only a couple of hours ago," he moaned. "The black and white film of the moon landing is in better shape than this."

"Here comes Blessing's Micra," said John. "The Land Rover pulls out of the junction behind her and speeds up.

He's right on her tail with his headlights on full beam when they pass this place."

"Are you sure there's nothing else?" asked Gus.

"You saw where Blessing's car was, Gus," said John. "This garage is one mile away. There are only a handful of properties between here and there. If one of them has any security cameras, they'll be the same as yours, concentrated on access points to the property, not the road."

"Dad's right," said Suzie. "Where would Wallington take her?"

"He lives on the other side of Chitterne," said Gus. "We should try there first. I was with him this afternoon; maybe something I said or did spooked him. We'll use your Land Rover, John. Tell the lad on the till we'll collect Suzie's Golf later."

One minute later, they were en route to Lodge House.

"Did you suspect this bloke already?" asked John.

"Suzie put a crazy idea in my head," said Gus. "I spoke to Corinne Wallington after her husband left to drive to the manor house. A witness reckoned Collett, Thornton, and Wallington stared at the barmaid, Rosie Ritchens, when she cleared tables in the bar on Saturday night. Suzie asked whether they were in it together. Alf Collett's actions after the murder seemed to fuel that idea. I asked Corinne where her parents lived, thinking she would tell me they'd retired to Majorca. Instead, they still live in the same house near Portadown, County Armagh, where Oscar met Corinne while stationed in Northern Ireland."

"You thought Wallington flew to Palma on the same plane as Rosie?" asked Suzie.

"He was in the bar on the twenty-seventh when Collett told him where she was going. It made sense at the time.

Wallington was meant to travel to Portadown on the thirteenth, the night of the murder. The family was spending half-term with Corinne's parents. Corinne told me this afternoon that Oscar flew to Belfast for a weekend on the twenty-eighth. It was a boozy reunion with several of his colleagues. He returned on Tuesday morning. Rosie's death was what the police believed. A hit-and-run involving a drunken tourist at the wheel of a hire car. I got it wrong. Look, John, the Lodge House is on the right in one hundred yards."

John slowed and turned into the estate entrance.

"No Land Rover Defender in sight," he said. "I guess the Vauxhall is the wife's car?"

Gus jumped out of the vehicle and ran to the front door. It was just after eleven o'clock, and the house was in darkness. Gus kept ringing the bell and waited on the doorstep, praying Blessing was still alive.

"Who is it?"

Corinne Wallington wasn't opening the door to strangers.

"Gus Freeman, Corinne. We met this afternoon."

Corinne opened the door.

"Are you looking for Oscar?" she asked.

"Do you know where he is?" asked Gus.

"I haven't seen him since he left this afternoon. He told me something needed his attention at the manor house, but I discovered he'd packed a bag and taken it with him when I went upstairs later this evening. He's not answering his phone. I have no idea what he's up to."

"Where would he go if he was running, Corinne?" asked Gus.

"What do you mean? Why would he be running?"

"We need to speak to him urgently. He has one of my

colleagues with him. We found her car abandoned on the outskirts of Tilshead."

Corinne shook her head. Gus could tell that the news about her husband had come as a shock. They were wasting time standing on her doorstep.

"Am I in danger, Gus?" Corinne asked.

"Where are the boys?"

"Patrick, our eldest, shares a house in Salisbury with two friends from university. I could take Charles and stay there until this is over."

"That sounds like a good idea. I'm sorry, I can't tell you more, Corinne," said Gus. "We've got people looking for Oscar at ports and airports. We aim to search the most likely areas on the Plain he might have gone after taking my colleague hostage."

"Good luck with that," said Corinne. "He knows the Plain like the back of his hand."

"Where were your married quarters, Corinne?"

"We were at Upavon when we first moved here, and when the boys came along, we moved to a bigger house at Bulford. I can give you the addresses."

Gus left Corinne Wallington to wake her son and try to explain what the heck was going on. Once he was back in the Land Rover, John Ferris set off towards Bulford Camp. Gus checked his phone. Still no reply from the SIB contact.

"How do we get onto the camp to check whether Wallington is there?" asked Suzie.

"Come to that, how does he have free rein to come and go four years after he retired?" said Gus.

"We won't get to Bulford before half-past eleven, Gus," said John. "Upavon is ten miles further on. Time is ticking."

"Perhaps I should call Geoff Mercer," said Gus. "He can get people to Upavon. Then, if he's got people closer to

Bulford already, we can get these addresses searched while we're driving."

Gus cursed.

"What's up?" asked Suzie.

"Have you got a signal on your phone? Mine's dead."

"Me too," said Suzie.

"Make that three," said John. "Reception comes and goes out here. We'll get back in service before you know it."

Gus hoped John was right. They continued to head towards Bulford.

The ringtone on his phone suddenly rang out, making him jump.

"Gus Freeman."

"Jamie Barnes-Trewick here. Sorry I didn't reply earlier. I hope I didn't wake you?"

"No chance, we're on our way to Bulford. One of my detectives is missing. We believe a suspect in a murder case took her hostage."

"Blimey, I was with Blessing earlier. I stopped her car because she was trespassing. When she explained what she was doing, I stayed with her until we'd driven to Durrington and back. Blessing said what she'd learned had solved a mystery. I reunited her with her car, and she was driving back to the main road, heading home. That was half-eight, give or take."

"She didn't get home, Jamie. We found her car on the Worton side of Tilshead. Based on the evidence we've gathered so far, Oscar Wallington took her."

"The name rings a bell. Wasn't he one of ours?"

"He left Bulford Camp four years ago and is the estate manager at a place between Chitterne and Warminster. We suspect he murdered a guy called Kendal Guthrie in 2015, and Blessing worked it out."

"Blessing didn't mention the guy's name. I got called away to a suspicious fire in derelict married quarters at Upavon and walked in the door just this minute. I told her the Plain was dangerous."

Gus heard Jamie smack a hard surface with his hand.

"You okay, Jamie?" he asked.

"I remember who Wallington is now. He set up dozens of urban warfare scenarios. Wallington wrote the manual. If he's running, he won't want baggage. He'll ditch Blessing and get moving. I know where he's taken her, Gus. It's Copehill Down, three miles from where you found her car. Thank goodness I got your message and didn't wait until morning. The place will get lit up at 0545 in the morning. The major exercise on the Plain starts at 0900 hours because the heavy artillery disturbs the locals. But the assessors insisted they upgrade the Copehill exercise to a dawn raid. I can get there with a team to start a house-to-house search for Blessing in twenty minutes via The Packway and the A360. Where are you now?"

"We just drove through Shrewton, so we should arrive a few minutes ahead of you."

"Leave it to the experts, Gus," said Jamie.

"We need to head back to Tilshead, John," said Gus. "Then we're going to Copehill Down."

"I know the area well," said Suzie. "I've ridden around that town a hundred times. Stop at the garage, and I'll pick up my car."

When John Ferris reached the training site, the place was in darkness. Suzie's Golf was parked five yards ahead of the Land Rover. Gus and his daughter had gone on ahead.

"Typical," said John. He grabbed a torch, got out, and made his way to the site perimeter. Behind him, he could hear the sound of vehicles approaching at speed. The cavalry had arrived.

John spotted Gus and Suzie twenty yards ahead.

"Wait, you two," he shouted. "Although you've ridden around the perimeter, Suzie, do you know how many houses are here, let alone cargo containers?"

"It's difficult to tell in the dark," said Gus.

"They have a variety of detached, semi-detached and terraced properties to match every eventuality. Jackie and I counted eighty properties when we rode these tracks. They have added more since those days. Your RMP colleague will know what's required. Unless you stumble on Blessing in the first house, working alone will take hours."

Gus and Suzie reluctantly walked back to the Golf and the Land Rover.

"You must be Gus Freeman," said a voice. Suzie watched as a handsome young man in fatigues trotted towards them. Was it possible to have shoulders that broad?

"Jamie BT, your SIB contact. My guys are sweeping the town sector by sector. We'll check every house, every room, every container."

"It's already gone midnight," said Gus.

"I want to find Blessing alive as much as you do, Gus," said Jamie.

"Wallington's killed once," said Gus. "He could have done it again."

"Not giving up yet," said Jamie. "Can I ask a question?"

"Of course," said Gus.

"Why did Wallington kill this farmer Blessing mentioned? The guy who owned Glenhead Farm."

"The motive was unclear," said Gus. "Guthrie had a go at several people in the bar with Wallington that night. One witness told us Guthrie said something that appeared to faze

Wallington, but we haven't learned what that could have been yet."

"I may be able to help," said Jamie. "The fire I investigated in Upavon was at a property once occupied by Wallington and his wife. The damage wasn't great. My guess is he was destroying evidence. Those properties have been unused for several years."

"Did SIB ever investigate Wallington during his time at Bulford Camp?" asked Gus.

"A rookie recruit went AWOL back in 1997," said Jamie. "Wallington was one of his trainers."

A green flare lit up the sky.

"They've found her," he cried. "Follow me, but watch where you're going."

Jamie set off towards the far corner of the site. Gus struggled to match the young man's pace. John shone his torch ahead of them to guide them towards the sector that fired the flare.

Blessing Umeh was sitting on the back step of an Army ambulance. Jamie sat on one side, with a medic tending to her on the other. She looked dazed.

"I'm sorry, guv," she said when she spotted Gus. "I listened to my gut instinct, which landed me in big trouble."

"Don't worry about that now, Blessing," said Gus. "I'm just relieved you're alright."

"Your colleague was bound, gagged, and semi-conscious when we found her, sir," said a young soldier who stood nearby. "Someone had placed an ISIS target between her and the door. So when the raid started at dawn, the first guy through the door would have killed her."

Gus left the medic to continue caring for Blessing. There appeared to be no permanent damage done, thank goodness. He called Geoff Mercer with the news.

"What a relief, Gus," said Geoff. "I'll call off the people I have on standby and step up the hunt for Oscar Wallington. Any clue where he might run?"

"His wife has family in County Armagh, near Portadown."

"Did he do a tour of Northern Ireland?" asked Geoff.

"In the late Eighties, yes," said Gus.

"We must make sure we catch him before he leaves the country. Kenneth will insist on getting in touch, too. I'll talk to you tomorrow. Goodnight."

"Good morning, more like," said Gus.

John and Suzie came across to speak to him.

"Dad's going to wait to drive Blessing back to the farm," said Suzie. "I can take you to Blessing's Micra. Do you think you can cope driving that to Worton?"

Gus gave her a look that was wasted in the semi-darkness.

"I'd like to chat with Jamie before we leave," said Gus. "He was about to tell me something before the flare went up."

"Jamie BT is busy," said Suzie. Gus looked across the street to the ambulance. The SIB contact and his Detective Constable seemed unaware of anyone else in this urban warfare setting.

"Funny how things work out sometimes, isn't it?" said Gus.

Suzie laughed, and Jamie looked up. He left Blessing and came over.

"Sorry, Gus. I was going to tell you about Wallington. He came under scrutiny for allegedly carrying out brutal initiation ceremonies. A Private John Winslow, nineteen, disappeared one night several days after this hazing was thought to have occurred. Winslow was reported as Absent

Without Leave the following morning. We searched for him in the local area and his home town of Chester, but he never surfaced. Wallington always protested his innocence. He got posted to Kosovo eighteen months later and switched to Afghanistan in 2001. After he returned to Bulford, he resumed his duties as a trainer, retiring in 2011. An audit in 2012 revealed that training and complaint documentation records for 1997 had been altered, possibly removed. Does that help at all?"

"I should say so. What do you know about Durrington Down?" asked Gus.

"It's between my camp and Larkhill. Why?"

"Three years ago, the MoD decided they didn't need five farms they'd acquired half a century ago. Guthrie bid for all five. Because of Larkhill's proximity to Durrington Down Farm, Guthrie told an audience in the Traveller's Rest that when the Army withdrew from Germany, they would need married quarters for families of returning soldiers."

"It makes perfect sense," said Jamie. "The ground there isn't great for farming. That was one reason for buying the farms in the first place. So, you're thinking Wallington realised if Guthrie was successful with his bid, he could start building on the lower reaches of Durrington Down and discover something Wallington wanted to remain hidden?"

"I suggest you call someone at Swinton Barracks at Tidworth, rustle up a few Royal Engineers, and start digging, Jamie," said Gus.

"Can I leave that until morning?" asked Jamie. "It's been a long day."

"You can say that again," said Gus.

Gus and Suzie walked to the ambulance where John Ferris was waiting to drive Blessing home.

"All clear?" asked Gus.

"The medics have told her she could go home and rest up," said John.

"Take a couple of days, Blessing," said Gus. "I'll see you on Monday morning."

"I've learned my lesson, guv," said Blessing.

"I'm glad to hear it. When you return to the office, I was hoping you could teach the others what you know about dead reckoning. I believe the basic elements are direction and distance. Am I right?"

"There was no logic behind it, guv," said Blessing. "I asked myself, what would you do, and went with my gut."

Epilogue

SECURITY AT BOURNEMOUTH AIRPORT arrested Oscar Wallington as he queued to board an EasyJet flight to Belfast International.

When they searched his Land Rover Defender in the Long Stay car park, they found a twelve-inch long iron bar hidden in a compartment under the driver's seat.

ENGINEERS WORKING under Jamie Banks-Trewick recovered Private John Winslow's remains from a gully near the boundary of land belonging to the farm on Durrington Down. John Winslow died from blunt force trauma to the skull.

BLESSING UMEH ATTENDED St Peter's Church, Englishcombe, on Sunday, the second of September. Her parents, Kelechi and Maryam, accompanied her, but Ekene Kanu was indisposed.

Blessing sent Ekene a selfie on Friday evening taken in the orchard at Worton Farm, where she entertained a visitor keen to help her recover from her ordeal.

Jamie BT was a great kisser. Ekene Kanu was surplus to requirements.

GUS FREEMAN HAD DRIVEN to the Old Police Station office first thing on Thursday morning, explained what had happened, and sent the rest of the team home until Monday.

"There's no point getting our files updated before Blessing can provide her invaluable contribution," he said. "We deserve a break. So please make the most of it. Who knows what our next case will bring?"

vinci-books.com/normalnovember

In November's chill, a killer lurks in the shadows.

Detective Gus Freeman and the Crime Review Team investigate
the perplexing murder of recently wed garage owner Richard
Chaloner. With time ticking away, the team must navigate a
labyrinth of secrets and lies to unmask the killer before they strike
again.

Turn the page for a free preview…

A Normal November: Chapter One

Thursday, 30 August 2018

Gus Freeman arrived at the Old Police Station office first thing. He had a list of things he needed to deal with after the excitement of last night.

John Ferris had delivered Blessing Umeh to the safety of his Worton farm once he'd persuaded her that Jamie Banks-Trewick and his men had work to do. His wife, Jackie, was waiting patiently in the kitchen to shower Blessing with a lengthy cuddle, a hot drink, and the offer of food despite the lateness of the hour.

"We were so worried," said Jackie. "Thank goodness you're safe."

"I was stupid," said Blessing. "I thought I could prove how someone had done what seemed impossible. How would I know the killer would drive past the main road and spot my Micra on the skyline? Perhaps, I was unlucky, but I should never have gone onto the Plain alone."

"Where are Gus and Suzie?" asked Jackie.

"They should get here in a few minutes," said John. "Gus is bringing Blessing's car back. Although, you won't need it for a day or two, young lady. Do what your boss said and rest up before returning to work on Monday."

Blessing sighed.

"I'll miss out on the fun," said Blessing. "A good night's sleep, and I'll be raring to go."

"You've had a shock, Blessing," said Jackie. "That's bound to catch up with you when the adrenaline rush fades. Gus is right. Take your time, enjoy a long weekend, and you'll be firing on four cylinders again."

"That sounds like Suzie's VW racing up the drive," said John. "Will she never learn?"

Jackie coughed a warning. Gus and Suzie had told them about the baby, but there was over a week before Suzie's twelve-week scan and any official announcement. John sat down and waited for Gus and Suzie to come indoors. He knew his place.

Jackie didn't let her daughter and partner escape her kitchen without questions and refreshments. Gus had groaned as he realised it was two o'clock when he and Suzie reached the bungalow in Urchfont.

Suzie seemed content to write it off as good training for next year.

Gus hadn't been surprised to be the first to arrive in the office today. Sleep hadn't come easily last night. He knew they could so easily have lost a valued team member. One by one, the rest of his Crime Review Team rode in the lift to the first floor.

"No sign of Blessing yet, guv?" asked Neil Davis, who was last to put in an appearance for a change.

"Now everyone's here, Neil. I'll explain what happened to her last night," said Gus.

Neil, Luke, Lydia, and Alex sat quietly and listened as Gus told the tale.

"Blessing's okay; that's the key thing," said Lydia.

"We no longer have a case to solve," said Neil. "I didn't expect to hear that this morning."

"No," said Luke. "Every lead we followed went nowhere. So I wonder what prompted Blessing to go it alone?"

"It's not something I recommend," said Gus. "Blessing knows now it was an unnecessary risk. She won't do it again. There's no point getting our files updated before Blessing can offer her invaluable contribution," he said. "We deserve a break. Please make the most of it. Who knows what our next case will bring? I suggest you clear the decks to prepare for next week and then get off home. I don't want to see any of you until Monday morning. I need to make a couple of phone calls, and then I'll follow you."

It did not surprise Gus that there were no objections to a brief holiday. Everyone was as shocked as he was at the sudden turn of events and naturally concerned about their absent colleague. As he searched for the contact details for Corinne Wallington, his phone rang. Geoff Mercer had heard from the security people at Bournemouth Airport.

Oscar Wallington was queuing to board an EasyJet flight to Belfast International when a vigilant officer spotted the fugitive and arrested him. Security personnel later searched his Land Rover Defender in the Long Stay car park and found a twelve-inch long iron bar hidden in a compartment under the driver's seat.

"Many thanks, Geoff," said Gus. "I'll pass the good news onto the team."

"The killer didn't make his escape then, guv?" asked Luke.

"No," said Gus. "If he'd reached the countryside near Portadown, his chances of evading capture would have improved markedly. Wallington knew the area well after serving there as a soldier and spending holidays with the family at the property owned by Corinne's parents. That brings me to my next task. I must put his long-suffering wife in the picture."

Gus called Corinne and relayed the details of Oscar's capture, but he didn't mention the discovery of the murder weapon. Life had changed dramatically for Oscar's wife and two sons in the past twenty-four hours. He didn't need to rub their noses in it.

"Thank you for calling, Mr Freeman," said Corinne. "No doubt, the police would have officially sent someone to inform me in time."

"I thought you deserved to hear it from me. What will you do now?" asked Gus.

"We'll get out from under Patrick's feet," said Corinne. "I'll take his younger brother, Charles, back to the Lodge now the danger has passed. Oscar's employers need to know what's happened. That's not a conversation I expected to have. I enjoyed our time there and hoped we'd stay for many years."

Gus tried to think of something positive that might come of the sorry affair but failed. The manor house needed a new farm manager, and the accommodation at the Lodge went with the job. Her husband was in custody, about to be charged with the murder of Kendal Guthrie. With other possible charges to follow.

Corinne Wallington thanked him again and ended the call. Gus imagined her first call would be to her parents. She and Charles would need a roof over their heads before too long. At least some of the family would make it to Ireland.

Neil was the first to leave the office.

"I changed the filters in the Gaggia, guv," he said. "Alex and Lydia wanted to work on the maps we had on the walls. More than my life's worth to get between those two."

"We'll see you on Monday, Neil," said Gus. "Give our best wishes to Melody."

"Fingers crossed the temperature drops, and she can get a good night's sleep, guv,"

Neil was soon in the lift and heading for the car park. Gus looked around the room. The others wouldn't be far behind him.

"Shall I hang onto these maps, guv?" asked Lydia. "Divya went to a lot of trouble producing them. They might come in handy if we have another murder from the Plain to solve."

"Remove the items we added," said Gus. "Clean one up as best you can and store it in the stationery cabinet with the rest we've gathered over the months. The rest can go into the recycling bins in the corner of the car park downstairs. It won't hurt our image if the locals see we're doing our bit."

Alex and Lydia left together ten minutes later. Luke Sherman wandered across to join Gus.

"Something on your mind, Luke?" asked Gus.

"I had a phone call last night from a former colleague. He transferred to West Mercia Police eighteen months ago. We attended the same weapons training course. They've got a vacancy for a training officer, and he wondered if I was interested."

"Salary-wise, it wouldn't attract you, surely?" asked Gus.

"No, but the hours would be more predictable, which

solves Nicky's problems," said Luke. "He wouldn't have any trouble finding employment if we re-located, and there's more nightlife in the Midlands."

"Have you spoken to anyone at London Road?"

Luke shook his head.

"I'll use the extra free time this weekend to think things through," said Luke. "If I decide to put my name forward, I'll tell DS Mercer."

"I don't want to see you leave," said Gus. "You're three years younger than Suzie Ferris. With the breadth of experience you've gained since becoming a sergeant, I'm sure Geoff Mercer has a career path in mind. But don't make a hasty decision. We've all suffered relationship issues because of the unsocial hours we work, but something usually turns up that offers a solution."

"Let's be honest, guv," said Luke. "If a DI role popped up from London Road, Alex would be first in line. Either that or they would bring someone in from another region, as they did with Grace Packenham. I'll see you on Monday."

As the lift doors closed behind Luke, Gus sat in the office alone and wondered what had possessed him to return to work. He'd left this angst behind him four years ago. Gus thought back to his first evening in the Bear Hotel with Geoff Mercer when the Detective Superintendent outlined his hopes and dreams for the Crime Review Team and urged Gus to come and work for him.

Gus had decided to give it a whirl. Retirement wasn't all it was cracked up to be, especially after Tess had died. So when he'd met with Alex, Neil, and Lydia, he imagined the first to fly the nest would be the fiery red-haired female.

Because of her qualifications and background, Kenneth Truelove had already warned him that the university graduate was on a fast-track programme. The modern police service pushed for a more diverse image, and Lydia had plenty to offer on that score.

Perhaps it was inevitable following the team's early run of successful investigations that the pressures would grow. Both internal and external pressure, as teams around the county and beyond spotted talent they could use. Any team member might want to spread their wings, and who was he to stand in their way if that was their decision?

A second phone call interrupted his gloomy vision of the future.

Geoff Mercer had another update.

Engineers working under Jamie Banks-Trewick had recovered human remains from a gully near the boundary of land belonging to the farm on Durrington Down. Subject to official confirmation, the Military Police believed the remains were those of Private John Winslow. He died from blunt force trauma to the skull.

Gus listened to Geoff Mercer's upbeat report in silence.

"Everything okay, Gus?" he asked. "I thought the second piece of good news in one day would be a matter to celebrate."

"What do you make of Luke Sherman?" asked Gus.

"An excellent young officer with a bright future," said Geoff. "Why do you ask?"

"Are you planning to move him to a more senior role soon?"

"I don't know what you've heard, Gus, but no, Kenneth and I are delighted with where Luke is at present. We're in no rush to change a winning team."

"Luke's partner would prefer they spent more time together. Nicky works nine to five. You know how it goes."

"We've been there, Gus. Christine had the same reaction to the long hours and sullen moods when I was younger. It's something Luke, Neil, and the others have to go through at certain stages in their careers."

"Luke heard of a vacancy in West Mercia," said Gus. "It would be a step sideways at best, and at worst, it could harm his progress for good. So I'd prefer him to stay with us for the foreseeable future."

"Look, you know Kenneth's role as Chief Constable is a stop-gap measure to calm the storm after the rapid turnover Wiltshire Police experienced in that role. Who knows what will happen when he retires? In eighteen months or two years, what will you feel like? Maybe you will be ready to hand in that consultant's ID card and return to your allotment full-time. If the new boss wants to keep the Crime Review Team, it will need a DI at the helm. That's a carrot to dangle in front of Luke Sherman."

"Luke thinks Alex Hardy will be more likely to get a promotion before him, Geoff," said Gus. "Or you might bring someone in from outside, as you did with Ms Packenham."

"You needn't fret about Grace getting the lead job with CRT, Gus," laughed Geoff. "She's good, but not that good. Alex always expressed a wish to return to his old job as a motorcycle pursuit rider. That may be too big an ask, but Alex is a good number two. He's more of a plodder, like Neil Davis. I won't write the two of them off as having got as far as they're going to get, but Luke and Lydia are much better prospects."

"Despite having done something reckless last night," said Gus, "DC Umeh is one to watch. I reckon Blessing has star quality at twenty-two for what it's worth."

"If you rate her highly, Gus, then Kenneth and I will listen. Keep me in the picture with Luke Sherman. We need to help him decide to stay with you for at least eighteen months. I guess the next time I'll see you will be Monday lunchtime?"

"That's the plan, Geoff," said Gus.

"Have an enjoyable weekend then, and well done again this week. Another rotten apple removed, and another case that won't haunt the original detectives until they reach the Pearly Gates."

Gus decided there was nothing to keep him in the office today. As for what he might say in eighteen months, that was a different matter. Gus took one last look around and headed for the lift. He had the entire afternoon to himself. The weather was fine, and the allotment was as good a place to spend it as any.

Friday, 31 August – Sunday, 2 September

Blessing Umeh had spent two lazy days on the farm at Worton. Jackie had been right about delayed shock. Blessing stayed in bed most of Thursday morning, and when she wasn't sleeping, she sat in the kitchen with her landlady, drinking coffee and watching Jackie baking.

Jackie had asked Blessing if she was going to call her parents.

"They won't have heard what happened on the Plain," said Blessing. "My father would drive here and insist I quit my job at once. So no, it has to be our secret."

When Blessing received a text on her mobile phone late on Thursday afternoon, she had hoped it was Gus relenting, saying she could return to work on Friday. The text wasn't from Gus.

Jackie heard the delighted squeal and turned to see Blessing punching the air.

"That was good news, I take it?" she said with a smile.

"Jamie wants to know if it's okay to visit me tomorrow afternoon," said Blessing. "Do you mind?"

"Not at all," said Jackie. "I can't wait to meet him. John told me he was a charming young man, and even Suzie had to admit he was handsome."

"Jamie's just what I was looking for," said Blessing. "My knight in shining armour."

"What about the young man your family wanted you to meet on Sunday?" asked Jackie.

"Ekene Kanu? He needs a woman who will look after him day and night, bear him children, and never speak out of turn. It wouldn't work between us; we're from different worlds."

Jackie smiled to herself as she kneaded her pastry dough. John didn't know it yet, but they were going to make themselves scarce on Friday afternoon. Blessing and her dreamboat needed to be alone.

When Blessing wandered into the kitchen on Friday morning, Jackie was taking a well-earned break.

"I don't need to ask if you slept better last night," she said. "I was just going to make myself a coffee."

"Is that eleven o'clock?" asked Blessing. "Half the day's gone."

"What time did Jamie say he would get here?"

"Between two and three," said Blessing. "He's working this morning and hoping to get away early for a change."

"Do you want any breakfast?" asked Jackie.

"I'm starving," admitted Blessing, "But I'll wait until lunchtime now. Coffee would be perfect for the time being, thanks."

"John's driving me to Amesbury this afternoon," Jackie said. "We'll not get back until late. Do you think you can cook something for the two of you? Or will you venture into Devizes for a meal?"

"I don't know how long Jamie can stay," said Blessing. "He's on call in case there's another incident like the one he responded to on Wednesday evening."

"John will be in for his midday meal in an hour," said Jackie. "Have you got your appetite back, Blessing?"

"You bet," said Blessing.

"Why not spend the afternoon in the orchard?" said Jackie. "It's cooler, and you know there's plenty of food in this kitchen to snack on if the two of you get hungry."

John and Jackie left in the Land Rover before one o'clock. Blessing showered and tried on half a dozen dresses before deciding which one to wear. At two o'clock, she stood by the kitchen door, trying to hear the sound of an approaching car. She didn't have long to wait.

Blessing's heart flipped when Jamie got out of the car and walked towards her. The tight-fitting white t-shirt, black jeans, and aviator shades were a look to grace the catwalk in Paris or Milan. Jamie removed his sunglasses and smiled.

"It appears you've fully recovered from the other night," he said. "You look stunning."

"So do you," said Blessing. "I wondered what you looked like out of uniform."

Jamie laughed.

"So, this is where you live? Do I get the grand tour?"

"You've spent ages on Salisbury Plain," said Blessing. "Once you've seen one farm, you've seen them all. So why don't we visit the orchard at the back of the farmhouse? It's shaded, quiet, and the perfect spot on a warm afternoon. I often sit there to read or to chat with Jackie, my landlady. Can I get you a drink?"

"A cold beer would be great," said Jamie as he followed Blessing along the path at the side of the farmhouse.

Blessing turned around to look at him.

"Well, I didn't plan to drive back to Bulford for ages," Jamie said.

"That's a relief," said Blessing. "In that case, I'll have a glass of wine too."

Time flies when you're having fun, and it was early evening when Blessing snapped a selfie of her and Jamie lying on a rug under the branches of an apple tree.

"Facebook?" asked Jamie.

"No," said Blessing. "I thought I should send it to someone my parents know."

Blessing sent the photo with no words. The message was simple. Ekene Kanu was now aware he was surplus to requirements. Jamie BT was a great kisser, and Blessing Umeh was not looking for a make-do husband.

When John and Jackie Ferris returned to Worton Farm later that evening, the farmyard was empty.

"I'd better wander around to check everything's secure," said John. "See you in ten minutes."

Jackie went indoors and found Blessing sitting in the kitchen.

"How did it go?" asked Jackie.

"It couldn't have been better," said Blessing. "I hope my parents forgive me."

"The heart wants what the heart wants," said Jackie, hugging Blessing.

"Did you and John get what you wanted in Amesbury?" asked Blessing.

"We drove around for a while, drank in a pub, and then sat on a park bench like we did when we were sixteen. We just wanted to give you two time alone."

On Sunday morning, Blessing drove to Englishcombe village, her parents' house. She attended morning service at St Peter's Church with Kelechi and Maryam, then returned home for lunch.

"I thought you told me Ekene Kanu was going to be there this morning," said Blessing as her father carved the roast beef.

"Ekene called yesterday," said her father. "He said he was indisposed. I said I hoped he got well soon. I got the distinct impression his indisposition could be permanent. Do you know anything about that?"

"I never met the man in person," said Blessing. "How could I know what made him change his mind?"

"We didn't have time to speak much on Wednesday evening," said Maryam. "I hope Mr Freeman's not working you too hard?"

Blessing squeezed her mother's hand. Maryam hadn't told Kelechi that she'd asked her mother for Ekene's phone number.

"Mr Freeman is looking after me, don't worry. I have much to be grateful for, and my trip on Wednesday evening bore fruit. I hope my work-life balance will improve in the months ahead."

Monday, 3 September 2018

"What's on the agenda for today, Gus?" asked Suzie as she popped two slices of bread into the toaster.

"We didn't hear any negative reports from John and Jackie over the weekend," said Gus, "so I expect to see Blessing fighting fit and back in the office. She needs to update our digital files on the Guthrie case as soon as possible. Then, it won't take the rest of us long to fill in the blanks. I fully expect to take the completed files to London Road before noon. The office is as tidy as it's been in weeks, so while I collect our next case file from Kenneth, the others will probably relax and pepper Blessing with questions about her few hours of excitement."

"We used to call that skiving in the old days," said Suzie. "I can't recall the last time we had free time at London Road."

"That's the Packenham effect, I presume?"

"Grace's relentless," said Suzie. "She wants to turn the place into a lean, mean crime-fighting machine."

"Ms Packenham reports to Geoff Mercer," said Gus. "A man who has carried more than a few extra pounds for the past two decades. I never thought Geoff would be the sort to follow the 'don't do as I do, do as I tell you' principle. The lady is a loose cannon. Someone needs to have a quiet word in Geoff's ear."

"I wonder who you have in mind?" laughed Suzie.

"Has Geoff found anything new to add to your workload?" asked Gus.

"On Friday afternoon, he mentioned the PCC had raised the subject of thefts from vehicles," said Suzie. "Statistics showed an increase from nine to ten per day across the county compared to last year. Most of these incidents occur in beauty spots and are from insecure vehicles or those that have valuables on display. He asked me to run a crime prevention campaign urging motorists to lock their vehicles and keep belongings out of sight."

"It will keep you out of mischief," said Gus.

"Even if it's Common Sense, Room 101," said Suzie. "Are you going to eat that second slice of toast?"

"Not today," said Gus. "I may bump into Ms Packenham later. I don't want to give her any ideas."

They left the bungalow at eight-fifteen on the dot and drove in convoy towards Devizes.

When Suzie turned into the London Road car park, Gus gave her a wave and carried on towards the Old Police Station office seven miles away.

He had achieved a lot since Thursday lunchtime. The allotment was now on par with Bert Penman's plot for the first time in months. All the jobs he'd put off for weeks had been finished. Tess's climbing roses on the side of the bungalow could now enjoy a controlled flourish with a newly added wire framework. The wooden bench on the edge of the front lawn had gained a fresh coat of wood stain.

Gus had stood in the doorway of the second bedroom on Friday afternoon, wondering whether to make a start on re-decorating it, ready for the new arrival. But instead, he decided against making unilateral decisions until Suzie reached home.

Suzie had accompanied him to the allotment, as the weekend weather had been conducive to spending time outdoors. Gus persuaded her to sit and watch him work. Suzie agreed, as long as Gus let her drive into Devizes on Saturday afternoon to pick up an armful of brochures from various DIY stores.

"If I'm to sit and watch you work for several hours today and tomorrow, I can plan for the first weekend when the weather forces us indoors," she said. "Do I have a budget?"

Gus had stopped weeding and thought for a second.

"I've ignored every budget London Road has ever set. I told Geoff Mercer when I returned to work that if they wanted the job done right, it would cost what it would cost, and I don't see any reason to work to different limits at home."

"That's the right answer," said Suzie, dropping the cheaper brochures onto the grass beside her chair.

Although Gus knew he had earned brownie points with Suzie with his reply, he spent much of Saturday afternoon thinking of Luke Sherman and Geoff Mercer's comments when he'd spoken to him on Thursday morning.

Somehow, he had to persuade Luke to stay.

Geoff thought Luke was a potential Detective Inspector and the prime candidate to succeed Gus as head of the Crime Review Team when the time came. Gus couldn't fault the logic. After all, Kenneth Truelove was under orders from his wife to retire as soon as possible. The thrill of being the wife of a Chief Constable would only last so long. Geoff's view was it had a lifespan of eighteen months, two years at the most.

The storm clouds would gather, and Gus's protection would become vulnerable once Kenneth's protection disappeared. However, DI Sherman could confidently take things forward if the team had proved it deserved to stay in existence through a string of solid successes.

Geoff's other comments had given things Gus hadn't considered an uncomfortable clarity. Gus had never been a fan of the annual appraisals introduced at Bourne Hill during the latter part of his time there. Gus believed a team was like a car with four wheels. None of those wheels was worth any more than the other.

Now he had learned that the top brass at London Road viewed people like Alex Hardy and Neil Davis as less valuable than Luke Sherman. That gave him a problem he didn't need. How could he tinker with the team dynamic, so Luke felt the love while keeping Alex and Neil happy too?

They weren't daft. He'd always treated everyone alike since they started working together. Those two would soon wonder what was behind any changes, no matter how subtle.

As he slowed at the traffic lights near the village of Seend, Gus thought about Lydia and Blessing. Geoff Mercer intimated he was more likely to find openings for those two. They had tremendous potential. Ten minutes later, Gus parked the Focus in the empty bay behind the Old Police Station and steeled himself for what lay ahead. As a young lad, he'd never mastered the art of juggling, and at sixty-two, he was unlikely to be able to add it to his skill set.

Gus found the rest of the team gathered around Blessing Umeh's desk. He heard his young Detective Constable mention Jamie Banks-Trewick twice and wondered whether the Second Lieutenant from the Military Police Special Investigations Branch had visited Blessing since the early hours of Thursday. It had been hard enough prising them apart and persuading her to get into John Ferris's Land Rover.

"Morning, guv," said Lydia. "All present and correct. Blessing solved the murder and found a boyfriend. All on the same night."

"It's good to see you looking refreshed and ready for a new challenge," said Gus. "Have you started updating those files yet?"

"We only arrived a minute ahead of you, guv," said Neil. "We've hardly had time to do much more than hear about Blessing's weekend."

"How were your parents, Blessing?" asked Gus.

"What they don't know about the details of Wednesday night won't hurt them, guv. I was a dutiful daughter and attended church in Englishcombe, and then I spent the afternoon with them before returning to Worton Farm. I should finish my updates by eleven o'clock if that fits your timetable."

"That will be perfect, Blessing," said Gus. "How about the rest of you? Any problems with meeting that deadline?"

Nobody protested, so Gus got stuck into completing a report on his contributions to the case from Wednesday afternoon onwards. One hour later, Alex and Lydia offered to get coffee for the team. Blessing was still recounting her adventures in the middle of Salisbury Plain while Neil and Luke read through the Guthrie case notes for the third time.

"Has anyone notified the detectives from the original investigation?" asked Neil.

"Keith Porter is still at Bourne Hill," said Luke. "Gus and Blessing visited Maxine Coleman last week at home with her baby."

"That's right. Maxine's a Devereux now, married to that rugby player. Gus might think she'll want to learn we've wrapped up the case. I'll ask him before he shoots off to Devizes."

"I'd like to know what Helen Guthrie made of it," said Luke. "The files show Gus heard from Geoff Mercer after we left here on Thursday. The SIB people found human remains on one farm Kendall Guthrie submitted a bid for before he died. Wallington had killed before. He must have suspected Guthrie would discover his secret. I was reading an article at the weekend, and if Helen Guthrie had plans to carry on what her father started and sell that land to developers, she'd have to think again. The MoD built dozens of temporary buildings near the garrison camps during WWII. Then, after the war, they bulldozed the site and buried everything underground. The farmers who lived and worked there struggled to grow anything, so they used it for grazing sheep and cows. The article I read reckoned asbestos and lead have tainted the land. No way could anyone build on it."

"You know what that means," said Neil. "Wallington didn't need to panic when he heard Guthrie mention the farm was among the batch he'd applied to buy. The odds of anyone testing soil samples and then uncovering those remains were tiny. Gus's report said they found the remains in a gully on the edge of the property. Private Winslow was reported as AWOL twenty years ago, and nobody had ever thought to look for a body."

"So, Kendal Guthrie didn't need to die," said Luke.

"If Oscar Wallington hadn't done it, someone else would have," said Neil with a shrug. "He was universally disliked. That's not something I would want on my headstone."

"My report is ready to go, guv," said Blessing.

"With ten minutes to spare," said Neil. "Luke and I wondered whether you wanted us to inform DI Porter and Mrs Devereux, guv?"

"I don't think Keith Porter will bother Neil," said Gus, "but call him, by all means. Call Maxine too, for definite. It might convince her to return to work after her maternity leave. We live in hope."

"How do you think Ms Guthrie will react to the news that the farmland opposite Glenhead Farm is riddled with asbestos and lead?" asked Luke.

"Which renders it unsuitable for development," added Neil.

"I think you can leave that one to me," said Gus. "I owe her one."

A Normal November: Chapter Two

Gus skipped into the lift with the Guthrie file folder and whistled a cheerful tune as he emerged into the car park. He stood by the open driver's door of the Focus, waiting in vain for the temperature inside to drop to bearable. Time was pressing, so he reversed out of his parking bay and headed for the exit.

It was fifteen minutes to twelve when he turned off the London Road into the Wiltshire Police HQ visitor's car park. He sat and thought about Maxine Devereux. What if she decided to be a stay-at-home Mum? Nothing wrong with that, of course, if that was her choice. Even if she was depriving the county of the services of a first-class detective.

If Maxine decided she would enjoy a return to work eighteen months or two years from now, where might she be a good fit as a Detective Inspector? Perhaps he should start dropping hints to Geoff Mercer that Maxine would make a better replacement for him and the CRT when he finally got put out to grass.

Did that mean he was coming around to the idea Luke

could transfer to West Mercia? These personnel problems were a nuisance. His sole focus needed to be on whatever case the Chief Constable handed him in the next half-hour. Gus would never admit to Suzie that multi-tasking was easier for her than for him, but he found it impossible in this arena.

Gus trotted up the steps to the main door and spotted an older face on the Reception desk. This morning, access to the first floor without pranks or mishaps should be a breeze. Within seconds, he signed in and took the stairs two at a time.

"It's a warm one this morning, Mr Freeman," said Kassie Trotter. "Did you hear? August was the warmest month on record in England."

"Too warm for baking, I presume?" asked Gus.

"I'm into skinny-baking these days, Mr Freeman," said Kassie. "I told you last week."

Gus had tried to rid himself of the image Kassie had planted but failed.

"The end product tasted better than ever, Kassie," he said. "I left work early to allow myself time to enjoy the experience. You're a genius."

"Do you want to know what I have for you in my drawers, Mr Freeman?"

"That's not what Kassie meant, Gus," said Vera Butler, who suddenly appeared on his left-hand side. "Kassie concentrated on a lighter bite in deference to the warm weather. I'm sure you'll enjoy a slice of her summer berry cake."

"I'll keep an eye out for the office mafia and collect my treat after meeting with Kenneth," said Gus. "How are things in your world, Vera?"

"Monty's having issues with several of his tenants," said

Vera. "I'm glad I'm out of it. You remember what he was like; a prince one year and a pauper the next. He's panicking over what the eventual Brexit deal will hold."

"I'm guessing several properties he bought to let got snapped up by people from Poland and the Baltic states," said Gus. "If the divorce is painful, there's a risk they'll return home, and he'll lose a significant proportion of his income."

"Exactly," said Vera. "Some younger women have jumped ship already without clearing their rent arrears."

"I'm surprised Monty stood for any arrears based on what you've told me."

"He's a single man these days, Gus," said Vera. "I suspect he had an ulterior motive."

"Has he contacted you?" asked Gus.

"Monty knows better than to try anything like that with me, Gus," said Vera. "No, he's sneaky. He dropped by my parent's home to give them a sob story about how hard life was for a hard-working businessman in the UK."

"Monty didn't ask for financial help, but he sowed the seeds," said Gus.

"That's typical of Monty," said Vera. "It's always someone else's fault when a get-rich scheme turns turtle. My father sensed Monty felt this latest downturn in his fortunes wouldn't have happened if we were still married."

"No doubt Monty got short shrift from your father?"

"My father bailed Monty out frequently, as you know. He won't receive any more help from that quarter. I feel sorry for Monty, but he brings it on himself."

"You were married to the guy for half the time you've been on this earth, Vera. So it's only natural you still take an interest in what's happening with him. He's the father of your children. What's done is done. You have your life to lead now, and Monty has to fight his own battles."

"You'd better get over to Kenneth's office," said Vera. "You'll be late. Thanks for taking the trouble to listen."

"What are friends for, Vera?" said Gus. He spotted Kassie Trotter pointing to the second and third drawers on a filing cabinet by her desk and gave her a reassuring wave.

Geoff Mercer emerged from Kenneth's old office and caught Gus before reaching the Chief Constable's door.

"Any progress?" he asked.

"With Luke Sherman, d'you mean?" asked Gus. "I haven't spoken with him this morning."

"Don't leave it too long, Gus," said Geoff. "West Mercia was keen to secure a deal when they put the feelers out to me a while back. So if they hear a whisper Luke's unsettled in his CRT role and interested in a move to the Midlands, they'll snap him up before you can say West Bromwich Albion."

"We've got ages then, Geoff," said Gus.

The Chief Constable was at his desk when they walked through the door.

Gus handed the Kendal Guthrie file to Kenneth Truelove.

"Another one bites the dust, sir,"

"Mercer tells me this success could have come at a high price, Freeman. It would help if you kept better control over your people. That's not your only fault. At the outset, I said you needed to take a serving officer with you whenever you interviewed a witness or a suspect. I received a complaint from Helen Guthrie at the weekend. She thought your manner surly and confrontational."

"It takes two to tango, sir," said Gus. "She started it, wheeling in her farm manager and solicitor for what was supposed to be an informal chat. They weren't interested in offering any help to find her father's killer."

"I hope you won't make a habit of flying solo, Freeman," said the Chief Constable. "It sends the wrong message to the junior members of your team, evidenced by the calamity that almost befell DC Umeh."

"I'll be more cautious in the future, sir," said Gus, deciding not to mention he'd also visited Dave Vickers and Oscar Wallington alone the same day.

"How is DC Umeh now?" asked Kenneth.

"Fighting fit, sir," said Gus. "Blessing had Thursday and Friday off work. I believe she drove to visit her parents yesterday and seemed fine this morning."

"You should remind DC Umeh that her well-being is important to us, Freeman. If she needs to speak to someone about the emotional arousal from the events of Wednesday evening, then you must make sure that happens. Blessing may look fine on the surface, but frights such as that can lead to PTSD."

"Got it, sir," said Gus. "I understand she's spoken to someone already. From snatches of conversation I caught in the office this morning, good progress has been made, and someone has a firm grip on her emotions."

"Right then, perhaps we can park that matter for now. I want you both to watch this CCTV clip. That's if I can remember how to work this blessed remote control. The quality of the image isn't great, but you will get the gist of what's occurring."

Gus and Geoff watched the screen, and Kenneth provided a running commentary.

"We have a couple of likely lads, bold as brass, stealing a catalytic converter in broad daylight. This white van pulls up behind the target vehicle; its driver and passenger get out. The passenger walks by to look at the car and check for nosy passers-by. Then the driver fetches a jack from the back of the van. He sets to work at the side of the car. The passenger removes a saw from his hooded jacket, and off he goes. You don't need to put a clock on it. Thirty-one seconds for a piece of kit that could fetch at least one thousand pounds depending on the damage caused as they remove it."

"Inside two minutes, they were in the van and driving away," said Geoff Mercer.

"Although the image was poor, even I could read the number plate of the van," said Gus.

"False plates," said Kenneth, "belonging to a VW Passat reported stolen seven weeks before the theft. Both men wore hooded jackets, which proved impossible to identify."

"Both men were white," said Geoff. "The driver was perhaps six feet tall, while his colleague was six to eight inches shorter. Despite the baggy clothing, we can make assumptions about their build, but there's nothing for the Hub to use to match them with anyone in our databases."

"When and where did this theft occur?" asked Gus.

"Towards the end of October, two years ago," said Kenneth.

"There must be more to this than the theft of a few car parts," said Gus.

"They may not look much," scoffed the Chief Constable, "but it's big business. Those catalytic converters contain two valuable metals, rhodium and palladium, and the price of those metals is on the increase. That's attracted the interest of organised crime gangs who have acquired specialist tools to remove converters from cars. We've visited the local scrap metal dealers, warning them to be mindful when offered converters or exhaust systems. Some will contact us if they suspect they could have been stolen, but other dealers aren't so scrupulous."

"Where did the theft take place?" asked Gus. "Those buildings in the background look familiar. Are we in Swindon?"

"Just off Station Road," said Geoff.

"That is brazen," said Gus. "Right. Can you tell me why I had to watch this CCTV clip?"

"I want you to take a second look at the murder of Richard Chaloner," said Kenneth, handing Gus a copy of the file. "He owned a garage, perhaps half a mile from where this theft occurred. Chaloner was forty-four years old and had recently married a forty-one-year-old divorcee, Eve Allsopp. Chaloner had been a single man until the wedding, which took place six months before he died. The victim was last seen alive at ten to six on Monday, the seventh of November 2016. Chaloner ran a small business that handled car body repairs, MOTs, that sort of thing. He had two employees. Matt Merchant, twenty-nine, and Harry Simpkins, sixty-one. Both men had worked for Chaloner for over ten years. Simpkins left work at the usual time at half-past five and walked to his home in Alfred Street."

"I wonder why Merchant stayed late?" asked Gus.

"I'll come to that in a moment, Freeman. Chaloner cycled to and from work," said the Chief Constable. "Richard and Eve Chaloner had moved into a house on Shrivenham Road, the other side of the County Ground from the railway station."

"The County Ground is where Swindon Town play, Gus," said Geoff.

"I'm not a fan," said Gus, "but I know where they play, Geoff. Gary Mallinder and Ian Hewson went to watch a match there. The stadium is only ten minutes from Gentle

Touch, the massage parlour where Laura Mallinder worked. I'm familiar with the district."

Kenneth Truelove continued with his introduction to the new case.

"As Merchant was leaving, he spotted Chaloner's bicycle had a puncture. He returned to the office, where his boss checked invoices and completed worksheets. Chaloner went outside with Merchant to inspect the damage. It wasn't a puncture; someone had deliberately slashed the tyre. Matt Merchant offered his boss a lift home, but Chaloner told him he'd finish the paperwork, fix the problem himself, and he'd see him in the morning."

"Did Merchant see anyone near the garage when he left?" asked Gus.

"At ten to six on a miserable, wet Monday evening in November," said Kenneth. "What do you think?"

"Too early for dog walkers," said Gus. "Anyone with any sense would have been tucked up indoors eating a warm meal."

"Matt Merchant was first to arrive at eight o'clock the following day," said Kenneth. "it did not surprise him to see the boss's bicycle in its usual spot. He didn't give it a second glance, parked his car, and entered the garage by the side door."

"Did he have a key?" asked Gus.

"Both Merchant and Simpkins had keys for the side door and the office," said Kenneth. "Whoever arrived first went inside and got things ready for the working day. Chaloner was a good boss, according to his employees. His customers appreciated the warm, friendly atmosphere he encouraged, and repeat business kept the little enterprise busy. The side door was open, and Merchant looked towards the office, expecting to find Chaloner sitting at his desk. The office was empty, but the lights were on. Merchant heard a sound outside. It was Harry Simpkins arriving for work. Simpkins flicked the light switches to illuminate the main part of the building as soon as he stepped inside to join Merchant. They saw Richard Chaloner's body lying between two cars they had worked on the previous afternoon. Simpkins walked towards the body, but Merchant told him to stay clear. He went outside and used his mobile to phone the police."

"It makes a change for a member of the public to preserve the integrity of a crime scene," said Gus. "Merchant sounds like an upright citizen, am I right?"

"He had a few brushes with the law as a juvenile," said Kenneth, "but marriage and three kids have had a positive effect."

"He hasn't had time to go off the rails," said Gus. "Hold it a moment. I'm forgetting someone. You said Chaloner married six months before he died. So why didn't his wife raise the alarm when he didn't arrive home?"

"Eve was in Halkidiki with three friends from work on a seven-day hen night," said Kenneth. "They're all the rage these days. I was lucky to get a three-hour stag do."

"Me too," said Gus and Geoff in unison.

"That must have burst the party balloons when news filtered through," said Gus. "Who caught this case from Gablecross?"

"The SIO was DI Raj Sengupta," said the Chief Constable.

"Ah yes, the cybercrime team leader," said Gus. "He worked with Jack Sanders. Our paths have crossed."

"I wouldn't want this to escape these four walls," said Kenneth, "but Sengupta is in a better place these days. He performs a valuable role with the cybercrime team but was hopeless out in the field."

"Colonel Sanders was an old-school copper," said Gus. "I can't see him and Raj seeing eye-to-eye. Who else did Raj have on his team?"

"DS Tom Spencer," said Geoff Mercer. "He's from the same mould as Jake Latimer. Rough around the edges, plenty of local knowledge, and not afraid of hard work."

"When you read the murder file, Freeman, you'll see that DS Spencer did most of the leg work. Stuart Fitzwalter was the police surgeon who attended the murder scene at the garage. He determined Chaloner died from a single gunshot to the chest. His killer was no further than three feet away. The time of death was between six and seven in the evening. The killer must have turned off the main lights as they left the garage but left the office lights on."

"Any evidence left at the scene? What was the motive?" asked Gus.

"Forensics found no fingerprints," said Kenneth Truelove. "One possible chance would have been the light switches, but Harry Simpkins obliterated any hope of that. DS Spencer always believed the killer wore gloves, so maybe Simpkins was off the hook. As for motive, Chaloner's wallet was stolen, which his wife believed would have contained less than one hundred pounds. A gold chain her husband always wore around his neck was missing. The killer took a bank card for the garage's business account from the victim's desk and used it to withdraw four hundred pounds from an ATM in the town centre later that evening. Merchant stopped the card on Tuesday morning. The killer never attempted to use it again."

"What happened? Did the victim reveal the PIN without a fight?" asked Gus.

"There were no signs of a struggle," said Kenneth. "Remember, when Merchant left on Monday evening, Chaloner worked in the office. So the card was likely lying on the desk when the killer walked in. Matt Merchant confirmed Chaloner had the PIN written on a scrap of paper pinned to the notice board," said Kenneth.

"Terrific," said Gus. "Chaloner was a very trusting boss. With lax security, both employees could have helped themselves whenever they pleased."

"Come on, Gus," said Geoff. "Merchant said it was a happy work environment. Someone withdrew the money on Monday evening. If Chaloner hadn't died, he would have spotted the missing money once he checked his business account. Small firms such as that live hand-to-mouth these days. I doubt the working balance would have hidden a four hundred-pound black hole."

"How did DI Sengupta approach the case?" asked Gus.

"He treated it as a robbery in the first instance. It seemed logical," said Kenneth.

"An armed robbery in a busy part of Swindon isn't an everyday occurrence," said Gus. "Why did the killer slash the bicycle tyre?"

"The police believed that was a tactic to keep Chaloner from leaving with his employees," said Kenneth. "The killer waited until Merchant left the premises. He wanted to guarantee Chaloner was alone."

"What was Sengupta's first move?" asked Gus.

"Sengupta organised his uniformed officers on a house-to-house, searching for eyewitnesses. Not to the murder, but someone tampering with Chaloner's bicycle or acting suspiciously in the garage's vicinity."

"Why didn't Chaloner wheel his bike indoors?" asked Gus. "There must have been room, surely?"

"Force of habit," said Kenneth. "Before the wedding, he'd lived in Pinehurst. He had made the two-mile journey every weekday since he opened the business. His bike wasn't one of these top-of-the-range items that demand the rider wear lycra. Instead, it was a bog-standard machine with a comfortable saddle and panniers. Although Chaloner secured it to a metal fence while working inside, he never dreamt anyone would want to steal it. The bike was visible from the pavement, but whoever slashed the tyre had to walk past Merchant's car to reach it."

"Where does Merchant live?" asked Gus.

"Elmina Road, with wife Jess and their three children," said Kenneth.

"Matt Merchant was young and presumably fit," said Gus. "Why drive to work from Elmina Road? It can't be further than a ten-minute walk away. Harry Simpkins walked from Alfred Street, which was as far in the opposite direction."

"Merchant played six-a-side football on Monday evenings," said Kenneth. "He had a fifteen-minute drive out towards Wootton Bassett via Great Western Way. His teammates confirmed he was at the Gerard Buxton Sports Arena between six-thirty and eight-thirty. His alibi was set in concrete, as was Harry Simpkins. Harry's wife, Thelma, said he reached home at twenty minutes to six, as usual, and was eating his dinner at six. They walked the dog together at six-thirty and sat in front of the TV to watch The One Show at seven o'clock. Harry never left the house until ten to eight the following day to walk to work."

"Okay, so what did the interviews with the employees and the house-to-house enquiries throw up?" asked Gus.

"Three persons of interest," said the Chief Constable. "The first man was white, thirty-five to forty-five years old, wearing white overalls. Simpkins told police he turned up at the garage on Monday morning at around eleven o'clock. He hadn't made an appointment and asked Richard Chaloner to look at an intermittent electrical fault on his van. Chaloner pointed out all three of them were busy at present on jobs booked in for regular customers. So they didn't have time to stop. Simpkins was underneath the car he was working on and couldn't see what happened next, but raised voices suggested the guy in white overalls wasn't happy with his boss's reply. When Simpkins next stood up, the van and its driver had left without getting what he wanted. Chaloner was in the office, calling a customer to say his car was ready to collect. He didn't elaborate on the argument with either Merchant or Simpkins."

"Did the police find this painter and decorator, or whatever this tradesperson was?" asked Gus.

"Harry Simpkins was lying on a trolley under the car, Freeman," said Kenneth. "Hardly in a position to identify anyone or spot any writing on the side of the van. Merchant gave a general description of the unexpected visitor to the police. He, too, continued working towards the rear of the garage on a customer's car while the man stayed on the premises. Although he overheard snatches of the conversation, he couldn't give the detectives a name."

"It could be something of nothing," said Geoff Mercer. "Richard Chaloner forgot the episode quickly and got on with his busy workload. It doesn't strike me as being the catalyst for what occurred later that day."

"I'd still want to find out who drove that van," said Gus. "Who else did they put in the frame?"

"The second person was a twenty to twenty-five-year-old white man," said Kenneth. "He was a short, stocky individual with short blonde hair, wearing a navy bomber jacket. This man stood on the opposite side of the road from one o'clock to a few minutes before two."

"Was it Merchant or Simpkins who saw him?" asked Gus.

"It was neither," said Kenneth. "A Mrs Catherine Fryer returned home from her morning shift at a care home in Dean Park and had to step off the pavement to get past him. When she came out again at ten to two to post a letter, the man in the bomber jacket still stood in the same spot. Mrs Fryer returned ten minutes later, and the man had gone."

"Was he another one that got away with no one identifying him?" asked Gus.

"I'm afraid so," said the Chief Constable. "The description was more specific than for the white van man, but Swindon has its fair share of twenty-something white men. The uniformed officers who did the house-to-house were certain he didn't live on the same street as Mrs Fryer, but that was about as much as they could say. Now we come to person of interest number three. He was Afro-Caribbean, twenty-five to thirty, muscular, and wearing dark clothing. Mrs Fryer's neighbour, Stan Jones, seventy-one, saw someone standing on tiptoe to peer through the window on the front door of the garage at four o'clock in the afternoon. Mr Jones was pulling his curtains as the light was fading fast."

"Hang on," said Gus. "I got the impression when the white van man arrived at eleven, he parked and walked off the street straight into the garage to speak to Richard Chaloner. How come the doors were closed?"

"Because of the rain," said Kenneth. "Simpkins and Merchant said that by half-past two, the strength of the wind had increased, and what started as a light shower soon became a downpour. However, the side door was still open if a customer wanted to check work-in-progress or book in a vehicle."

"How long was this chap peering through the window?" asked Gus.

"Only a minute or two," said Kenneth. "Stan Jones said a car pulled up outside his house, and the man ran across the road and jumped into the passenger seat. Because of the heavy rain, he pulled his jacket over his head, meaning Stan Jones couldn't get a good look at his face. The driver was a young woman with long, dark hair, but Mr Jones could only guess her age was between eighteen and thirty."

"I don't suppose he got a registration?" asked Gus.

Kenneth Truelove shook his head. Gus Freeman sighed.

"Nobody said it was going to be easy," said Geoff Mercer.

"What about the marriage?" asked Gus.

"They had only been married for six months, Gus," said Geoff. "They had hardly had time to recover from the honeymoon."

"I didn't mean Richard and Eve Chaloner," said Gus. "I meant her first marriage."

"Eve was married to John Allsopp for fourteen years," said Kenneth. "The couple lived in Westbury after they married in 2000 and moved to Warminster in 2008. John Allsopp began an affair with a younger woman from work after a Christmas party at the end of 2013. Eve wasn't the forgiving type, and the marriage ended. She moved to Swindon, bumped into Richard Chaloner in a bar in the town centre, and married within a year. As Geoff suggested, they were as happy as pigs in the proverbial. John Allsopp and the young woman had split up even before the decree absolute. He still lives and works in Warminster, and his alibi was solid for the time of the murder. Allsopp was aware Eve had moved to Swindon, but there was no evidence to suggest he knew Eve had remarried. Unless he fooled DS Spencer when he interviewed him, John Allsopp didn't have means, motive, or opportunity to murder Richard Chaloner."

"Let's try another angle then," said Gus. "I'm fed up with dead-ends. Was there any reason Chaloner hadn't married until he reached the age of forty-four? Did he have any other serious relationships? Was he hiding a secret from his new wife, perhaps? Had Richard Chaloner ever been in trouble with the law? If he'd been in prison for ten to fifteen years, that would have reduced his chances of wedded bliss."

"Chaloner didn't have a record, Gus," said Geoff.

"According to the case file, Richard Chaloner had never been in a serious relationship," said Kenneth. "He wasn't a keen sportsperson, but he'd joined various clubs and societies over the years. His friends and family described him as gregarious. It certainly wasn't the case that Chaloner was a loner, far from it. From everything I can see in this file, he spent his twenties and thirties working hard and enjoying his leisure time with a wide circle of friends."

"He wasn't happy to settle for second-best," said Geoff Mercer. "I think the reputation his business had earned was evidence of that."

"Chaloner acted quickly enough when the right woman came into his life," said Kenneth. "The couple had much to look forward to, but someone stole that dream."

"Another dead end," said Gus. "I can see why Sengupta and Spencer initially thought they were dealing with a straightforward robbery. It would be easy to imagine an attack coming from a junkie hoping to score enough money to satisfy his craving. A quick in-and-out to collect cash and a bank card by waving a knife or machete at a frightened business owner. A robbery that offered the opportunity for a few hundred pounds would be common enough in a large town like Swindon, but this smells different. Guns are more available these days, but the mere threat of violence is often enough to get a shop owner to open the till. In this instance, the intruder didn't panic after he'd shot Richard Chaloner."

"What are you saying, Freeman?" asked the Chief Constable.

"He'd done his homework; that was obvious," said Gus. "He knew Harry Simpkins always left at five-thirty. Matt Merchant's car was outside until ten to six. If he'd studied the men's routine over weeks, he knew Merchant needed it to drive somewhere other than his house on Elmina Road on Monday evenings."

"Surely the killer must have panicked when Merchant spotted the puncture, Gus," said Geoff. "What if Matt Merchant had persuaded Chaloner to accept a lift? The opportunity to rob Chaloner would have gone."

"If I'm right, and the killer made meticulous preparations, he knew how insistent Chaloner would be on cycling to and from work. He'd cycled every day from Pinehurst before he married, and nothing changed afterwards. Chaloner needed to repair the tyre somewhen, and the killer played the odds. He gambled Chaloner would politely decline the offer of a lift, stay behind to finish the paperwork, make the repair, and then cycle home to Shrivenham Road. His wife was on holiday, so nobody was waiting for him to get home. The weather was another factor to play into the hands of the killer. If Chaloner took the opportunity to hang around indoors for another thirty minutes, the downpour could have eased."

"If we accept that's what happened before the attack,

talk us through events inside the garage, Freeman," said Kenneth.

"Where was Chaloner when Merchant left?" asked Gus.

"Merchant fetched him from the office after he'd spotted the damage to the bicycle," said Geoff.

"The autopsy report states the body hadn't been moved," said Gus. "Chaloner was shot at close range in the middle of the workshop floor. Simpkins and Merchant found him the following morning lying between two cars. There were no signs of any struggle anywhere on the premises."

"The intruder persuaded Chaloner to leave the office," said Geoff.

"The cash was said to be in his wallet," said Gus. "Where was the wallet found?"

Kenneth Truelove scanned the report.

"On the floor, just outside the office door. It got kicked under a workbench."

"Merchant said it was common for the bank card to be lying on the desk," said Gus. "Chaloner might have kept his wallet in the back pocket of his trousers, but when you spend your working life under the bonnet of a car, it's usual to protect your clothing. The photographs of the murder scene confirm Chaloner was indeed wearing a blue boiler-suit with zipped pockets at the front and his day-to-day clothing underneath. In addition, photographs of the office show a pair of shoes he would change into when cycling home, a jacket, and wet-weather gear. Once he'd repaired the bike, Chaloner would have changed out of his boiler suit and work boots and cycled home."

"You think the wallet was in the inside pocket of the jacket in the office?" asked Geoff.

"That's why you believe the killer kept his cool and didn't panic," said Kenneth.

"I think he waited for Matt Merchant to drive away, walked through the side door, switched off the lights, and made for the centre of the garage. Richard Chaloner went to investigate. He probably thought it was kids messing around or an opportunist thief hoping to grab a valuable piece of kit and escape before Chaloner caught him. He had no idea the intruder aimed to murder him in cold blood."

"So, the killer waited in the dark until Chaloner got close and shot him," said Geoff.

"Do you not think there was an argument, Freeman?" asked Kenneth.

"There were no signs of a struggle. The killer coolly removed the gold chain, stepped over the body, strolled to the office, and helped himself to the cash. If Chaloner had the wallet on his person, the CSI personnel would have noted any disturbance to his clothing. The killer removed Chaloner's gold chain without leaving evidence, which supports the view they wore gloves. The bank card was a bonus, but they had ample time to look around the office, find the PIN, and add the four hundred pounds to whatever was in the wallet to cement the idea it was a robbery."

"How do you explain the thefts of the catalytic converters?" asked Geoff Mercer.

"At some point, Sengupta and Spencer linked the killing to the CCTV caper you made me sit through," said Gus. "Am I right?"

"That didn't happen until they had exhausted the other lines of enquiry," said Kenneth.

"My initial thoughts are that the two events were unconnected," said Gus.

"The team spent a long time trying to find the men responsible," said the Chief Constable. "They hunted for evidence linking Chaloner with the criminal fraternity."

"Without luck, I imagine?" asked Gus.

"I wouldn't be asking you to take a fresh look at the case if they had, Freeman."

"We'll check everything, sir, as we always do," said Gus, "but my guess is the killer was local. We're looking for someone who could keep watch on the garage without attracting attention. Mrs Fryer and Mr Jones would have spotted a stranger spending long periods on the street outside their window. The killer was someone they knew. He may well have been someone Richard Chaloner knew."

"You haven't had the file in your hand for thirty minutes, and you believe you're on the verge of solving it," said Geoff Mercer. "Have you got a bus to catch?"

"I thought you would be on the same page as me by now, Geoff," said Gus. "This wasn't a robbery gone wrong, nor does it feel like an argument over money for stolen goods. As for solving it, we're a long way from doing that. It is, however, imperative we catch this killer. How he behaved after the shooting suggests that Richard Chaloner wasn't his first victim."

A Normal November: Chapter Three

"Let's not jump to conclusions, Freeman," said the Chief Constable. "Raj Sengupta might not be the brightest star in the heavens, but surely someone on his team imagined the same sequence of events you've hypothesised. Moreover, as the team switched focus to the catalytic converter thefts, it suggests they found a good reason to discount your theory."

"You need to read this murder file in more detail, Gus," agreed Geoff Mercer. "If you were right, the killer struck again in the past two years. However, the streets near Swindon railway station have shown no sign of being home to a serial killer."

"You might be right," said Gus. "We'll follow the evidence Raj and Tom uncovered. They never found the link to organised crime, but that doesn't mean it wasn't there. Similarly, they never identified the three men seen in the garage's vicinity on the day of the murder. Whether that was unlucky or sloppy police work, we'll only discover by going over everything with a fine-tooth comb."

"An open mind, Freeman," said Kenneth. "That's all I can ask."

While Gus flicked through the appendices at the back of the file, Kenneth Truelove called Vera Butler and asked her to serve lunch.

Geoff Mercer leaned forward to speak to Gus.

"Has Suzie told you I'd asked her to run a campaign encouraging car owners to be more careful in protecting their valuables?"

"Yes, Geoff," said Gus. "Only a few weeks ago, you added hate crimes and victim support to her list of the latest hot potatoes. Can't someone have a quiet word with the Police and Crime Commissioner? Too many carbohydrates aren't good for you."

"The PCC aims to deliver an effective and efficient service, Gus. When he says jump, we jump. It stops him from looking in our direction when he's looking for further reductions in personnel. I'm only following orders from Kenneth. Has Suzie complained?"

"Not yet," said Gus, thinking ahead to next Tuesday's visit to the doctor.

There was a knock at the door. Vera and Kassie each wheeled in a trolley laden with today's goodies. Enough to feed a small army, let alone three people.

"I see you ordered the usual, Geoff," said Gus. "No signs of any reduction there."

"Don't worry, Mr Freeman," said Kassie as she paused by his chair. "I added your favourite to the order we submitted to the suppliers."

Gus accepted the proffered bacon roll and kept watch on a healthy-looking wrap. It was unlikely Geoff Mercer would grab it, but stranger things had happened.

He glanced again at the Richard Chaloner murder file

lying on Kenneth's desk. Had he jumped too soon? Where would they need to look for the missing link between the garage owner and the people behind the car thieves from that CCTV footage?

"I'll see you when you've finished your lunch, Mr Freeman," whispered Kassie as she wheeled her trolley towards the door.

"Have you had any further fanciful thoughts now you've demolished that bacon roll, Freeman?" asked Kenneth.

"Did the Gablecross detectives explore every avenue, sir? I've only skimmed the file's contents, but I couldn't see any reference to enemies Richard Chaloner made during his twenty-odd years in the garage trade. On the contrary, his two employees painted a picture of a splendid chap who went the extra mile for each of his clients. It was a pleasure to go to work every day. Yet Chaloner gave short shrift to the unscheduled visitor they had that morning. Why didn't Chaloner take fifteen minutes out of his busy day to check the intermittent electrical fault? It could have been an easy fix, and he would have gained another potential repeat customer."

"DI Sengupta didn't find anyone who had a bad word to say about Chaloner," said Kenneth.

"Each of us has collared dozens of rogues whose friends and family swore were as pure as the driven snow," said Gus, "and several of them have worked in this very business."

"I admit rogues exist in the motor trade, Gus," said Geoff Mercer. "Dodgy workshops in the back streets where they issue MOTs for vehicles that should never be on the road. The owner dressed in oily overalls, manually rewinding the mileage with a screwdriver. Many think that practice died with the demise of analogue. The reality is that instead of being a modern, secure solution, the digital versions have made it easier for a vehicle's apparent mileage to get altered."

Gus wondered whether his old Ford Focus had ever suffered the fate of getting clocked. It didn't seem likely. Every mile his Focus had travelled was etched into its daily performance.

"Although the practice hasn't disappeared, surely it's rarer than in the old days?"

"Clocking is on the increase," said Kenneth. He searched through the pile of reports on his desk.

"Have you read every one of those reports, sir?" asked Gus.

"I'm obliged to pay attention to trends, Freeman," said Kenneth. The seventh file down was the one he sought. "Two years ago, one in twenty cars in the UK showed a discrepancy between the actual and apparent mileage displayed. That has increased to one in sixteen. As a result, the potential cost to motorists has risen to around eight hundred million pounds every year."

"A not inconsiderable sum," said Geoff.

"A sum caused by the impact on second-hand values," said Gus. "Yes, I understand the maths. My Ford Focus has done over one hundred thousand miles. If I took it to one of these dodgy operators and they knocked forty thousand miles off the milometer, I might get an extra two thousand pounds if I was to sell it."

"Chaloner wasn't a second-hand car dealer," said Kenneth. "He only carried out repairs and MOTs. There's no suggestion he ever had a car for sale on the forecourt outside his garage."

"True," said Geoff, "but he must have had customers bringing cars to him for their first MOT after three years on the road. So I think Gus is right to pursue another line of enquiry."

"Ah," said the Chief Constable. "You're pointing fingers at the car owners, not the garage owners. That's because of PCP, the most popular method of purchasing cars in the UK in recent years."

"Exactly," said Geoff. "Finance deals for personal contract purchase, or hire, often come with strict mileage limits, where each additional mile can prove costly. If you say you're only going to do five thousand miles per year on a three-year deal and cover double the distance, it could cost you fifteen hundred quid."

"My car needs servicing each year to get it through the MOT," said Gus, "and has its mileage recorded in the service book."

"Yes, but did you buy that rust bucket from new?" asked Geoff.

"Keep your voice down; she might hear you," said Gus. "Yes, I did, but although I didn't need to pass an MOT, I still got it checked over, and they recorded the mileage."

"Many drivers don't bother visiting a garage until that first MOT is due. It's easy to get a car clocked before it goes to the garage."

"That's illegal," said Gus.

"It's illegal to alter the mileage and then sell a car without telling the buyer its mileage has changed," said Geoff. "The act of turning back the clock isn't illegal."

"If Richard Chaloner got involved in that business, what equipment did he need?" asked Gus. "The days of the screwdriver are long gone, I presume?"

"Just a laptop and software available online," said Geoff. "If he didn't fancy doing the job himself, he could arrange for someone to pop in and do it for one hundred pounds."

"We'll check with Merchant and Simpkins," said Gus. "What happened to the garage after Chaloner's death?"

"Merchant has continued running the business, trading under Merchant Motor Repairs," said Kenneth. "Harry Simpkins is still there, and they now have a young apprentice motor mechanic, Anne Marie Buckland. Chaloner's widow, Eve, was happy to let Merchant take over the unit's rental. She lives alone in the house the couple shared for six months on Shrivenham Road."

"As this murder occurred only two years ago, almost every person Sengupta and Spencer interviewed is living and working where they were at the time," said Geoff Mercer. "Even the CCTV footage came from the same postal district next to the railway station. So if the killer were local, you wouldn't have far to look, Gus."

"We'll see," said Gus. "Is that it for today, sir?"

"I need to attend another briefing in ten minutes, Freeman," said Kenneth. "I would welcome the opportunity to spend that brief respite in quiet contemplation."

"Message received, sir," said Gus. "I'll rescue that chicken wrap and get this folder back to the Crime Review Team office."

Grab your copy...
vinci-books.com/normalnovember